Praise for *A Scrambling After Circumstance*

"With literary legerdemain, first novelist Denman wins readers' affection for her demanding narrator, Eula B.; the reader's fondness for her is evidence of the author's prowess as she creates a seamless picture of a life in rural Mississippi that nearly spanned this century."
— *Publishers Weekly*

"*A Scrambling After Circumstance* is seasoned with experience. . . . Surprising and impressive is the voice of Denman's narrator. First novelists sometimes write with Denman's apparent confidence, but few achieve the consistency of control that distinguishes her book."
— *The Boston Globe*

"A modest novel that sets out to be — and succeeds as — a family chronicle told from the point of view of its oldest member."
— *Kirkus Reviews*

"This is her first novel. You'll find that hard to believe — and find yourself praying for another. . . . A glorious journey through an ordinary life well-lived"
— *The Charlotte Observer*

"Margaret-Love Denman is astonishingly successful in creating a complex, altogether believable and engaging character and in presenting a rich, complicated narrative that does have meaning. I admired the author's secure craft and I was moved by her combination of tenderness and stubborn toughness."
— *The Spectator* (North Carolina)

"Denman shines in her first effort to give voice to her thoroughly Southern characters. . . . A warmhearted tale of that all-too-familiar clash between the generations and the way things used to be"
— *The Orlando Sentinel*

"*A Scrambling After Circumstance* is an unusually direct and likable novel. The sweet befuddlement of the narrator, groping for the significance of her life, is both appealing and moving."
— Valerie Sayers

"Margaret-Love Denman eavesdrops on the interior monologue of a proud woman tricked by her aging body and her shifting memories. Denman's prose never scrambles. . . . The voice encompasses both plain talk and poetry as Denman moves deftly between the vivid past and the infirm present. Denman demonstrates careful technique and the talent to progress in her future fiction."
— *The Asheville Citizen-Times* (North Carolina)

"A remarkable first novel. Among the many delights of this novel is its fine, sure voice."
— *The Washington Post Book World*

"A warm tide of wisdom runs throughout. . . . Eula B. makes discoveries up to the moment of her death. The reader shares her sense of wonder and, even after putting down the book, can't quite put aside its sorrow."
— *The Philadelphia Inquirer*

CONTEMPORARY AMERICAN FICTION

A SCRAMBLING AFTER CIRCUMSTANCE

Born and raised in Oxford, Mississippi, Margaret-Love
Denman has taught at numerous colleges and universities,
and began writing only after her five children were of
school age. She is currently working on her next novel.

A Scrambling
After Circumstance

Margaret-Love
Denman

Penguin Books

PENGUIN BOOKS
Published by the Penguin Group
Viking Penguin, a division of Penguin Books USA Inc.,
375 Hudson Street, New York, New York, 10014, U.S.A.
Penguin Books Ltd, 27 Wrights Lane, London W8 5TZ, England
Penguin Books Australia Ltd, Ringwood, Victoria, Australia
Penguin Books Canada Ltd, 10 Alcorn Avenue, Suite 300,
Toronto, Ontario, Canada M4V 3B2
Penguin Books (N.Z.) Ltd, 182–190 Wairau Road,
Auckland 10, New Zealand

Penguin Books Ltd, Registered Offices: Harmondsworth, Middlesex, England

First published in the United States of America by Viking Penguin,
a division of Penguin Books USA Inc., 1990
Published in Penguin Books 1991

1 3 5 7 9 10 8 6 4 2

Grateful acknowledgment is made for permission to reprint an excerpt from
"Wind Song" from *Black Dog, Red Dog* by Stephen Dobyns. Copyright © 1980,
1982, 1983, 1984 by Stephen Dobyns. Reprinted by permission of
Henry Holt and Company, Inc.

PUBLISHER'S NOTE
This is a work of fiction. Names, characters, places, and incidents
either are the product of the author's imagination or are used
fictitiously, and any resemblance to actual persons, living or
dead, events, or locales is entirely coincidental.

THE LIBRARY OF CONGRESS HAS CATALOGUED THE HARDCOVER AS FOLLOWS:
Denman, Margaret-Love.
A scrambling after circumstance/Margaret-Love Denman.
p. cm.
0-670-83534-X(hc).
0 14 01.5399 3(pbk.)
I. Title.
PS3554.E5336S37   1990
813'.54—dc20   89–40808

Printed in the United States of America
Set in Janson
Designed by Francesca Belanger

For my father:
without whom I would not have had the stories

Acknowledgments

As with any made thing, this book owes its final form to many people. There were the early encouragers. Grandma' Sally, Kay, Jean, Laura, Liz, and Joanne, who read first drafts and said keep going. There were the middlemen, Roland Tapp, John Pilkington, and Martha Lacy Hall, who saw my work as a possibility. But especially there were those who plodded with me through week after week of endless revisions: Peggy Parris, Geraldine Powell, and Elizabeth Squire. To them and to Alex Hoole, Louis Rubin, Louise Shivers, Rhoda Weyr, Kate Simpson, and Mindy Werner, I must say thank you.

And he wondered if all he had seen as progress
Was merely a scrambling after circumstance.

Stephen Dobyns, "Wind Song"

A Scrambling After Circumstance

$\mathcal{I}$ was eleven when the new doctor came to Sumner County. Prettiest man I ever saw. Came around to the school, looked at everybody in the class. When he got to me, he said, "You're mighty tall to be in just the sixth grade." I hunched over and made an S out of my backbone. But he could not spell my name. He said, "Speak up, girl," and I had to say it three times.

"Eula B. Eula B. Eula B." Only when he wrote it, he wrote "Euler Bea." I didn't tell him it was wrong.

I saw him again later, the summer after the sixth grade. "Burning with fever," Mama said, so hot she couldn't rest her hand on my head. The days and nights wound around the bedposts in the front room. Time passed me by, sliding down a muddy slope. It was a Sunday. Papa was getting ready for church. "Harlon, we're gonna lose Eula B. if we don't get some help. I've tried every cleanser I know, and she's still too hot to touch," Mama said. And the worry weaved around the edges of her voice.

Mama and Papa put me in the wagon with a feather comforter, even though it was summer and I was burning with fever. The feather points pushed up into my skin, so many little needles. Like all of me was sleeping, trying to wake up.

The doctor was in his room at Mrs. McCall's boardinghouse. He came out to the wagon half-dressed, pushing and shoving his white shirttail down into his trousers. Halfway up in the day on Sunday, and he still didn't have a belt on. Told us to meet him at his office.

It was over the drugstore. The stairs were dark and uneven. Papa used the toe of his boot to feel along the back of the step to make sure he didn't fall. I heard the scrape, step, scrape, step that took us to the top. A single yellow light bulb dangled from the ceiling. Our shapes made two sets of ghosts to follow us. They darted from one wall to the other. At the top, there was a wide hall with dark, uneven floors.

An old church pew stood on one side. Looked like a moaners' bench to me. A sign over the back said "colored." Papa and I sat down anyway. He smiled a little bit in the shadows and reached over to pat my hand. Papa wasn't much good at talking. I tried to smile back at him, feeling like I was going to be called on in class and not sure I knew the answer. My body feeling two ways at once. Waiting for the doctor, wrapped from head to toe in that feather comforter, half of me wanting him to come, the other half fearing that he would. He did. Splendid as before, the only man I ever saw except the preacher in Sumner City who didn't wear overalls and boots on a weekday. His shoes had shiny toes ending in a point like he didn't have toes like ordinary people. Square in the middle of his waist was a belt buckle. Shiny, golden, a winner's medal, bigger than any they ever gave at Field Day in Columbia. It was a blazing star with the word "*etoile*" written below. I wanted to put my fingers on the star and the letters to see if heat or light came out from them. When Papa put me up on his shoulder to take me into the office, the doctor said, "She's a mighty big girl for you to be carrying like that."

I curled into an S again.

"Just put her in that first room yonder while I wash up."

When he came in the little white room, he said to me, "Can you get up on the table so I can look at you." I tried and fell. He had strong white hands to help me, not coarse or stained like Papa's. I laid against the cold white table and he lifted the tail of my dress above my waist. He pushed the top of my step-ins down and asked me questions while his fingers pushed and poked against my body. His fingers asked questions I couldn't understand.

"Does it hurt here?" Then, "How about here? Does it feel funny when I press right there? How about when you go to the bathroom? Does that bother you?"

The questions filled up the space above me while his fingers poked and the star shined. He turned to the door, and I watched the belt buckle swing around out of sight.

Then he called Papa. I whispered "*E-toile,*" so he could not hear. The word felt round and good in my mouth.

"Mr. Harlon, I think she's got nephritis."

Papa did not answer.

"Some folks call it Bright's disease, it's a kidney problem and it can be pretty serious. I'm going to give you a prescription, and we'll start with that and see how she gets along. It'll be a while before we'll know. She'll have to have bed rest, too." Papa's hand was dark against the white paper. He held it out, even with his chest, careful that he didn't drop the mysterious words.

I could hear the doctor washing in the next room. He switched his white doctor's coat for a blue seersucker one. He buttoned it, walking toward the door. Leaving, he called back over his shoulder. "I'll check on her about Tuesday." Then he was gone. The room filled up with shadows again, the light from his belt buckle led him away. The dark upstairs fell back around Papa and me.

That summer was a long one. Hot days and fevered nights, his visits with the shining buckle, the sound of Mama shelling, canning, and drying in the kitchen. The mason jars new-filled and hot, lined up on the sills. The windows in the kitchen like the stained glass in the First Baptist Church in town when the morning light came through them. Yellow cream corn and canned tomatoes made virgin hair and red robes for the saints. From my cot I could hear the quiet hum of her and Mattie, talking.

That summer, 1914, I learned to hate my body. I heard I was supposed to. The doctor came and left. I thought about how beautiful he was. A preacher came for a rivival and talked about hating your flesh. He said to be full of the spirit you have to crucify the flesh. All the grown-ups in the church said "Amen." The doctor caused me a kind of sweet pain I still remember. But then I called it shame.

"Toy, can you come fix this bed so it stops moving?" Not Toy, but Edward Earl's heavy steps coming down the hall make the whole trailer shake. He always comes into a room belly first. He wears a big belt buckle with a Stetson on it snuggled under his belly. Edward Earl's buckle tries to hold in all his fat. The doctor's fit clean and easy against his flat stomach.

"What's the matter, Mama?" he wheezes. The slightest effort and Edward Earl wheezes. I hate it when he calls me "Mama." I warned Toy. But she never listened, always been hard to handle. Started off that way, two days in labor with Mama helping me.

"I was scared."

"What's that, Mama?" Edward Earl busts in on those long, hard days with a wheeze. His head sits down on his shoulders, and the fat on the sides of his face hangs like a rooster's bib. When he moves his head just a tad, it wiggles.

"Turn out the light, please, it's making the circles start up again."

"All right, Mama." He oozes back out the door. His big wide behind leading the way.

They start up in the living room soon as he gets back.

Toy will be standing there with her fists wedged in tight against her waist, making a roll of flesh on either side. Pushing her face into the air above him. Edward Earl making a spread-out V in the dark plastic of his recliner.

"It seems to me one night a week, you could stay with Mama. You don't seem to mind when we get her social security check to add to my check every month." Toy's voice comes down hard on *my*. "But you get mighty busy when it comes to staying here with her just every once in a while."

Toy's voice has a sharp edge to it when she gets mad. She is a lot like Q.C. that way. She gets mad, and holds it in just like he did. Then explodes, white-hot all over everything. The voices in the next room rise and fall in rhythm with the circles on my bed. This place is so small and hot it makes me catch my breath. Their voices float in and out on hot waves of air. Too hot for this double-wedding-ring quilt. Mama Two pieced it when Gus and me married. It is heavy, heavy on my feet and heavy on my stomach. Big yellow circles sit hard on me. They twist and twirl and make me ache.

"Trailers is for gypsies and carnival folks, we never was like that, we always stayed put, had land, kept cows and chickens, we are not trailer folks."

Talking to myself again. Toy always hollers in here, "Huh, Mama?" That way she calls attention to it.

*

"Toy, Toy," I call her, making my voice strong against theirs. "Come here and lift this quilt up off my stomach. It's weighting me down something awful."

"I'll be right there in a minute, Mama," she answers, and her voice slides in under the door.

The light above me looks like a wagon wheel, only smaller, with three bulbs and bumpy brown shades on the bottom. Wagon wheels go on wagons, not lights. I told Toy that. Toy asked me how I liked it and I told her. Got to be careful now, my thoughts float away from me and make wide, clear balloons just below the light bulbs.

"What are you wanting, Mama?" Toy asks just before she opens the door. She sounds tired and mad. But Toy was raised right, learned to hold her peace early on. She won't get smart-alecky with me, her mama. The wind from the door causes the balloons to shiver, just above me.

"I want you to move this cover, it's too hot and heavy on my stomach, and them wedding rings keep swirling around over me."

"Okay, Mama." Toy rearranges the cover, and I hear her sigh. She moves slow. Heavy people do. She starts out the door, looks back to see if I'm comfortable. I nod just a little, to tell her it's all right to go. "The balloons was interrupting my thinking." Toy holds still for a minute, then closes the door.

Gus was glad about Toy, he always wanted children, always wanted us to have a house full, but Toy was the only one. Gus wanted to name her Eula Faye after me and his mama, the one we called Mama Two. But I said, "No, if I go through with all this, I'll name her." She was a funny little drawed-up thing, and I called her Toy. That was not her real name.

No, I named her Etoile, but nobody ever called her that except Mama. It got to be Toy right away.

"Toy." The puffs of air I use to call her name makes the sheet hop up like a frog's under there.

"Coming, Mama." Toy's bedroom slippers make swishing noises on the linoleum in the hall. She opens the door and comes to rest against the door frame. She leans instead of standing. Says she's always tired. She's just been to the beauty parlor. It must be the night she goes to bowl. Always does them on the same day. Never does her hair on Saturday to be ready for church. No, she gets her hair ready for bowling. The curls, tight and screwed down on her head like a pig's tail, are browner now than this morning. She don't tell Edward Earl she colors her hair. The bottles hide right behind the towels. I think Mattie colors her hair, too. It still had red highlights the last time I saw her. Not a touch of gray.

"Toy, I hear you and him going on in there and I want you to know I don't need nobody to stay here with me. Why, I stayed at home in the country by myself for fifteen years after your daddy died, and I'd be there right now if you hadn't got this idea about bringing me to town so we could rent out the place. Now, you let Edward Earl go and do as he pleases. I don't want him staying here with me, stomping up and down that hall, wheezing and keeping me awake. You hear me?"

"Mama, you know you can't stay here by yourself. You can't even get up to go to the bathroom, and Edward Earl can stay with you just every once in a while."

"I don't want Edward Earl helping me to go to the bathroom and I won't die while he's the only one around. I guarantee it." I won't let my body play that trick on me, showing out so I have to depend on Edward Earl.

"Well, Mama." The "well" takes a long time coming out.

"If you really think you'd be all right just long enough for me to go to my bowling league, I'll be back just as soon as we finish."

Toy stands away from the door frame and pulls the knit top down over her doughy body, front and back, then sucks in air to make her middle look smaller. Sitting all day, doing piece work in a factory, that gives you a middle. Not farm work. I just see her now, having a fit to ride into Richardson with a carload of girls to get on at the shirt plant. Esther Mayfield picked her up, smacking gum with bright red lips stuck out further than a pouter pigeon. Her face painted up like an Indian. I told Toy there was not any point in it. We would get by. But Toy's like my sister Mattie that way, too. Always wanting to move up in the world, not satisfied with what we got. She met Edward Earl there, in town. He was a security guard at the plant, right after the war. The soldier boys from Camp McCain had all gone home. Well, Edward Earl loved to saunter around with that big belly of his and that gun strapped to the top of his leg like he was somebody important, uniform and all. Toy just fell for him. I told Toy not to marry a fat man, lazy, I said, but she didn't listen. And I was right, soon as they married, no time really, he got laid off, probably for drinking on the job. Hasn't had a real job since. Toy's still at the plant. She's good, too, made production the first month she was there.

Just a while back her picture was in *The Richardson Star*, getting a pin or something. But after Edward Earl got laid off, he never even looked for a job. He just takes Toy to work and rides around to the café, I guess, drinking coffee and cussing, and telling jokes. That's what Gus said most of those town fellows do. He picks her up at quitting time.

E-toile, she toils all right. I crackle a laugh and make the frog do double jumps under the sheet.

I hear Toy getting ready, getting out her bowling shoes, her ball and bag, shouting at Edward Earl all the time about how he never tries to help anyway. I bet he's not even listening. A horn honks outside. Car lights turn the curtains into shadows.

The front door shuts, and Toy calls to the other bowlers. In just a minute I hear the refrigerator door open, and a corner of light flashes on in the hall. That'll be Edward Earl easing the leftovers out and setting them on the counter. He eats like a starved animal, like a dog left on the side of the road that eats until he vomits and then eats again because he's afraid when he comes back it'll all be gone. I noticed it when he first came out to the house, when he was courting Toy. He leaned over the table, his chest almost on his plate. Stuffing his food in his mouth and looking at the rest of the table, making sure no one else was getting a helping. I had field hands like that. They were no good for afternoon help, them kind. You work them in the morning, feed them, pay them off, and then let them go. I never hired them but once. But I got Edward Earl every Sunday after they married.

Gus said I was the best hand he ever had. "You know, Eula, you're stout as any man." He always grinned when he said that, it meant a lot to him. He never added the B. "You're a good stout woman, not to be no bigger than you are."

I was more than big, though, when I was like that with Toy. Mama never said "pregnant," always *like that*. Never again, I told Gus after Toy, that was plenty. I never let my body play that kind of trick on me again. Sickness is a trick, keeps you from doing all you planned, keeps you from canning and gardening and tending to your chickens. Sometimes it'll even make you lie to your mama. Like with the Watkins man.

If I had stayed on at the place, I could've tended to my chickens. Only had a few pullets, no roosters, I could've managed the eggs. Bruce Tillman at the Jitney Jungle wanted all my extras. I didn't have to fix nests or watch for ones that set outside the house, so I could have managed. Then Toy and Edward Earl got some crazy idea about me not being able to stay on out there by myself.

I had the cleanest yard of anybody on my route. Oscar

Coglan said so. The bricks around my flower beds were a perfect circle, painted white. Not one bit of grass. I kept it all myself, didn't have a single bit of help the last five years. Didn't need any really after we rented the pastures and the bottom land to Carroll Bickham's boy. I did fine. There wasn't no reason to move me, specially into this trailer. Trailer room's a cage. A cage I don't even recognize. Toy wouldn't let me bring any of my things from the country.

"Too old-fashioned, and besides, the trailer is completely furnished, even to the pictures on the walls. It's a complete house, Mama. You'll see."

"It's not a house," I said. "There's no room for my wandering Jew and beefsteak begonias. My beefsteaks won the blue ribbon only last year." Something's sucked the living out of trailer parks. No place to put important things. Toy didn't seem to notice.

"Mama, a plastic schefflera comes with the den and some red geraniums are fixed in the bay window in the kitchen. You'll get to like it." Toy set my plants back on the windowsill. "It's the best we can do, now, Mama."

I saw those plants. The sun baked the red in them to a dusty pink and cracked their plastic leaves.

But I packed up a box of crocheted doilies, starched and ruffled, to put under the lamps. Put the special one to go under the pink milk glass candy dish Gus brought me from the fair in Jackson on top. He took a fine bull calf to the fat stock show, sold it for a pretty penny, and bought me that candy dish. The Golden Rule Ten Cent Store carried some shiny variegated thread of blues and pinks, greens and yellows back then. I made up a pattern to fit under the bottom of that dish. Could have entered it in the fair, too.

"I got lots of pretty things, Toy. Things that'll look good in your house."

But Toy said, "No, the lamps in the trailer are all in one piece with the table they're setting on. Ain't no place to put doilies, or plants that are just gonna die. And we don't have any space in the cabinets for a bunch of old dishes. Just leave your stuff out here for the renters, Mama."

I did. I cleaned for two weeks before the renters came, restarched the doilies and the curtains, scrubbed the kitchen pine floor with a soapstone from the river and swept the yard. That was after Billy, Ed Barnes's boy, came and bought the pullets. He give fifty cents a piece for them, not hardly enough to buy a flat of eggs. The whole place was as bare as Judgment Day.

It took a long time to get the place ready. Cleaning the yard was the hardest. I had to watch where to put my feet. Years of sweeping the yard left little trenches, tricky places, beside the azaleas. Early, before the schoolbus ran, I worked with the metal walker that the county lady left. I could lean on the center of it and reach out over the top and clean a wide path with my hoe. I missed Gus the most when I hoed. He always took my hoe out to the shed and sharpened it to a fine point. I killed a yellow-bellied moccasin down near the well house thanks to that good sharp hoe. A dull hoe told me he'd been gone a long, long time. Two strokes, a house fire, and a tornado ago. So long I had to move into town.

Then the renters showed up, in an old van. Rust ran down one side and showed three different paint jobs. The tag said "Louisiana." Held on to the back bumper with a piece of baling wire. No windows along the side. I stood in the shadows of the front room and watched it drive up.

It honked. I pulled the walker toward me, eased my weight over the top so I could start the long path to the door, and then pushed it to one side.

"I don't have a dog. They could come to the door."

I picked up my cane, opened the screen, and looked out. I waited. The driver moved first, he leaned toward the van's door. It creaked. Then I pushed against the screen.

I walked slowly down the concrete steps. They were new, almost. Three years ago, I got Carroll Bickham's boy to replace the wooden ones. A wide crack opened up between the edge of the porch and the top step. Had to be careful not to catch my cane in it. Lots to think about when you got an extra metal leg. The new steps were tacked on to the front porch like a ruffle on a skirt that was too short. I thought they looked kind of make-do. Toy said, "Mama, it don't matter." I thought it did. When I get back, I'll fix them right, and get out all the doilies, too.

I started out toward the van. There the man and his wife sat, I guess it was his wife, can't always tell these days, and folks in a van, well. I nodded and looked in. All I could make out in there was eyes.

Wide, vacant eyes that belong to poor whites. I knew that look. Move-every-time-the-rent's-due eyes. On-every-government-program-they-can-get eyes. I knew the eyes, hooded and vacant.

I said to them, "I guess you the ones who come to look at the place. Get out and look around." They did. The man got out first. He spat. His spittle made a little brown curdle in the dust where I swept. Then it drew the dirt up into a bruise on the yard. No Jesus here to open a blind man's eyes.

The woman turned sideways and pulled her clothes together. The baby she was nursing didn't cry or whimper. He looked with a tired old stare at the commotion in the back of the van. Holding the baby on one hip, the woman pulled herself out of the van. She had a lean brown ponytail that hung out over the neck of a man's faded denim work shirt. Mama'd say she was "poor in body." The man offered her no help. Slowly, she unwound, and the eyes in the back found their bodies and started moving. Five in all.

"This place won't be big enough for all of you." I felt better knowing there was so many of them. "There is only one bedroom now and the sleeping porch we closed in for me and Mattie."

The man spat again and twisted his head in my direction without straightening his neck. He reminded me of that deformed crane downriver in the marsh. His eyes were hard, hooded, like his children's.

"That'll be all right"—he twisted his head back toward the children this time—"all of them can sleep out there."

"Well, there's another thing, too. On the second Saturday in August, you and yours'll have to give us the porch and yard so that we can have the family reunion here. No ifs, ands, or buts about that. That is how it has to be." I waited for him to say no. But he just kept looking at the ground, letting one of the little boys dance around him like a wild Indian. "We can manage that, I guess," he said.

"Well," I said, "I guess then you will want to look around." I started with the henhouse, fresh with new hay, took a full morning to bring it from the barn in the lower pasture. They followed me like a line of ducks, all those children, quiet as death. Jumping and dancing, making no sound.

"Good and safe for chickens," I said.

"Ain't gonna have no chickens," the man said. "But I can keep my motorcycle in here. I guess it's dry, ain't it?" He twisted his question back at me.

I nodded. Next I showed them the garden spot. Fenced, burned off, waiting for a new layer of manure and straw, waiting for a good plowing and the start of a new season. Little bits of green already showed around last summer's dead stalks. Mama called those "little bits of promise."

"You could feed all of you mighty fine from this garden.

Why, I used to can up to two hundred quarts out of it every summer. That was before I got my freezer." I waved my cane toward it standing on the porch.

The woman stared at me for a full minute and then sighed. The baby rode up and down on her hip like a leaf on a gentle current.

"I can't do no garden. Anyway, we get commodities and stamps." She waited and looked right at me, like I ought to say that was just fine.

"Say, how you heat this house in the winter?" the man wanted to know.

"Wood, got a good chimney in the front room and in the bedroom, too. Both got a good draw to them, and plenty of red oak in that bottom near the creek to keep you good and warm." The way they asked things made me try to get them to like the place. They must have, for they took it. Gave me three months' rent in advance, got the money out of a brown government envelope.

They came in three weeks and I moved. To town. To the trailer with Toy and Edward Earl. Left my things for the renters, just like Toy said. When the renters were gone, there was almost nothing left of me. The flower beds with the perfect circles of white bricks, so many little teeth guarding the azaleas, the fresh nests, hollowed out by a wide hen's breast, rich and thick, the doilies with their starched dancing skirts, fresh curtains smelling deep of sunshine, all of it had the renters' marks on them.

They were just the first ones, as it turned out. Now, unless he died, Louise Farr's old widower is out there. He gave his place to his children, and they put him over on my place. Toy says it's all right to do that. "Since he's missing his mind and don't know where he is, he don't mind living there."

Each of the renters took something from the place. Not so

much what you could see, but feelings and memories. When I went back just to look around, the last time, I was a stranger there. There was all kinds of sins against the place, and I was uneasy at visiting the rooms that held my life for so long. Me and Toy and Mattie's daughter, Eunice, went to clean things up for the family reunion. Mattie didn't set much store by the family reunions, stayed over on the other side of the river, building a whole life over there, on the outside somewhere.

Now, that was something that stayed the same. The reunion. Everybody came at ten-thirty. The men stayed under the big oaks in the front yard, telling what a bad year it was for cotton and beans. Too much rain, too little rain, or the rain was too late or it was too early. Talking man-talk under the trees. The women inside fussing over the food, waving a slow fan to keep the flies off. Unfolding the year's heartaches, shaking their heads in time with the fan, glad they didn't have to swap troubles.

A family meeting after dinner always decided where to have the next reunion. I don't know why we had a meeting. We always came back to my place. The last year, I asked them, "Where we going to have the reunion next year? Not here, not next year. I won't be able to get it ready again." I don't know how I knew to say that. I'm no prophet, but I had my second stroke ten days later.

When I was little, there was no need for family reunions. Nobody ever moved away. We had the first one in August, late August, after everybody's crops were laid by, because Ollie, my oldest brother, was leaving and everybody came to say good-bye.

Ollie was my favorite. He put the tire swing up for me the summer I was sick.

"Eula B., I'll hang it right outside your window, you can watch me. When you feel like it, you can go out and swing. You'll be better soon, I promise. And you can swing, high up, and see clear to the river."

Was it still there, he asked when he called. Fifty years later, he called and said to me, "Can you still see the swing, Eula B.?" Then he talked to me about holding up. "Can you make it?" he said. It must have been when Gus died. "I would have called sooner, if I'd known you had a phone," he said. "I thought you'd be the last person in Sumner County to have a phone put in, Eula B." He laughed. Old-fashioned, he called me.

"I wouldn't have one now. Except the new doctor in town said that with Gus's heart, I can't be so far away from civilization." I told Ollie that.

Civilization, that's not what I call living in town. Anyway, that new doctor, he was so young. He called me and Gus by our given names. I never did get used to that. I called him Dr. Simmons and he called me Eula. When I got confused, they say I called him Dr. Young. I never could get used to him calling me Eula, though. Anyway, living in town with a telephone always ringing in your ear don't seem like civilization to me. I told Ollie that and he just laughed, like he used to. Then he told me he couldn't come home for Gus's funeral. He called about Gus's passing. And the swing, he wanted to know about the swing.

On the long, hot nights when I couldn't sleep and the pain in my back caused the big fat bedposts in the front room to shimmer like the sun on the hard-packed dirt in the backyard, Ollie sat on the end of the front porch and played his harmonica. "Shall We Gather at the River?" he asked with a long, lonesome sound. Him playing helped me through the nights. Shame he's not here now. He played "Oh, Susanna" real slow and dreamy, and at the end, when it came to "Don't you cry for me," he blew that harmonica just like a long, lonely train whistle in the dark. Ollie was planning to leave. The sound of that train whistle was already calling him. He was seventeen that summer and he was ready to leave.

Ollie, his real name is Oliver, worked a man's job from the time he was about twelve. He was good in school, but Papa thought eight years of schooling was enough. It was all Ollie had. He hadn't gone to school regular since he was about fourteen. Nobody really argued with Papa. So Ollie left.

At least he told us he was leaving. We got to say good-bye.

That was why we had that first family reunion. To say good-bye. All of Mama's people come, and Papa's, too. and all their children. Mama's mama and papa were both dead by then, but Papa's mama brought chicken pie in a big silver-colored washbasin. The dish was so big I had to put my arms around it to bring it in to the table. The heat from the pie turned the tops of my arms pink.

That reunion, Mama cried. We never had anybody leave home before. The house where we lived, where all of us were born, was Mama's mama's and papa's. Mama was their youngest. When she and Papa married, they just moved in with her folks. Papa Taylor died the winter Q.C. was born. Mama said, "Winter is hard on old folks. If Papa'd made it through that winter, he'd lived at least another year." When I was born, Mama T. helped out with me and with Q.C. since he was still just a baby. Mama said, "Poor Mama, she was already wore out and getting up with Q.C. and his croup and getting you in for me to nurse, well, it was just too much for her and she followed Papa Taylor to the grave in less than two years. Lost 'em both in less'n two years," she said, and then she cried.

That summer, 1914, she cried a lot, too. Maybe I had time to notice. Ollie put me on a cot on the back porch, where it was cooler and I could watch the swing. I can still feel Ollie coming up on the back porch after supper and carrying me in, gentle as a mama cat with a kitten, and putting me on the bed in the front room. During the day that old live oak shaded the back porch and kept it cool. I laid there and watched the swing, hanging straight as a plumb line. The backyard still as a picture. Sometimes the sun made the air above the hard-packed dirt dance before my eyes. There, on the porch, I heard Mama crying. I wondered why. Now I know. Just living is enough to make a woman cry, tending to birthing and dying is bad enough, but all that goes on in between is sure enough to make you cry. Sometimes, you got to turn your heart off just so you can make it through.

A goose walks over my grave when I think like that. The wagon wheels shiver just a touch. Toy is home. She just slammed the trailer door. Somebody told them to put some concrete footings under the trailer and brick it up all around the bottom like some little dancing skirt, then that shaking would stop. That's all a bunch of foolishness. First they leave a house that doesn't move to get a house that has wheels on it. Not that a house with wheels on it is really a house in the first place, but then they take a house with wheels on it and puts bricks all around it so it can't move anyway. A bunch of foolishness. I told Toy and Edward Earl so. They don't listen. Edward Earl just said, "Oh, Mama." I don't like him calling me "Mama."

I can hear Toy tiptoeing down the hall. I can just see her. Her bowling shirt hugs the rolls around her middle. Looks like ripples on a washboard. Her hair ripples too flat against her head since she got that permanent wave. She walks funny. Trying not to put her whole weight down, like tiptoeing would make her seem smaller somehow. The door of the room cracks and I make slits of my eyes, trying to look like I'm asleep and still be able to see Toy.

"You awake, Mama?"

"Yes." Now I have to talk to her. I can't put anything together right now and Toy will want to tell me about bowling even though I think bowling is another bunch of foolishness.

"Mama?"

"Hmm?"

"Guess what?"

"What?"

"I bowled my best game tonight. Our team made it to the league finals. Looks like we'll be bowling against the women from First Baptist, downtown next week." She sounds like a little girl who's just won at Red Rover.

"Well, that's fine, Toy. I'm glad for you."

Toy never talks about anything important. What did Mama and I talk about? Recipes, the garden, patterns, crocheting, all those things, but when we sat together when I was tending to her before she died, we really did talk. Mostly it was just remembered things. Mama would tell me about the times when we were all little, when Ollie and Mattie, Q.C. and me were babies, when her house was full and her heart did not hurt. Mama remembered and I listened.

Maybe that's what's wrong. Maybe I can't remember what to tell Toy.

"Toy."

"Ma'am?" Her voice sounds hurried, impatient.

"We've got to remember the important things."

"Oh, I know, Mama. I filled out all your cards for the home care nurse. She needed your social security number and your Medicaid number. But I took those to her last week. And the social worker, you remember when she was here? She called back and said to tell you that you were eligible for everything since the farm isn't in your name anymore. Isn't that good?" Toy leans into her talking, trying to pull me along with her.

"I guess so. I got the farm from my mama and daddy, just like you will. You take care of your folks and you get the land. You know that, Toy?"

"Yes'm. The social worker took that all down. You remember when she was asking about the farm?"

I remember that little girl all right. She had on blue jeans and some kind of pretend-like cowboy boots. And a fancy sweater, too tight, I thought. And a lot of blue color on the tops of her eyelids. She asked so many questions. And had a briefcase, like a lawyer or an insurance man. I guess that's what it was. I never saw a woman carry one. And a big book, about the size of the New Orleans telephone book, was inside it. Every time Toy or me told her something, she would look it up in that big book and then write it down on her papers. She licked the end of her fingers and curled the corners of those thin papers. Her fingernails were wet-shiny and too red. Miss Thornhill was her name. I asked her if she was kin to the Ocie Thornhills from Silver Creek. She didn't think so. She carried her papers attached to a bright yellow clipboard and asked nosy questions, too, about wage earners and dependents and property ownership. Miss Thornhill was a wet-shiny one, slick like those plastic geraniums.

While she was here I began to have those pains again. Different ones, in my dead leg and arm. They say I really can't feel anything there, but I know hurting. The hurt was from another time, hurting right into now. I'm sure about one thing. While that little question girl was here, Toy had to call the doctor to ask him about the pain.

"Mama, I can't get the doctor to answer now, I left a message on his tape recorder. It said he'll call back later. I'll just get you some more aspirin until he calls, is that all right?" I nodded yes. But it really was not all right. Doctoring must not remember about important things, either, if you have to leave a message with a tape recorder when you're hurting. It wasn't that way when I was sick that summer. The doctor came every Tuesday and Friday to see how I was doing. He'd pull up in the yard and the dust would puff up all around his car. It was the first car I ever saw. Folks in the county said he drove fast, made the chickens squawk and fly, said he caused a terrible fuss wherever he went. I don't know about that. When he drove up in the yard, the dust would make a cloud for him and he would come down out of it and float into my room. Always he would ask me questions. "Well, Euler B., how's my girl feeling today? Does it still hurt here?" With that he would push against the hollows in my back with fingers as strong as milking fingers. The bad part was when he moved to the front. He pushed and asked how did it feel. "What about when you pee?" I always said "just fine," even though it burned so bad and I would wait too long and wet the floor getting to the pot. Always questions. How did I feel? Did it hurt here? Or here? What about pain? And when he asked me how I felt, I knew that it was important to him. Maybe the pain was coming from then, from that summer. The little question girl didn't make me embarrassed with her questions, just tired was all.

"Mrs. Freeman, I know these questions are a bother to you and I'll try to get through them as quickly as possible. Do you know when the property in Sumner County which was assessed to you in the last tax rolls became yours?" She stopped. Then she started again.

"When did the farm on Route Six get to be yours?"

I heard the question, looked at the little question girl, and turned to the wall. And closed my eyes.

Toy kind of giggled, like she was nervous and embarrassed by me.

"I'm afraid you'll have to come back or we could go into the den and I can try to answer the questions for her. When she does that"—Toy mocks me, closing her eyes and looking at the wall. I see her through the slits I make in my eyelids. Like looking through the boards in a barn door. I could just make out her mocking me. Q.C. was a mocker, called me "Miss Priss"—"she's through talking. The doctor says she can't concentrate very long since the strokes. It's just too hard for her to think."

I heard that all right. I can think just fine. Toy ought to

know better, but I just was not sure I wanted to tell that little girl all about the farm. When did the farm get to be mine? Mama said all along Gus and me would get it. I took care of her and Papa. Mama got it the same way. Whoever takes care of their folks gets the home place. Everybody knows that. Everybody, I guess, except that little question girl. That is the way it ought to be. Toy and Edward Earl will get the place. I guess they already got it. I think that paper they brought in here and I signed means they have it now. It was something about getting help from the government. I know you are not supposed to move off and leave land. Not if you mean to get it. You are supposed to take care of your mama and your papa and then the land is yours. You do not move off into a trailer and then move your mama off the place and into something with wheels on it: moving off just brings heartache and trouble. Ollie, Q.C., even Mattie left.

"There." I puffed a little puff and made the quilt dance again. Like when it rains in the dead of August, drops falling into fine red dust. Little dust waves dance up all around the drop. August drops are big and fat and tease the dust into dancing. Only a breath of a shower, nothing to water your dahlias. Just enough to puff up the dust and fool you. Summers can be full of false promise, like that.

"There, I knew if I worked at it I could remember it. That's one of the important things. You don't move off land. You stay and the land is yours." I could feel myself smile, like a one-sided jack-o'-lantern. Only one side of my face moves since the last stroke. I heard the doctor say that. He thought I wasn't listening. But I was. That other side of my face refuses to do a thing. Stubborn as a tea stain, it is.

"You cannot let your body play tricks on you." That is another important thing. Saying it out loud keeps it from getting away from me.

That first thing, about the land, made Mama cry that summer. It was Ollie leaving the land, going away to a place where he had no people. He only had a postcard about it and he just left. On the strength of a postcard, he left. Now, that's something. Hard to believe, even now. The postcard came from Ray Graham, he was a second cousin of Mama's. He left the fall before, caught a ride on a freight. "Hoboing" is what Mama called it. Anyway, Ray left in September, after the crops on their place were in, and he sent Ollie a postcard that Christmas. Oscar Coglan, no, it wasn't him, it was the postman before him, when he delivered the postcard, he waited for Ollie to read it. The card said:

> Ollie,
> It's all we dreamed it was. There's plenty of work.
> Why don't you come?
> Very Truly Yours,
> Raymond L. Graham

I still see every word. The printing seems as big as the letters in the primer, not shrunk down like they would be to fit into a trailer court. We thought it was funny Ray signed his whole name and made it sound so fancy. We wondered if California did that to you. The picture on the front was in color, the brightest blue sky and the greenest trees I ever saw. Trees loaded with oranges stretching out as far as I could see, and the opposite side of the postcard said "California's second gold rush." We took the card in to show Mama. She just pushed it to one side and said, "I don't have time to be wasting on California."

She cried when she made dressing for the chicken. When I asked her what was the matter, she said, "Nothing, I just cut all the onions up for the dressing and they got in my eyes." I knew different, and I got the little paring knife out to help her. Soon we was both sniffing and using the backs of our hands to wipe the tears away. Both acting like it was just onions. All that winter Ollie kept that card sticking up on his chest of drawers. Once when I went in to ask him to help me get the stove going, he was laying across his bed, his long old legs sticking out almost to the door, reading that postcard. I asked him what he was doing, and he said dreaming of gold. I thought that was a bunch of foolishness, and I told him so. He just smiled. "You don't need to be so serious, Eula B., that you can't even dream." He poked a long, skinny finger at my stomach and smiled. That same old dreamy smile that went along with "Oh, Susanna" and his harmonica.

When Ollie was not working for Papa, he was always dreaming. Mama said he was a real Ferguson. They were all dreamers. Mama's Grandpa Ferguson barely made a living on the farm even though everybody said it was one of the best pieces of land in the county. "The Fergusons was all dreamers," Mama said. Ollie was named for Grandpa Ferguson. "I guess I marked him, naming him for Big Papa," Mama said. Ollie and I were the Ferguson ones, she says, built like them. Like Mama, too. Tall, thin, kind of scarecrow-looking. Shaped just like a bean pole, Mama says. Mattie and Q.C. was shaped like the Taylors. Round, short the Taylors ran to fat when they got older. Maybe that was why Ollie and me were closer to each other than to Mattie and Q.C. Ollie was a Ferguson dreamer, not me. I learned early about dreaming up big plans. I put those away and got on with real living. I had too much work to do.

That summer, 1914, when I was sick, Ollie and me got to be best friends. He sat on the porch and played his harmonica and said to me, "Eula B., you ready to try that swing?" After he left I couldn't get in that swing for the longest time. I would pull that wooden slat back with my hand and just let it go. It would swing crazy, one-sided, and bump into the tree. But I couldn't get in it. Swings go up and back and up and back. But they come back to where they started. Brothers do not. I cried for Ollie at the swing, and Mama cried in the kitchen. So we had the first family reunion that August before Ollie left for California. It was hot and still and the air shivered with the heat. We made lots of jokes about how he was going to get so much of that California gold that next summer he would be back for another reunion and bring us all kinds of fancy presents. I laughed, too, but I knew he wouldn't be coming back. That's another important thing. When you care about somebody a lot, you know what is really true about them, no matter what they say. I knew Ollie wouldn't be back, he didn't have to tell me. He didn't have to tell Mama either. I think Papa believed him. All that next spring he said, "If Ollie don't hurry up, I'm going to have the whole crop put in before he gets here." Then, as the summer wore on, he said, "If Ollie don't come on soon, I'll have everything laid by, and he won't get to do nothing but help me harvest this year." Then by late November, Papa said to Mama one night, "You know, Mamie, I never spent a year of my life that I didn't make a crop. Neither did my papa. Now, here's Ollie, only eighteen years old, and he's spent a year without so much as putting a seed in the ground. Somehow that just don't seem right." I heard him in the front room. Mama didn't say a word. I think she was crying.

Maybe that was where the trouble began, the kind of trouble you don't see for a long time, the kind of trouble that finally moves you off your land and rents it out and winds you up in a trailer.

I'm glad to be getting some of these things straight. While Toy goes bowling, I lift my bad arm up with my good arm and scoot sideways and move my hips and legs toward the edge of the bed. Just as soon as she goes again, next week, I'll get to the bathroom by myself. Once I do that I can go back to the farm. Get out the dishes, root me some begonias.

That is important. I try and rest on it.

Weak bands of sunlight come slanting in through the bottom of the lower panes. Afternoon sun. I slept a long time. Maybe there was two naps instead of one. The weight of my bones feels set somehow. Gus will be here, and I'm not ready. What was I going to get up and do? I wanted to go to California to see Ollie. But there was something else.

The bathroom. Going to try to do it without one of them. That was it.

Take my dead elbow and push my shoulder and hip toward the edge of the bed. There, a little jerk in the direction of the door. The bed creaks just a tad, so I must have jarred it a little. The dead side of my face is not smiling. Sometimes I dribble down that side and don't even feel it. Toy always tells me about it. I'll rest for a minute. Seems a terrible trick to play on somebody like me, somebody used to being up and going from daylight to dark.

Get that elbow moving again and jerk. Those big yellow wedding rings resting on my stomach jump and jerk right along with me. Careful not to wet the bed. That little question girl asked Toy if I was still continent. I heard that. Toy said to her, "What does that mean?" The girl said, "Can she still control her kidneys and her bowels?" She asked that right in front of me. Asked Toy like I wasn't even there. And Toy answered her, said yes. "That's good," the little question girl said, "because so often when old people lose that, well, you simply have to put them in a home." Toy nodded like she knew just what the girl meant. That's why it's important to get up and get to the bathroom on my own. Somebody's in the house, but I won't call them.

There's the side of the bed. Now I can stop jumping and

jerking and get the covers back and my feet down on the floor. I used to sing, "Get along home, Cindy, Cindy, get along home. Shoes and stockings in her hand and her feet all over the floor." I got to do that next.

When Toy was born, the doctor said my feet couldn't touch the floor for two weeks. "Fourteen days," he said. And they had not. Mama moved into the room with me, and she was there every minute. Once or twice, Gus lifted me onto the bedpan. But mostly it was Mama. Mama said, "You ain't cut out to have many children, having such weak kidneys and all."

One of the important things that we talked about, I remember. Mama said, "It's only another woman who really helps you with having babies." That was why I found that conjure-woman.

Mama said, "No man really understands." She said, "I never knew how much you could miss somebody, Eula B., until my mama was gone. You know your daddy and I come home from our wedding and moved in with Mama and Papa. I never had no home except this one. And then when Ollie was born, it just tickled my mama to death that we called him Oliver after her papa. Mama was such a blessing then, too. I didn't have enough milk, and she made hot poultices for my chest and kept a chicken stewing on the stove for broth for me to drink so I could make milk."

Mama said, "When Mattie was born round and fat like a little doll, Mama Taylor was just the same, always there. I did better nursing Mattie, such a good baby she was. Then Q.C. come along, so puny and pitiful, kind of like your Toy, Eula B. We like to have lost him. I was often cross with him. Maybe that started his trouble. Seems like he was just born for grief, right from the beginning. Mama stayed up every night so I could get my sleep. Then she nursed Papa Taylor during the day. He was heavy when he got old, like all the

Taylors. Of course, Mama T. tried to lift him. Then when he died, it just took the starch out of her. She was glad enough to see you, Eula B., but somehow she just kind of gave up on living, just wore out. But, Lord, I never knew how much you could miss a body until Mama died, Eula B."

I hear Mama talking about her mama. Maybe keeping track of bedside talking between mamas and daughters is more important even than the land. Finding out who you can depend on and who you cannot. Mama said, "You won't bear up under many children." I said to Gus right soon after Toy was born, "I am done with this, Gus." It all went back to that summer, 1914, when I had nephritis. Only I can't always remember what that lovely shining doctor called it. It was a name Papa didn't know. He called it Bright's disease. That's easy for me to remember since it makes me think about his buckle, bright and shining, and drawing me into some kind of other world. One time, that summer, before he stopped coming by, I asked him about the buckle. "I bought it in France," he said. "After I went to medical school, I spent a whole summer in France," and he called out the names of the towns where he went. They sounded like some kind of music. He said, "It's not like the France that's in the papers now, in 1914. It was a peacetime France, beautiful. I wanted to stay there, but the war broke out and I got a letter from my father that made me come home."

He talked to me just like that. "You must be something like Ollie, longing for some faraway place," I said.

"Maybe," he said. "I bought the belt just before I got on the boat to come home."

He came most of that summer, every Tuesday and Friday. Each week or so, he stood at the front screen door—it did not sag then—and left another piece of white paper for Papa to take in to the drugstore in Richardson. Then he got into his car and drifted away in a cloud of red clay dust. Shining in the middle of hot August days. Then Papa made a special trip to town, he wouldn't wait until Saturday, but he left just as soon as the doctor drove out of the front yard and the dust died down. While the doctor was there, he and Mama sat at the big kitchen table with the oilcloth cover. They waited like two schoolchildren, feet flat on the floor, until the doctor called them. Mattie did the dinner dishes by herself, fuming over the sink, fussing about the extra chore. Mama pushed all the jars she canned that morning to one side and she said, "Dr. Thompson, would you like a glass of ice tea?" She saved back some ice from dinner when he was coming. "No, ma'am," he'd say. "I got to be on my way, but I do want to try another medicine for Eula B. this week." Then, when he left, Ollie got the wagon ready for Papa headed for town. On those days Ollie and Q.C. did Papa's afternoon chores.

Sickness is a bad trick, hard on everybody.

When Papa got back, it was nearly always night, and he started giving me the medicine right away. Every dose was worse than the last. By the end of July I was wasting away to practically nothing, Mama said. On a Wednesday night, before the revival, Fanny Graham, Ray's mother, saw Mama at prayer meeting. She asked about me. "She's no better," Mama said. "I'm afraid we're getting nowhere with the doctor, too. He just comes and tries some new tonic, and Eula B. still burns up with fever at night, and the pain in her back and bladder is almost more than that little thing can bear." Mama cried when she told me that story, years later, while we was waiting for Toy to be born. We talked about the pain of that summer and the pain of birthing, and Mama says, "It seems sometimes all your pain just rolls up into one big whirlwind and almost sweeps you away." Mama pulled up the corner of her apron to pat the tears away while I listened. She was right.

After that service Mama said, "Fanny asked me what about trying some of the remedies that Quester Franklin used." Quester was the only nigger who lived in the white part of Sumner County. Her folks lived there before her. They was all good niggers. She could cure anything, knew more about herbs and weeds and doctoring than any doctor in that part of the world, Fanny said. "I'd try her, I sure would, Mamie. You got nothing to lose."

That next Friday, Mama did not sit at the kitchen table when the doctor was there. She waited in my room, the front one we made into a sickroom over the summer. I could hear Mattie banging the pots against the sink's edge. Mama sat fidgeting on the chair at the foot of the bed. When the doctor finished with his questions, she did not offer him a glass of tea. She pleated the bottom edge of her apron in her fingers and then made a little twisted case out of one pleat. The worry lines around her eyes seemed deeper, like the dry summer wind was pushing them into her bones.

"Doctor," Mama says, "when is Eula B. gonna get any better? That little thing's been sick going on seven weeks and she's no better, in fact, she's a whole lot weaker. What are you gonna do?" Mama looked him right square in the face. Like she wasn't scared of nothing. I wanted her to be quiet. Don't talk to him like that. Don't you see he's not like us, he won't understand. He'll leave and take his shining with him. Leave him alone, Mama. I feel my throat getting tight now, just like it did then, like I was going to cry and trying hard as ever not to. Mama just got bolder and bolder when he did not answer right away. She looked him right in the eye, and she was tall, like the Fergusons. Stood almost even with the doctor. Then Mama said, "Do you think you can cure her?"

I feel how still that room was. Nothing moving outside and no sound, not even breathing, in the front room. The back door banged shut, Mattie was through with the dishes. Then the quiet in the room folded back around us. I wanted to holler at Mama for coming in and asking questions of the doctor in all his shining and wonder. He didn't say a word, he just shook his head. Finally, he says to her, real slow and sad, "No, ma'am, Mrs. Carpenter, I don't think there's a thing I can do for Eula B. I've tried everything I know. If she's strong, she'll just wear this thing out, but I'm afraid she'll have some damage to her kidneys, damage she'll carry with her for the rest of her life. We just don't have a cure for nephritis yet. Maybe someday."

He sounded so sorry, so hangdog, like it was his fault or something. I wanted to cry and tell him it was all right, I didn't blame him in the least. He done the best he knew. He took his shining and his wonder and left and I hurt for the rest of the summer.

Those leftover days were swept clean of wonderment.

Afterwards, in the week of the revival in late August, Mama asked the elders of the church to pray for me. "Pray for a healing for that tired little body," Mama said. There was a visiting preacher, not the regular one from Sumner County, but one who come up from the Coast and had a funny-sounding name. He said to Mama, "Miz Carpenter, I'll be glad to lead the whole congregation in prayer for the Lord's will for Eula B.'s life. Of course, I can't rightly ask for healing since I do not presume to know the mind of the Lord, but we will pray, of course, we will pray."

Mama said, "When he told me that, sitting in the front pew of the church, soft ladylike hands folded just so across his big fat stomach, I was mad enough to spit." I heard her and Papa talking after they went to bed that night.

"The very idea," Mama said, "that the Lord's will for a little eleven-year-old girl would be anything but healing. I never. Everybody says that this is some fine preacher and some fine

revival, but I won't be going back to listen to no man who
can't see his way clear to pray for healing for a little child."
Mama was mad. Papa tried to quiet her down. But the next
night when he got ready to go—he went early because he led
the singing—Mama was not ready. He called her from the
front porch, holding the door open, making it easy for her to
change her mind. "Mamie, Mamie, you 'bout ready?"

Mama said, "Harlon, I told you last night I'm not aiming
to go back to hear that man. I'm easy about you going, but I
don't need no fancy-dan from down on the Coast telling me
that he don't know what God's will is for a sickly child. You
go and be blessed right along. I'll stay here with Eula B. and
do my own praying."

She done just that, Mama did. But, she was quick to say,
she put shoe leather to her prayers. She went to Quester Franklin's before the week was over. She stopped by the doctor's
office in Richardson on Saturday, the week after she asked
him all them questions in the front room. He told her again,
"Mrs. Carpenter, I just don't think there's a thing we can do
for Euler B."

"Well, then," Mama says to him, "I'm aiming to take over."
I heard her tell Papa, "Harlon, I told him not to come back.
I told him just as sure as I'm standing here before God and
everybody." I hurt when I heard Mama say that. Still in all,
I knew it would be all right.

I cried, quiet-like, over losing the doctor. When Mama did
the doctoring, there was no cloud in the front yard with questions coming out of it, there was just her everyday nearness.
She moved quick and steady with no questions, no hurting in
my heart. There was pain, sure, but it was only the pain in
my flesh, there was no soul in it.

Mama made an exception about Quester Franklin. Most of the
time she didn't have any time for niggers. Good ones or bad

ones, she just didn't have any time for them. She never worked them, never had them in her house. It was not like Mama hated them, like some did. She said to Papa, "Harlon, I'm going to Quester Franklin's tomorrow. I'm going to see if she has any remedies for Eula B. I know I've never used her before, but this feels like the last chance. I know she's a good nigger. Lots of white folks uses her. Fanny Graham, for one. Besides, you can look at her and tell she's got a lot of white blood in her. She's clean and she stays away from the rest of the niggers, and she might be able to help Eula B. I'm going. Tomorrow." Mama didn't usually say hard, finished things to Papa. Only a few times do I remember her saying them. That night, the night that Q.C. disappeared, not many other times.

That long day, in 1925, when we waited for Toy to come, Mama told me all about that trip, all about that summer when I was so sick. It was good to hear what Mama remembered. She didn't remember the swing, or how I slept on the porch on a cot in the daytime right outside her kitchen window.

"I got up before sunrise, Eula B., and I got Ollie to drive me. We wanted to leave before the sun got too high. Lord, I do remember the day as hot, and there was a chance of a storm on over in the evening. Ollie wanted to go, he always was just crazy about you, Eula B. He was better to go to a nigger's house, better than Q.C. Q.C. was always so hotheaded. Q.C. was a Taylor, every bit of the way.

"It took most of an hour to get there. The road was full of ruts and places that could break an axle in a hurry. Ollie drove safe and steady, dodging around them holes as easy as you please. When we drove up in the front, I told Ollie to put the wagon under the tree and wait. He was such a good boy, Eula B. Did just what I told him. Where did I fail Q.C.? He always had the bit in his mouth. I knew Quester was out back. I saw smoke from a wash pot drifting up behind the house. The road circled around to one side, and I saw the shadows from the fire dancing on the back wall. Kind of like ghosts. And I felt funny, I don't guess I'd ever gone up to a nigger's front door before. I didn't want to holler, but I didn't know what to do. I finally just went up on the front porch and knocked. I don't think it was wrong, do you?" Mama said. And I said, "It wasn't."

That was one thing we got settled.

Mama said, "The visit with Quester was not hard at all. After I got over being in a nigger's house, it wasn't bad, Eula B. It didn't smell or nothing, why, you could have your baby there just as good as you could have it here. It was clean, clean. And she knew so much. She asked me all kinds of things. About your pain, your kidneys, about your fever. She asked if your pee was yellow, yellow as a buttercup or yellow as a bitterweed. She said in a low, soft voice that seemed to match her skin, 'That tells me a lot.' We talked for a while. Just as nice as you please. Sitting there in her kitchen, with her, tall and fine-looking, I mean. She didn't seem a bit different. Just a little darker, really, than Gus and Ollie after a summer in the fields." Mama stopped, fluffed the pillows under my head. "She had a big old Bible on the kitchen table, just like Mama's, and a white oilcloth cover, like the one we use. She said to me, 'You want a glass of ice tea, Miz Carpenter?' Now, you know, Eula B., I never had a drink of nothing with a nigger, but I took that glass of tea as quick as you please. She wanted to fix a glass for Ollie, but I said to her, 'No, we'll be going soon and he'll be fine till we get home.' She was just as nice as you please.

"She sat awhile at the kitchen table, running her shiny pink palms—they was so pink, I never knew niggers had such pink palms—down the tops of her legs, pressing out her skirt and apron to her knees. Then after the longest time she says, 'Miz

Carpenter, I think I know what might help Eula B. I've used it, and it always done a lot of good. The time of the year ain't just right, it being summer and all. This works best in the spring, but mebbe we can find some even now. In the woods. If you can find some uva-russel grown in the sun and ain't wilted yet, make a tea out'n that. Brew it strong, roots, stems, and leaves, and give her a glass ever' hour till her pee is the color of the first shoots of jonquils. Then keep the uva-russel tea up for another week or so, a big glass before ever' meal. She should clear of fever and start getting her strength back.' I finished my tea and thanked Quester. I didn't know how much I owed her, whether she had a regular price or what. Quester just stood there for a long time, not rushing. She stood there, still as everything, watching me. Then she said, 'You don't owe me nothing, Miz Carpenter, I'm glad to help. I only charges when I delivers babies. What I told you is just friendly help. I'm glad to do it. Now I got to get back to my washing. I want this hot sun to bleach out my midwifing cloths. I got three babies coming this month.' She made that visit so easy, so natural-like, Eula B. Like I told you before, we wouldn't have no trouble at all with niggers if they was all like Quester Franklin."

That was the day that Toy was born. Mama said, "You remember drinking that uva-russel tea every hour for a week, and before ever' meal for the rest of the summer, Eula B.?"

I tried to, but I couldn't.

"But you do remember, Eula B., by the time school started in the middle of August, you was fit to go?" Mama said.

When Dr. Thompson came to the school that fall, I nodded to him only once and ducked my head. He didn't say anything about me being a big girl or tall for my age. Or anything. He asked how I felt, real polite-like, and says, "How are your mama and papa?" Nothing else. He wore his belt buckle that day. I saw it when I turned to go back to my seat. It did not draw me this time. It lighted the way down the aisle, back to my desk. I went back and sat down between my sister Mattie and Mary Wortham. I sighed. Mattie looked up from her composition book. She was practicing her Jackson script. She put her hand to her mouth and giggled, then cut her eyes up to the front at the doctor, then back at me. There were no questions this time. The star had gone out.

*A*nother summer, when we thought Ollie was coming home, that kind of shining came back to me. Mama was happy then, singing in the kitchen while she shelled peas and canned tomatoes. "I just got a feeling that Ollie's been saving his money so he can see his way clear to make a trip home, Eula B." But Ollie had been gone so long by then, three years or so, I had to stop and think hard to make a face come up in my mind when Mama said "Ollie."

"Oh, he won't look like you remember him, Eula B.," Mama said. "He's been doing a man's work for several years now, and I'm for certain that he's filled out real good and he'll be sunburned from working in them orange groves."

I tried to fill out Ollie's lanky frame in my mind and paint his skin the color of the Indians I saw in *The Indians of the American West*. My teacher, Miss Johnnie Logan, let me borrow it from her desk since I had a brother in California. Ollie's face would not come clear when I tried all these new things on him.

If Ollie is coming home, Toy and Edward Earl ought to be busy in there helping get this place ready. We're all needing to work on that. Mama'll be waiting for me to go to the garden and pick some corn. Ollie always did love sweet corn better than anything. I got to get up and get myself out of bed. This old dead shoulder's got to move.

"Mama, whatever in this world are you doing, scrunched way over here next to the edge of the bed like that? If you don't stop that scooting and squirming, I'm gonna get one of them hospital beds with sides on it and put you in it."

Toy's voice drives away all hope of that other summer. The day Toy was born, Mama and I were getting some important things settled, and Toy interrupted then, too. Mama and me got back to settling those things only when she took sick and I was waiting on her. Toy's got a way of disrupting things. Like now, pushing Ollie and the shining summer away. Coming in the midst of things, always pushing for her way. Getting Gus to do whatever she wanted.

"Mama, we had a real good night. I never heard you once. Do you want to get up and go to the bathroom now? Or do you want to have your breakfast first?"

I try to bring Toy into focus. Why does she talk so loud? She must think because one side of me is dead that my ears are, too. When I try to think about something else, she just talks all the louder.

"Not hungry this morning. I can wait and eat after you get back from the plant."

"Now, Mama, you know we can't do that. The lady from the home care health service will be here today, and if she came and found out that we hadn't had any breakfast, why, what would she think of us? Come on, we'll eat and then we'll get up."

I don't know why Toy always says "we" when she's really

talking to me and telling me what I need to do. That home care woman does the same thing. She always says, "Well, how are *we* doing today, Eula?" Calls me by my given name. Forgets the B. I know people who talk to babies like that, too. Babies may not know enough to care, but it seems silly to talk to an old woman that way.

Toy is struggling, huffing and puffing, to put her arm under my shoulder and then swing her other one under my knees. I could do it myself if I only had a little more time.

"Edward Earl, Edward Earl," Toy bellows in my ear. I'm all bunched up with my butt hanging down in front of Toy's knees and her just hollering.

"We can make it without him, Toy," I whisper just to show her that old ladies can hear whispering. "Watch, I can help."

"Now, Mama, there's no sense in breaking my back when Edward Earl is right here."

"I don't like for Edward Earl to help me," I whisper again.

"I swear, Mama, you never did like him. I know that. But he's not a bad man, Mama. He's no farmer like Daddy, but then, I'm not a worker like you, either." She laughs a little laugh in my ear. "But for the life of me, I can't believe you'd go so far, not even letting him help you up and down. At least you could let him help me save my back."

Right then I need to tell Toy that you learn early who you can count on. I don't ever want to be counting on Edward Earl. You simply cannot count on a fat man, not too many skinny ones either. I think that's a true thing, an important thing. You could count on Gus. He was that kind. Mama always said, "Steady, that's Gus, steady." And he was. Mama said, "If Gus Freeman says a thing, you can count on it."

"Edward Earl, that's okay, I think I've got her." Toy gives in. I push all my weight over to the good side and let Toy hold up the side that drags along like a worn-out slipper, one that came unglued from the upper. Slap-flap, slap-flap, we shuffle down the hall. I am taller than Toy, I need to stand up straight, carry myself proud, like Mama did, not all folded over on stomach fat, the way Toy walks. It makes me grunt to pull up like that. One side comes up nice and easy, the other, where Toy is holding on to me, just drags along, slap-flap, slap-flap.

"Mama, I'm having enough trouble without you jerking on me like that." Trouble—mamas aren't trouble, Toy.

Toy doesn't understand that standing up and holding your-self right is important. It always was to Mama. She said, "Eula B., stand up, be proud of your height. It's the Fer-guson in you." I wish I could make Toy understand that. Maybe it's because she's short and squatty, built just like a Taylor.

"Here we are, Mama. Here's the bathroom. Remember the potty chair the health nurse left? It's right here. Now, let's get ourselves all ready and we'll just have a set. Okay?"

There she goes again with that "we" business. Something wrong with children putting their mamas on a potty chair.

"Let's get our gown and robe out of the way. There now, just set down and relax." Toy giggles a little, steps back, and looks at me. Like she never seen me before.

"Come on, Mama. Let's pee so we can have our breakfast."

"Get out for a minute, Toy." I give each word just the amount of air it needs to get to Toy's ears and no further.

"Well, yes, ma'am." Toy snorts.

That was almost smart-alecky. But then, watching your mama pee is smart-alecky, too. I can hear her outside the door, drumming her fingers in an impatient rhythm. I wait longer than I need to. Since she was a little thing, she's been tapping her fingers, tapping her toes, pushing, wanting more than a body ought to ask out of this life.

"You can come in now."

"Are you sure you're ready." I hear the mad in her voice.

Q.C.'s voice used to do that. Say the right thing but be all iced with anger.

"Yes." I answer them both.

We jerk back into the hall again. Toy steers me toward the kitchen. An oval table made to look like oak sits in a small bay window. The red geraniums have a powdery film of dust on them. It sifts in from the unpaved road just outside. Only plastic flowers could live with all that dust. Toy's voice is still a little tight, holding in her anger.

"Mama, I've got your oatmeal fixed, but you're gonna have to let Edward Earl put you back in the bed. I've got to go on to the plant. We're starting early every day this month so we can get out earlier in the afternoons, since the weather's better."

She's watching to see if I can understand that. She must think I'm a little silly.

"Mama, I want to get back here so I can talk to the home care nurse when she comes. I want to punch in early. Okay?" I hold her there just by looking at her and not answering.

"I've asked Jimmie Lee to come over as soon as she gets the kids off to school. She'll change your gown and brush your hair. Okay?"

I still hold her to her place.

"Mama, I've got to go." I nod slightly. That's just like Toy. Always got to go. That's why she got that job at the plant in the first place. Got to go, got to go. I never did understand why she didn't want to stay at home and help us there. First it was New Orleans with the school trip, then it was singing lessons in Richardson, then the play and costumes, then it was wanting that pretty Yankee soldier boy, then Edward Earl. Don't know the meaning of the word *content*. We could have made it on the farm. And not had to count on nobody that was not family.

That second summer, when we got ready for Ollie, Aunt

Lena came by to help Mama when the cucumbers came in. She told Mama about the Watkins man.

"He's really not a Watkins man, Mamie," she said. "He's got all kinds of tonics and stuff. You ought to see what he's got for kidneys. He's liable to have something good. Maybe something to build Eula B. up. You ought to check on it, Mamie."

Soon as Aunt Lena left, Mama called us. "Q.C., you and Eula B. drive over there this evening and see if he's got any kidney tonics, something to flush out the kidneys. And that's all it's for, you hear me, Q.?" Then she gave him the money from the little cotton sack that she kept in the pantry. It was enough to get the kidney tonic and two sticks of horehound candy. Q.C. made me promise not to tell Mattie. She was always a counter. "I did the dishes last, I fed the chickens twice, I ironed three shirts to your one." A counter, she'd tell Mama if she found out that we spent the change on candy. Couldn't tell Mattie.

There was a lot I didn't tell. That Watkins man, Lord, he was beautiful. Just like the doctor. I just stared at him for the longest time when he was waiting on the lady in front of me. Stared and wondered. His face seemed to have a light behind it. When he talked about the cures he carried in his wagon, he shined even more. When it was our turn, I shoved Q.C. in front of me.

"What's the matter, little lady, don't you want to talk to me? I promise not to bite." Then he laughed, and I felt my face burn just like I had a fever.

"Tell him what we want, Q.," I whispered, watching the toes of my shoes.

"Well, sir, we was wondering it you might have some kidney tonics, something to flush out the system?" Q.C. remembered how Mama had said it, just right. Then he stepped to one side, and I stood directly in front of the Watkins man. Inside the wagon there were shelves of bottles, brown mostly, and lined up, in rows by sizes. Big ones in the center, petering out to small, snuff-sized ones on the ends. I stared at the shelves so that I wouldn't have to look at him. But I could feel the shining, just flooding all over me.

His name was Ned Framington, he said. I found that out later when I met him in town. He asked me to come back to town and meet him, and I did. It was the only time I ever told Mama a lie. But I did. I told a lie for the Watkins man. Men who made you lie you cannot count on. Does Toy know that?

"Mama, you just staring at that oatmeal. Better start eating it before I have to go."

I met Ned on my own. I must have told a fancy lie to get Mama to let me go. Q.C. went with me a piece of the way, but then he went on into town by himself, up to no good, I reckon. He told me good-bye at the corner of the depot. We left the wagon there. He was in a big hurry, I know that, and he smelled of harsh lye soap and some kind of toilet water. I wonder where he got that. Papa never would have used anything like that. Q. put it on after we got in the wagon. Then he stuck it up under the seat. "Q., you got a girl?" I asked him.

"That's for me to know and for you to find out." He did not smile. "And don't you go telling Papa you think so, you hear?" The tops of Q.C.'s ears got red when he was mad or shamed. I don't know which feeling made them red that night. "You be back at the wagon by nine o'clock, and don't you be looking around for me, you hear me, Miss Priss?" Then he turned the corner. I don't know where he was going, probably went into the Elite Café, on Railroad Avenue. Papa said that gambling went on there in the summers, after harvest. Papa knew some men who lost their whole crops at the Elite.

Ned was sitting there, on Main Street, near the alleyway that ran between the courthouse and the jail. A terrible moaning coming from the third floor of the jail. The sound filled the narrow space.

"What is that?" Ned wanted to know.

"Just some ol' nigger, I guess, one the sheriff got for bootlegging, I suppose."

"You're mighty brave, walking down a dark alleyway with somebody you hardly even know."

"I ain't scared of much," I told him. Only of what I was feeling inside, scared, but like a daredevil all at the same time. Ned put his arm around my waist when we got out of the glare from the streetlights, near the end of the alley. I can still feel how easy and fierce his hand felt resting on the top of my hipbone. I wore a little cotton print dress, white with lilacs on it and with sleeves to cover up the red streaks that I always got when I'd been in the sun. Mattie wore long sleeves and a bonnet when she picked the garden. Ned began to move his hand in rhythm with our walking, down my hip when our left feet hit and up toward my ribs when our right feet hit. Up and down, up and down, a kind of warm comfort. When we turned the corner and felt the lights of Main Street on us again, he stopped. Turned away.

"Is something wrong?" I asked.

"Nothing, really, just that I wanted to see you by yourself, I mean really by yourself, without your brother around the corner and half this town watching us. So I could tell you all about me and you could tell me all about you. You know, private, like real sweethearts."

"You could park your wagon out by the church. I could meet you easy there." Lord knows I don't know how ever in the world I thought I could get away from home again.

I did though. I told Mama that I was going to spend the night with Aunt Lena's girls, and I got Q.C. to take me to the end of their road. He jerked the horses to a quick stop. Dust rose up around the spokes. Q. looked straight ahead. "Here you are." He didn't move when I got down off the high wagon seat and reached back to pick up the little sack of clothes I'd brought.

"Well, 'bye, Q.," I said.

He only grunted, didn't ask me why I was getting out this far from Aunt Lena's house, just grunted and popped the reins over the horses' backs. The wagon started up and the muscle in Q.'s jaw pushed out against his cheek.

" 'Bye, Q.," I said again, and waved to his back. "See you sometime tomorrow." He didn't turn around. "Will you pick me up?" I called louder this time. The sacks of feed in the back of the wagon swayed like fat pillows on a giant's bed. Q. still had work to do.

I watched his back get smaller and smaller, a brother so full of anger, somehow lost to me, even then. I hurried down the road, making little dents in the dust with my feet. Aunt Lena's house stood off the road a ways. The sack of clothes fit right under the rock that kept their mailbox standing up straight. They were not expecting me until after prayer meeting. I had plenty of time.

It took only a quarter of an hour or so to go from their driveway to the edge of the churchyard. Salem Baptist called off prayer meeting in the summer. I knew that. Mama should have. He was already there. Waiting beside the wagon. As beautiful as ever. Just shining there in the late afternoon sun. I thought he must have been close to Jesus, he looked so fine. He ran right out to the end of the road to meet me. Said he had been waiting, hoping I would come.

"Like there was any chance that I would stay home." I laughed, looking right up at his face.

He said that I looked pretty, prettier than all the girls he knew in St. Louis. "Mississippi lady," he called me, "I know now why the South lost the war, the men were too busy staying at home taking care of their women." That is exactly what he said. I can hear it now, just like he was telling me all over again. Calling me a Mississippi lady.

The sun just slipped off of the edge of the sky, like it will do in August, and left behind a soft, easy powder, not quite light and not quite dark. We sat on the tailgate of his wagon for the longest time and talked.

"Do you stay here in the wagon at night?" I asked him.

"When I'm traveling, I do. But in St. Louis I have a big house on a paved street and a room where I keep all the bottles and tonics. A separate room to mix them all up before I head out again. You know, you could come to St. Louis on the train." He waited a minute to see what I would say, I guess. "I could meet you at the station. You'd be lost if I didn't. Why, the station in St. Louis is so big that all of Richardson would fit under its roof." I didn't tell him I'd never seen the inside of a train. "One comes through Columbia, I could catch that one," I told him. I saw a picture postcard of it. Papa brought one home when he put Ollie on the train. I wasn't up to making the trip to Columbia that summer. Mama stayed home, too. Neither of us felt like going to say good-bye. Q.C. and Mattie told me all about it. Papa didn't say a word when he came home. Just hung up his hat and went out to milk. That night at supper, Q.C. and Mattie had run on for the longest time about the train and the station, and how Ollie had bought his ticket and who else was getting on. A lady with two children and a picnic basket, going to join her husband who was in the service somewhere out west. She said that she'd give Ollie something to eat. Mattie said she had the fanciest clothes she'd ever seen. And a wide-brimmed hat caught up on one side with a feather and an onyx pin.

"I'd love to see me fixed up like that, one day. Fancy hat and silk stockings to make my legs shine like a reflection on water." Mattie threw her head back in a pose like we'd seen on the picture show advertisements in Richardson. Half-closed her eyes and crossed her hands over her bosom.

Mama and Papa just looked at her.

"You and me and Eula B. probably gonna be stuck here from now on is my guess," said Q.C. He looked down at his plate, pushing the corn on his spoon with a wide, stained thumb. "Mr. Ollie's left us all, with a heap of work and one less soul to do it." He jammed his thumb against the edge of his spoon and spattered the corn over the front of his overalls.

That picture postcard was as close to a train ride as I ever was. But I just nodded like I knew how I was going to work out getting over to Columbia and getting my ticket to St. Louis, finding him in that big station, figuring out how to tell Mama another lie.

"You could help me with my tonics, even learn to mix them up yourself. I bet you're handy as everything, aren't you?"

"Mama says that I am the best worker in the family. If I was big as the boys, she said, I could handle twice what they do." It was bragging, but that is what Mama said. He went on and on about St. Louis, how they had the fair there and some folks made $600 in one week.

"Of course, I could marry you right now before I go back to St. Louis." He told me that right off, at the beginning.

"That would be fine," I answered. He waited a minute.

"No, I will not have any wife of mine riding to St. Louis in a wagon when she could ride on the train." I thought that was so nice. His face was so beautiful and so hurt when I said that I would be glad to ride all the way to St. Louis with him in the wagon. I never heard anybody talk so pretty, so hopeful, as the Watkins man.

When the sun finished falling off the edge of the sky, we plain and simple laid down in the back of the wagon, and that Watkins man began to talk to me in the sweetest way I ever heard, telling me how being around me made him fierce and wild, like a young bull. I knew what that meant, I'd seen bulls on Carroll Bickham's place break down the fences between his pastures when their lowing and bellowing got the best of them. It was that way with him, he said, driving him crazy with wanting me and wishing that I could make him rest easy. It seemed like such a little thing to do for him. To help him with how he felt. He said we were going to get married, that made everything all right. "After all, Mississippi lady, I've already made all the arrangements for you to come to St. Louis. What are you waiting for? This will seal our promises." His voice was as fetching as his looks, and that night it made perfect sense to me. To undress underneath the powdery night sky and wait for him to come and take me away first that time, and then later to St. Louis. It made perfect sense to me. To ease his pain and to seal a promise, it seemed to be right. He undressed slow and easy, showing his pretty body to me, this way and that. I'd never seen a man before, it scared me, seeing that shadow raising up like some wild knife, waiting to create and destroy all at the same time. Made in the image of God, creation and destruction, I thought. He was easy about being naked, took his time. The final light pierced the back of the wagon and made his flesh turn golden as an egg yolk. Shining there in front of me, not a bit ashamed.

The Bible calls it "knowing" a man. Like when Joseph did not know Mary. That was what it was for me. I knew that Watkins man like I never knew Gus. The rough boards of the wagon bed he covered with a blanket. "You'll have to bring some of them pretty Mississippi quilts to St. Louis and show us city-folks how to make them," he said. Then he laughed when he spread the blanket out. I dropped my dress and step-ins to the side, and he pushed them under the blanket to make a pillow for me. Easy and sweet was the way it was for me. I've heard a lot of talk around a quilting frame about the terrors of the first time. Not for me, sweet and easy was the way he took me, telling me all the time he rose and fell above me, "This is so right for us, Mississippi lady, you'll see, so right." And then he exploded within me and let out a cry that shook me and the wagon. Like a shower of stars that comes in August, during the dog days, that's what it was. Bits of light piercing the darkness, filling that whole wagon with shining.

"Hush, you'll have half the county out here with such a noise," I told him. He laughed and reached under the blanket to hand me my clothes. It was over in just about the time it takes for me to remember, but in some ways it was never over. Later I thought, I was fruit, ripe for the picking. He was a wonderful harvester. I have always thought that. I never blamed him.

The weeks after Ned left were the hardest. A summer of
waiting for the mailman. Waiting for Ollie to write and tell
us he was coming. Waiting for Ned to write and tell me to
come on to St. Louis. The letter from Ned never showed up.
I thought maybe he had lost my address and I thought about
writing to him, but I didn't know anything but Ned Framington, Easy Street, St. Louis, Missouri. Soon I knew that
I had to make some plans. My monthly show didn't come
when it was time, and then I had to decide. Mama wouldn't
understand. After all, I did wrong by her when I lied, so this
was one time I knew that I had to do the planning on my own.
She was busy with getting ready for Ollie. When I was sure,
I went down to the river edge to think it all out. Some of
Jimmie Lee's stories on the TV show where a girl in trouble
thinks she will maybe kill herself or some such awful thing.
But sitting there on the river edge, I never did think of anything
so silly. I knew I had a bad trick played on me and I needed

to take care of it. I sat in the shade at the end of the sandbar.
The current had cut a deep hole up under the bank. The river
tried to cut back on itself and all it did was make a big hole.
I watched a leaf, caught there, swing round and round. Sitting
there still as death, making no ripples at all, I saw the big blue
heron in the shallows. The sun shone on his white head and
the water reflected up against his black underside. His twisted
beak was open like he wanted to talk. He stood there quiet as
me, waiting for a silly fish to swim his way. I splashed both
feet and hands in the still water of the hole.

"Hurry, you silly fish, hurry, don't you see that quiet, beautiful thing about to catch you sure as you're born. Hurry!"
The heron turned, looked away, and unfolded his wide blue
wings. A great swell lifted him right up over my head.

Mama and Papa were going to town over on a Saturday
afternoon, taking Mattie and Q.C. "I want to stay home and
just be by myself today, Mama, and get myself ready for
Sunday." See, one lie always makes another. Mattie thought
I was crazy to stay home. Soon as they left, I took one of the
field mules, threw a burlap sack across his back, and got one
of Papa's extra bridles off the nail by the barn door. That old
mule jerked and snorted over a bit, and I had to kick him hard
in the flanks to get him started down the road for Quester
Franklin's house. I was glad I knew the way, no place to ask
a neighbor, they would want to be knowing why it was that
I was heading out to a nigger's house on a Saturday evening.

Her cabin set back off the road and looked like a little knot
stuck up on a red hump there in the summer sun. What if she
wasn't home? I never thought that maybe niggers went to town
on Saturday evenings, too. The road curved off to the left and
then to the right, oozing up to her door, real easy. When I
got to the edge of the bare yard, I slid off the mule and tied
the bridle to a piece of privet hedge. I saw the tree Ollie must

have sat under while he waited for Mama. The house and yard stood still as a picture. I figured she wasn't at home.

I started across the yard in the hot pink dust. Walking soft and easy, trying not to make any marks at all. I didn't want a trace of me being there. It was dead quiet. No dogs. No rooster or hens, just me and the dust.

"What you wanting, girl?"

She about scared me to death. Standing in that doorway, tall as the frame almost, wearing a long white apron, white nurses' shoes peeping out from under it. She had a white rag tied tight around her head. She was yellow-brown, the color of a pecan just out of the hull. And pretty. That surprised me.

"Ma'am?"

"I said, what you wanting, girl?"

"I'm in trouble. I need you to help me get rid of a bad trick."

"Who are you, anyway?"

"You know my mama, Mamie Carpenter. You gave her some tonic for me once, a couple of years ago, when I was sick with Bright's disease. Her and my brother come over here, and you gave her a recipe for uva-russel tea. You remember her, I know you do." My voice was moving up higher and higher. She kept looking hard at me, not moving even the slightest bit. Finally, she nodded. The two white tips of her head rag tipped forward, like a little wave from two doll's gloves. "What kind of trouble you in, girl?"

"Bad trouble. I haven't had my monthly flow since, well, since a long time. That's why I think that I got to get rid of this bad trick."

"You asking me to help you get rid of some baby you don't want?" She stayed so still, like some kind of dead woman, not moving, only her mouth was saying these hard words.

"Is that what you want, girl?"

"Yes'm, that's just what I want."

"You know that's against the law of God and man, girl."

"Yes'm, I know, but there's just no way I can have this baby. He forgot to send for me and Mama would never understand. It would just kill her. With Ollie leaving and Q.C. so mad that he seems like he is going to explode any day now, and Papa so quiet grieving over Ollie going. I just have to get rid of this thing. And you just got to help me. That uva-russel tea cured me before, and I know, Miss Quester, that you can do it again. You got to, please." I was crying by then, and the words kept falling out. I tried to wipe my eyes with the back of my hand, and the mule sweat made them sting, like strong salt in a wound. My stomach started jumping, jerking like a chicken with its neck wrung. The weight of my words pushing all the air out. She just stood there, looking, piercing me with a kind of strong brilliance behind her darkness. Not moving even to breathe. I was stuck to the spot in front of the porch steps, jerking with the end of my crying, feeling the dirt and tears run down my face. Finally she moved just a touch, the little doll-gloves nodded toward me.

"When you want to do this?"

"You mean you will? Oh, thank you, ma'am."

"I ain't doing this for you, I'm doing it for your mama. She got her hands full, and she don't need no little bastard running around the yard and her trying to explain to other white folks just how her little girl done got in to some kind of deep trouble. But you remember this, girl. Delivering living babies is my job." She stopped, like she was hearing her words again for the first time. Then she nodded just a bit again. "But sometime we got to decide which way will cause us all the least trouble. Getting rid of this baby may be the best thing to do. But I don't never want to see you back here. You hear? I don't never touch nobody but once. When you want to do it?"

"Now. Mama and Papa went into town for the evening. They won't even know that I come over here if we do it now."

"Uh-huh. You know how bad this gonna hurt?"

"No'm."

"Well, it is. And you gonna hurt for a while in your body, and they say for a long time in your heart. Me, I don't know about that. I know the body hates to give up on a little one, but we best get at it if you gonna get home before your mama and papa get back."

She looked down at me, still standing in the pink dust.

"Well, come on."

I started up the steps and saw dusty pink outlines of my feet running opposite the grain in the wood. A complete set stood on the bottom step, but the outlines grew weaker and weaker as they followed me up the steps. By the time I reached the porch, they were gone, erased. Maybe I could get by and not leave a trace here after all.

She held open the screen door behind her and led the way through the front room and into the kitchen. The floor of the kitchen sloped slightly toward the back door. I looked down to see if I was tracking in. I couldn't see a trace. Quester took the bucket off the table by the door and headed outside, toward the well.

"I got to boil some water before we start. You get a sheet off that shelf in the other room. Then just try to relax. It don't take no longer to get rid of one than it took to get it in the first place. Ain't near as pleasurable, but don't take much longer. How far along you think you are?"

"Ma'am?"

"I say, how far along you think you are? How long's it been since you been with your man?"

I didn't want to tell her. It wasn't her business. "I just don't know, exactly."

"No sense in being shy with me, girl. Time to be shy was then, with him. I got to know how big a job this is gonna be. Now you remember while I get this water."

I could figure easy. Eight weeks. The days between then and now were just standing there. Waiting to be filled up with his letter and a train ride and a house on the longest street in St. Louis. Eight weeks. I knew.

"Eight weeks, ma'am." I told her when she came back with the bucket full.

"Well, it could be worse. Soon as that water boils, you cover the table with that sheet, strip from the waist down, and I'll get this thing over with. Here"—she handed me a bar of lye soap—"undress and wash your privates good." She turned toward the stove to get me a dipper of water. "So you don't get no infection."

Quester was right. It didn't take any longer to get rid of it than it took to get it. There was no soft powdery August night or Ned making a pillow for my head. Just the hard table in Quester Franklin's kitchen, covered with a nigger sheet, rough and sun-bleached. She put another sheet on the floor and brought another bucket in to catch the blood. She worked quick and never said a word that she didn't need. Mama said that in the Bible the prophet Samuel never let a word of his fall to the ground. Quester was like that. I wanted her to say something to me that would help. All she said was "Lie still, try to relax. This will be the worst part, you can scream if you want to. Folks around here used to hearing a woman scream. It takes screaming to bring them out, one way or the other."

I didn't. I bit my lip so hard it bled and bruised. I thought it served me right, hurting like that, after lying to Mama the way I did.

"You better stay here for a spell, until you get your strength back."

"I got to go back right away. Mama and Papa will be home from town soon, and they'll wonder where I am. I got to go just as soon as I'm able."

Quester made me some pads from a stack of torn sheets and helped me dress.

"Put cold compresses on your stomach tonight and all day tomorrow. Then switch to warm ones the next day. The cramping will last about eight days. Just like regular flow. Your mama'll think that's what it is. Take care that you don't get any infection. That'll kill you. Now, I'll help you to your mule." She put her strong hand under my elbow, guiding me to the door. Outside, the steps held no signs of my dusty footprints. We crossed the yard in silence like two stiff dancers. She gave me a leg up on to the mule's back. I looked down, to thank her. She waved her hand to one side. "And, girl, don't you let me catch you coming back here."

"No, ma'am."

I got home before Mama and Papa, just barely. I was putting the mule out in the back pasture when I saw the dust rising from the main road. Fast as I could I went to check my clothes, to see if they were stained. I crawled into my bed just when Mama came up on the front porch.

"Eula B., you here?" Her voice came down the hall. "Well, you missed a good afternoon in town. We saw everybody from church, and talk is that we'll have a good crowd at prayer meeting to get ready for the revival. And the store had a whole windowful of school supplies already. Be time for school to start before you know it. I got you a present. Look." She walked into my room, holding up a new box of pencils.

When she saw me in the bed, she began again. "Why, Eula B., whatever in the world is the matter? You look awful. You feeling okay? It's not your kidneys again, is it?"

"No, ma'am, I'm cramping something terrible."

"Well, I thought it was about time. Bad as cramps are, one or two babies and you'll never have them again, that's for sure." Mama plumped up the pillows, the way she always did when I was sick. "Why, you've bit a blood blister on your lip, poor thing. I'll get a cold cloth for you." Then she started fussing around the room. "Maybe you need a cleansing, Eula B. Sometimes that will help. The tonic you got from the Watkins man might do the trick." She kept on fussing with the room, picking up and straightening, getting all of life in order. "You never did try that before. This might be a good time for it. Where'd you put it? The tonic from the Watkins man?"

"No, no, I won't take that one, Mama." I started crying when she said that. Cried and cried and told her I couldn't come to the table for supper.

I heard her talking to Papa. "Harlon, I don't know what's got into Eula B. She just ain't been herself lately. She was off all yesterday evening, till nearly dark. Then today, not going with us. Mattie says Eula B. don't talk to her at all, just broods when they're working. That's not like her. Then she told me she was at the river yesterday, but Q.C. said he never seen her when he went to run the trot lines. Now she's been in the bed most of today. Crying with cramping in her stomach. I'm tempted to go to Quester Franklin's to get some female tonic for her. She refused to take the one she bought from the Watkins man."

The silence between Mama and Papa stood for a minute, then worked its way around the kitchen. Papa didn't make any answer. "Not much of a talker, your papa, none of the Carpenters are," Mama always said. "Brooders, they are, not talkers. Q.C.'s like your papa that way."

The cramping and the blood was terrible. Eight days and I could hardly stand up straight. My body cast aside that burden, not because it wanted to. And me, I cast off counting on the shining ones. I could count on Mama and Papa and Ollie. I never was too sure about Q.C. After all, he never even warned me about the Watkins man. Maybe he noticed how he shined. Maybe he thought he was beautiful, too. But mostly, I think he was just too busy wondering if he was ever gonna get a chance at life with Ollie gone and Papa mourning him so. I don't know much about how men think. Papa never said much, and then afterward, Q.C. was gone. And I spent such a lot of my life waiting for Ollie.

The first morning I felt like getting up, I told Mama, "I'm going to make this place look so nice, beautiful even, maybe then Ollie will decide to stay here and not even go back to California. Do you think that'd work, Mama?"

I pulled a kitchen chair up beside hers, careful to sit easy on the rough corn-shuck seat. She looked straight at me and just smiled. She didn't say anything right off, just kept on messing with the green beans she was snapping. When she looked back at me, she had tears in her eyes, and she said, "I don't know, Eula B. It seems he's mighty taken with that California life. We'll see, though, maybe he will see this place with a new set of eyes when he gets home. After all, he's got no people out there, and people, well, being with your people should make a difference. We'll see."

I got Q.C. to go with me down to the edge of the creek. There he cut me fifteen little scrubby plum bushes. I stripped off all the leaves, making a little green trail behind me all the way from the creek. It was a better walk than before, when I knew I wouldn't be getting a ticket to St. Louis. I ran and caught up with Q.

"Wait for me, Q., I'm coming as fast as I can. Your legs're too long for me." This time I kept myself thinking about Ollie and trying to get Q. to talk to me.

"Won't it be fine when Ollie gets home? Things'll be right again. Won't they, Q.?"

I could make it like the man from St. Louis had never been there. I would be well again and waiting on Ollie to swing. It could be like when I was little, when Ollie was there always looking after me. Q. stopped in the path, turning sideways, fixing his eyes hard on me. Twisted, like the crane.

"Hush up, Eula B. You sound just like Mama and Papa. When Ollie was here, when Ollie gets home, when Ollie, when Ollie, and I'm sick to death of hearing about Ollie this and Ollie that. If he's so wonderful, how come he ain't here to help, how come he ain't here busting his butt in the fields every day like I'm doing. How come? Answer me that." Q. let out a big sob, coming from somewhere way down in his soul. "Nobody here seems to notice that I'm still here, working from can till can't. All they see is Ollie's gone and maybe, just maybe, he'll be coming back. Why, we've never got the first letter saying he just *might* come back." When he said *might*, he kicked the rotted stump on the side of the path and stretched out those long legs of his and left me standing in the middle of the path. Watching him go, I called out, "Thank you for cutting the plum branches, Q., thank you."

I sat down on the stump, and the sadness of the summer washed over me in strong, hard waves. The sound of Q.C.'s moan went screaming through my ears and brought back all my troubles. Mama says a body's got to finish grieving before he can get on with living. I finished my first little bit in the path that evening.

I was shed of it by the time I got back to the house. When Ollie got home, it would be better. I got the twine out of the barn and tied the root ends of the plum branches together to make a yard broom. It wouldn't hold together like the ones that Big Mama made. I sat on the front steps and caught up the skinned ends between my legs and wrapped the twine as tight as I could. The sticky sap and the sharp places where Q.C. cut the bottom branches off made my legs sting and burn. Hurting like that was all right, though. I was in charge of what my body was doing now.

It took me most of the morning to get that broom to work. Same kind of broom I used later when I got ready for the renters. Sweeping things clean and putting them in order is good. Bible says sweep clean a wasteland and leave it empty and seven devils'll come in and fill it up. Devils from that summer been pecking away at me ever since.

I swept away all traces of grass and painted the rocks around

Mama's rosebushes white. Rocks from the river made a walk from the road to the bottom of the front steps. Little welcome posts for Ollie.

"Mattie, don't you want to help me get ready for Ollie?" I asked her while she stood at the kitchen window, daydreaming over the dishes.

"No, I got better things to do, Eula B. Besides, I'm saving my hands, as best I can. There was an advertisement in the paper that said you could get a cream that would whiten and soften work-stained hands." She picked hers out of the dishwater. Held them up before the light. "I'm gonna ask Mama to order some for me." She sighed a little sigh and shoved her hands back down into the suds. Mama ordered it, paid for with her egg money.

The preacher's wife gave me a cutting of some dusty miller. Aunt Lena had some prince's feathers seeds saved from the summer before. I planted them along the inside edges of the rocks. The soft gray velvet of the dusty miller drew pictures in my head of the afternoon with the Watkins man. Those bright tall prince's feathers, like some kind of fancy, prancing cock o' the walk, swayed back and forth in the wind I made with the broom's end. Swaying their deep red velvet plumes to the tune of my broom and scolding me for wanting finer things, like living on a paved street in St. Louis.

By late summer I was saving dishwater and bathwater to keep those plants alive. Hauling it out from the kitchen in buckets after every meal and then again at night made my back hurt something terrible. But that hauling kept my heart steady. Sometimes I'd find a little tuneless whistle deep inside that kept me going. Mama reminded me that a whistling girl and a crowing hen always come to some bad end.

Mama and me thought Ollie might be home by late August. Maybe early September. We figured he'd come home between the harvests for them out there because he wanted to have a good long time at home, he said that once, in a card with a picture of the Capitol at Sacramento. Our garden was nearly gone because of the heat and the drought, but Mama saved everything she could in mason jars. Lines of them in the pantry and on the shelves on the back porch. She asked Bob Liggins, that old nigger who lived on Carroll Bickham's place, to make her an oak split basket, with low sides, not like a cotton basket.

"Eula B.," Mama said, "we'll pack up a lot of canned goods for Ollie to take back. If he thinks that he has to go back."

"Mama, they'll just get all broken up in the train ride," I told her. I'd tell Ollie just how close I'd come to taking a train ride myself.

"Well," Mama said, still thinking about those canned goods, "I think I'll wrap them in some of my sheets and quilts. That'll keep them from breaking and give Ollie some good bedclothes for his place in California."

Mama kept on planning. Planning on Ollie staying and planning on Ollie going back. And I just kept on working. After I finished the yard, I went to work on the chicken house.

"Q.C., you'll have to help me on this one," I told him.

"Chickens is for you and Mama and Mattie to tend to, Eula B. I got the big fields all on me now that Ollie's gone." He brought up how Ollie leaving made it so hard on him every time I asked him to do anything. I saw him kick the side of the section harrow once when he was so mad. I laughed, watching him jump on one foot, holding his other one, throwing his hat on the ground, making the dust fly. Tempers made you act that way. Q.C. lived by his temper. That summer we waited for Ollie was Q.C.'s last summer at home. I think that's right. Sometimes the past is so clear, clearer than today really, but then again those times will shimmer above the bedclothes and hang there just out of my reach.

"Mama Eula, you gonna lay in here and sleep all morning? I fixed you a hot bowl of oatmeal. You think you can eat it?" Who's keeping Ollie from coming home? I turn and look at the voice so I can tell.

"Mama had to go on over to the plant and she asked me to come over and sponge you off and get you a clean gown. You ready for me to do that?"

I know. It's Jimmie Lee, interrupting me again. Toy said she was coming. She breaks in because Toy told her to, a nice-looking girl still, slim and a fine head of brown hair, with red highlights in it, like Mama's.

Jimmie Lee gets me to the kitchen table easier than Toy. She stands and watches me eat. I push the spoon into the middle of the gray lump.

"I'm not through yet."

"Well, I'm in no hurry. I got the kids off to school and Darin goes to Head Start today, so I got nothing to do till he gets home at noon."

That was just like Toy's girls, got nothing to do till noon. I saw Jimmie Lee's trailer once. She moved hers to the same trailer park as Toy and Edward Earl after she and Royce separated. They pipe-lined for twelve years before that. Jimmie Lee says her trailer's been around the world, with her in it. When they separated, she had that trailer hauled right down here next to her mama, and that's where it stayed. Jimmie Lee must be on some kind of government program. She doesn't have a job, not even looking for one. I wonder what it is that she does all day.

"You just take your time, Mama Eula, I'd just as soon finish looking at the 'Today' show anyway. They've got a man on there this morning that catches alligators for a living and sells the meat to restaurants in New Orleans. I want to make sure I don't never go to any of them places to eat."

She laughed, and when she did, a puff of smoke blew out of her nose and her mouth. "I'll make a list of them, Mama Eula. That way neither you or me'll ever get caught in New Orleans, eating alligator meat." She laughs and slaps her hand against her knee. I feel myself smile at her. The ash from her cigarette drops on the floor. She spreads it out with the toe of her bedroom slipper. I hate the way she smells like cigarettes. Her kids, too. Those are my great-grandchildren. Smelling like cigarette smoke.

Something is wrong when you have great-grandchildren and you have to eat oatmeal. Not really breakfast. Breakfast is ham and eggs and biscuits and gravy and fresh plum jelly and coffee. Oatmeal is not for real people, either, like trailers. I know what's right and how things ought to be, but I can't figure out where I went wrong. Was it when I started sweeping the devil out of the front yard?

"Jimmie Lee, I'm ready."

"Yes'm, I'll be there in a minute. Show's just about over. I'll get you settled. Since you didn't eat much breakfast, maybe you'll eat an early dinner. Mama left some country fried steak and some potatoes from yesterday to warm up. I wish you would eat early. My stories start about eleven and I sure hate to miss them. When I had to take Darin for his physical at the health office, I missed them for two days. So I bought that little book at the grocery store, the one called *Soap Opera Digest*?" She pushes her voice up at the end to see if I know about her stories. I ought to since she talks about them all the time. Just like those folks was real.

"That was one thing I hated about pipe-lining. I would get so far behind on the stories that I like to have never caught up." She's looking over here to see if I understand. She looks a little like Toy and my mama. Got good hair. Shirley Earlene looks more like Edward Earl. Poor thing. Has that low-slung jaw, makes her face look weak. Mama says a low-slung jaw and big ears mean you can't trust a person. Jimmie Lee has the same habit as Toy and Shirley, leaning against the door-jamb, slumping over on herself. Wears those blue jeans all the time, tight as Dick's hatband. And boots. Never saw a woman I liked in a pair of boots.

"One reason I like coming over here is that Mama and Daddy have that color TV. My old black and white is about gone. Royce is three months behind on his child support. I was gonna buy a new TV before the kids got out of school. Lord, I can't imagine what it will be like in the summer and them with no TV to watch. I'll be crazy by September. I don't know whether to call the lawyer or not?" She slides her voice up again, asking me if I know about calling lawyers.

Her jaw pushes forward sometimes when she pushes the smoke out of her mouth in a little string of white. "I've tried to get him to do something, but he says that as long as Royce don't come back to the state, we can't serve the papers on him and it would cost me more money than I'd get anyway. I'm getting so far behind on my bills, I just don't know what I'm gonna do." Jimmie Lee lights another cigarette to help her worry.

"Well, I think you done about all you're gonna do to that oatmeal. Mama said you don't like it much. The home care nurse said you need to eat that rather than eggs and bacon. Me, I don't care much for neither of them. Me and the kids generally eat honey buns or cereal. That way I don't have to get up before they do. Too, they got a program now that they can eat breakfast at school. If you qualify. I filled out all the papers for them last year when school started. They told me then that I couldn't get the free breakfast as long as Royce was sending child support. I guess the way things look now, they'll be able to get them when they start back in September."

Jimmie Lee is just talking on and on, and I need to get my

good foot over a little ways to make room for the bad one. Then, once I clear a place for it, I can reach across with my good hand and pull the bad foot over into that empty space. With a little time, I can turn around completely and maybe get away from her. I can slide my hand over and push against the edge of the table.

"Mama Eula, what are you doing?" The scraping sound of the table legs moving against the linoleum makes Jimmie Lee sound just like Toy.

"Trying to get away from this oatmeal."

"Here, let me help you." With that, Jimmie Lee comes over and puts her hands under my armpits and drags me up, taller than her. Both of my feet stick straight out in front of me. Like two rag dolls, me and Jimmie Lee back down the hall, her dragging me, both of us looking forward, like we was expecting to see God Almighty coming in the front door. Her cigarette breath blows past my neck and up into my nose. I smell like cold oatmeal.

"Let's just set down here a minute, Mama Eula." Jimmie Lee drags me onto the edge of the bed. "Now, we'll just sponge off all the places that smell. Here we go." She unties my gown, drops it to the floor, and turns around to open the drawer of the bureau. Not a step taken, no wasted motion. That is what Toy thinks is so wonderful about a trailer. "No wasted steps," she says.

"No wasted steps, your mama says that's what good about a trailer." Jimmie Lee watches me while she wrings out the washrag.

"Well, Mama's like that." She twists the rag into a long white rope. "Always trying to get on to the next thing."

"Life in the country has lots of wasted steps. I think that's good. No wasted steps might mean you got no place to live," I tell her.

"Well, Mama was glad to get into town, that's for sure."

Jimmie Lee starts pushing the rag up and down my dead leg. No dirt there to scrub against. "Felt trapped, I guess, out there. No future, just lots of hard work." She rubs the same spot, over and over.

"I never quite understood that, you know, Jimmie Lee, I wonder where I failed her."

"No failing, Mama Eula. Just differences in likes is all I can see." She picks up the towel off the dresser just by turning around. Rubs up and down my side. Nothing wasted.

That summer I waited for Ollie, I wasted lots of steps—to the river to wonder about the tales he would tell about California, to the chicken house to freshen the hay, to gather eggs, to the road to check the mail two, three times a day.

"Eula B., you and Mattie gonna wear the path to the mailbox out. You know the mailman don't get here until twelve-thirty. I've seen you go to that box three times this morning. And Mattie's been twice. Besides, Ollie'll let us know soon as he can when he'll be home. And that hand cream won't come one bit sooner with you looking every fifteen minutes, Mattie. You two going to the mailbox ain't gonna hurry the mailman one bit. When he comes, he'll come. And not until then." But we both kept checking.

I played a trick on myself every day. I pretended, on first waking up, that the letter wouldn't come. That way I wouldn't be disappointed. Seems kind of backward thinking, but it worked for me that summer.

"Mama, do you think we should get one of Mr. Jake Billingsley's young goats and have a barbecue when everybody comes to welcome Ollie back home? Or will fried chicken be enough?" Mattie asked her while we were fixing dinner. "We could have a party to say 'Welcome Back, Ollie.' And maybe I could have a new dress. I saw material in Alford's window when we went in last Saturday. I could cut it out and work on it just a little every day. I could finish it by the time Ollie's train comes." She was watching Mama carefully, scrubbing the lid to a black iron pot over and over.

"I don't know, Mattie, maybe there'll be a little extra egg money. A new dress would be nice for everybody. I know how you love pretty things. We'll see." Mama sighed a tired sigh and I hated Mattie for her asking.

Mattie was fretting not because Ollie was coming home, but because she was hoping she'd be leaving, too. Hoping that Horace Bigham was going to ask her to marry him.

"Mattie's like an old sore-tailed cat," Mama said, and she laughed. But then she looked at Mattie and shook her head, kind of sad and slow, and smiled. Mama made it through Mattie's fretfulness and my pain and Q.C.'s anger that summer on the hope that Ollie was coming home.

Even Papa talked a lot for him. He bought a new matched pair of mules early in the spring and all summer he talked about how Ollie was going to love working them.

"They work good," he said, "Ollie'll be proud to work them. Work with just a touch to the line." Then he shook his head and smiled, drawing up a picture in his mind of Ollie plowing with the new team.

It was that matched pair that opened up the trouble with Q.C. like lancing a boil. Papa was just going on and on one night. Going on about those mules and how proud Ollie would be to drive them when he got home. It even made a picture in my mind, seeing Ollie, like before, working in the garden, then coming in to rest, just like nothing had ever happened. Papa and me could see it.

Suddenly Q. C. threw down his big spoon.

"I'm damn tired of hearing about Ollie and how he'd be so proud to work them mules—if you are so sure that he'd like to work them so good, then why in the hell don't you get him here doing it? It seems to me that he's off in California making all that money which we ain't seen one penny of—and we're here working our butts off getting ready for him to come back and he won't do nothing while he's here but be Mr. Bigshot. Well, I'm sick and tired of hearing about this whole thing. You can tell your precious Ollie to get his butt down in that stinking bottom first thing in the morning. Sun's so hot that your hair sticks to your hat and the dust so bad you can't hardly breathe. Yeah, get fancy-boy Ollie to help mow that field and help us haul up that last load of hay for the winter." He stopped eating his tomato gravy and biscuits and stood up. The big spoon shined right in the middle of Mama's white tablecloth. The tomato gravy moved off the edge of the spoon and made a spot against the white growing slowly into a big red patch with ragged edges. Q.C.'s fury knocked over his chair and he stumbled forward against the table. All the tea in the glasses moved in a wave, toward the sides. Nobody said a word. Q. turned and left. The stillness stayed on, hot and rigid.

The heat of Q.C.'s anger stung more than the heat of the Mississippi August sun. It scorched me and Mama worse than an iron on silk. But Papa, he just sat there, listening to Q.C. go on and on. He never answered Q.C., never said one word against Ollie. He just let the blast of Q.C.'s words hit him hard, like so many bullets. When it was over, the whole room felt scalded, a pig on the first cold day in autumn. I looked at Papa. He just folded up the dishtowel he always used to wipe his mouth, pushed his chair back from the table real careful, like he was not wanting to make a sound. He stood up, slow, like he was in a dream.

"That was a good supper, Mamie. I'm sorry we spoiled it."

He left the room and went out on the porch, I guess looking for the hot trail that Q.C. left. Me and Mattie started clearing the table, quiet, like nothing had happened. Mama sat, not moving, at her place.

"Mattie, I'll wash, you keep on saving your hands. That cream will be here soon, for sure. You put away the food, Mat, and Eula, you dry," Mama said into the quiet kitchen.

"Papa didn't do nothing to spoil that meal. It was all Q.'s fault. Him blaming Papa for Ollie leaving and blaming us for being glad he's coming home. Nothing about that makes sense." I dried that same plate, over and over again.

Mama just looked down into the dishwater. The remains of the tomato gravy turned it pink. Mama's tears made little clear circles in the pink sea.

"You gonna have to rub salt in the tablecloth, Eula B., and hang it in the sun tomorrow. Only way to get out tomato stains and blood."

"Yes'm."

Mattie and me went on to bed soon as we finished in the kitchen.

"Q. makes me so mad," I whispered to her. "Always mad, wishing things were different, making Mama and Papa hurt." Hot tears rolled down my face, remembering their faces at the table. "I'd like to punch him in the stomach, make him hurt a little, and him always calling me 'Miss Priss.' " Mattie didn't say a word. She turned on her side, kicked her leg out from under the sheet, and let out a little snort.

"Eula B., sometimes you can say the dumbest things. You just don't understand a thing." I didn't answer, and in a minute she was breathing steady, deep, dreaming about soft white hands, I guess. I wonder if she could understand about a Watkins man.

Later on that night I heard talking in the front room. Q.C.'s bed was in the corner.

"Q.C., Q.C., son, I want to talk to you."

"Huh," he grunted.

"Son, come on out onto the porch, where it's cool. I want to talk to you."

"Yes'm."

They settled on the porch swing right outside my window. The creaking of Q.'s weight against the lesser sound of Mama's. The swish-swish of her slipper against the wooden porch floor started the creaking chain.

"Son, tonight at supper, that was a terrible thing. You got no right to talk to your papa that way. He's got nothing to do with Ollie leaving. It like to have broke his heart, too. More'n anything else he wants him back here, helping us. But that's not the big danger. The worse part is what this thing's doing to you. You remember how in the story of the prodigal, it's not the sin of the boy who leaves that can't be forgiven. It's the sin of the boy who stays home and hates his brother. That's a terrible thing, Q.C., to hate your brother. It's as bad to break your papa's heart. Now, I want you to go back to bed and think on these things and get your heart right and make up with your papa in the morning. I'll have no strife at the breakfast table, you hear me, Q.C.?"

I guess he nodded in the moonlight, for Mama didn't say any more. What he did with all that she said, I don't know. Too much came in between.

The first big thing, I guess, was the letter. We'd heard from Ollie, for time to time before, but only postcards. Wonderful picture postcards of California. A place that really didn't seem as though it was. But if Ollie got home from there, then I could believe that there really was a place called California. A place had to be if somebody could come back from there.

That morning Mama called me and Mattie early.

"Get on up, girls, there's a real promise of rain before noon and we've got lots to do. I think this will be one of the last makings of squash and I want to can just a few more jars before I make squash pickles. Hurry on out to the garden and pick everything that's as big around as your thumb."

Me and Mattie rolled out of the bed and pulled on the cotton wash dresses that we laid on the chairs the night before. Okra stalks, tall as my head, made my arms itch when I walked down the rows. The creamy white trumpet blossoms opened wide against the sun. Archangel trumpets announcing a brother's coming home. Mattie slapped and twitched at the flies, like a high-strung mare.

We finished picking the whole garden and had the canner under steam by the time the mailman got there. Mama let Mattie go to the mailbox.

"You brought it in yesterday, Eula B. Now it's Mat's turn. Besides, her fretfulness makes the kitchen too small. I'm gonna use every chance I can to keep her moving."

We heard her whooping, hollering, running back from the road.

"Mama, Mama, it's here! We got the letter from Ollie. Can I open it? Please, Mama, please?" She didn't mention the hand cream.

Mama dried her hands on her apron and touched them to the sides of her hair. She did that when she got a letter. Wanted to look her best when she read important news. I thought she looked beautiful, standing there in the middle of the kitchen, the dampness from the canner's steam making her skin shine. She had good skin, Ferguson skin, she called it. The heat brought the color to her cheeks. Back then, her hair didn't have a speck of gray and it still had soft red highlights. She straightened her shoulders and pulled herself up from her ribs, standing tall. Mama always carried herself proud. She walked over to the doorway and called through the back screen to Mattie.

"Don't open it yet, Mat. We'll wait till Papa and Q.C. come in for dinner. That way we'll know together."

I about died. Mama took the letter from Mattie. Then she situated it right square in the center of the white oilcloth. There it lay.

> The Harlon Carpenter Family
> Route 6
> Mount Hermon, Mississippi

"Now, you girls, get back to work." Mama started slicing a few more squash, making each little yellow circle exactly the same thickness. She made a silent sigh with her shoulders, dried her hands, and went to the pantry. Pushing the curtain back with her shoulder, she brought in the big salt dish and set it in the center of the table. Then she leaned the letter against it. Like the signboard in church that announced the numbers present this week, last week, and last year. Me and Mattie and Mama spent the rest of the morning waltzing around that kitchen, watching the letter from every spot in the kitchen.

Papa and Q.C. were late, some kind of trouble with the hitch on the single tree. Q.C was going to ride one of the mules into town after dinner to take the broken part to the blacksmith. Papa came in first. I heard him climb the back steps. He was slow today. He walked to the shelf that ran along the wall beside the back door. A basin of water stood there with a piece of Octagon soap and a shred of a white towel. Nearby was a pitcher with the rinse water. Ever since I could remember, I'd been the one to fill both the basin and the pitcher at 11:30 when we had folks in the field. "It's too hot to come in and eat if you don't wash off in some cool water," Mama explained to me every morning when she sent me to the well.

Papa always washed the same. He took off his straw hat and laid it on the far end of the shelf. Then he bent over at the waist, closed his eyes, and filled both hands with the cool water from the basin. He splashed it all over his face and neck, sputtering as he did. Then he washed his hands, fronts, then backs, while his face and neck dripped. He wet his collar and the shoulder straps of his overalls.

"Keeps me cool while I take my nap." He told me once when I asked him why.

Papa was careful with water. After he finished, he carried the basin to the edge of the porch and poured it out on one of Mama's dahlias that grew there. Papa worked his way down the dahlias, watering one each day until he reached the end of the row. Then he'd start next to the steps again. Mama said he carried water for his mama when he was a boy and he knew how to make every drop count.

Papa never used the towel that Mama put out fresh every morning. With a dripping hand he'd grab the bandanna handkerchief that he kept in his back overall pocket and rub his face and neck with it. Poking one corner back in the pocket, he'd let the damp rag fly behind him for the rest of the afternoon.

Q.C. wasn't so careful. He splashed water everywhere. Didn't use the soap, either, so when he used the towel for one washup, I had to get a clean one. The red clay streaks left by his hands and neck had to be bleached out with salt in the sun, just like the tomato gravy. Q.C. always left splotches behind him. Seemed to bruise and scald everything he touched.

Took them both forever to get in for dinner that day. Mama and Mattie and me had everything ready. No last-minute scurrying around to find the salt or sugar or syrup. We got seated and Papa said the blessing. The same one he always used.

"Bless, O Lord, these gifts to our use and us to your service, for Christ's sake, amen." Mama said it was a Methodist blessing, for his mama was a Methodist before she married his papa. She taught him that one. Papa said, "for Christ's sake" like it was one word.

Mama started the meal. "I guess you see we got the letter from Ollie today. Guess now we'll know which train to meet. I know that Eula B. and me'll be able to get over to Columbia this time." She laughed and started passing the fried okra around. Crisp brown circles floating in the white bowl. "Won't leave the traveling just to you three." She laughed, Papa grunted a little, but Q. never even smiled. We sat around the table, passing the bowls of vegetables, wondering who was going to say "Well, let's open it." I kept watching it, growing there against the salt dish, drawing me toward it like there was some leftover light from California trying to get out and shed itself on this Mississippi dinner table.

When Papa finished, he reached over the bowls, still steaming, and picked up the letter. With one motion he grabbed the letter and pushed his chair back. He lifted one heavy work boot up on the opposite knee, scooted down in his chair to get comfortable. Papa wasn't much of a reader. He was a worker. Had only eight years of schooling, on and off, but he could read good when he worked at it.

We all sat, hardly breathing, wanting him to hurry. The whole summer of waiting was there in his hand, just within reach.

Papa slid his knife under the fold, and pulled out several pieces of lined paper. I saw Ollie's big, jerky hand sliding up and down the lines. His last year at school, he did a report for the teacher and he got me to copy it over for him.

"You've got such a pretty hand, Eula B.," he told me.

Papa started, shifting the pages around to get the best light.

" 'Dear Mama, Papa, Mattie, Q.C., and, of course, Eula B., I can't tell you how good California is. The last three harvests I have worked both shifts. Not much time for sleeping but I figure that I can make up on my sleep when there's not this kind of money to be made.

" 'Down the valley a ways there is some land that is soon to be put up for sale. It is just the kind of land to plant orange trees on. I am putting aside every extra bit, hoping I will have enough set aside to pay down and get them to hold me a piece by January. If the price is what I heard it was, I just may have enough. Think of it. Me owning some of this gold mine.

" 'I been pretty lonesome these last few years, but the money I got saved and the land I'm gonna buy will help me forget that, I guess. I have met a few families that come out here just like I did and most of them are doing okay now. I hope I will be as lucky.

" 'Since I'm saving every penny I can so I can make a bid on 130 acres in the valley, I'm not going to make it home this summer. This trip costs me so much and I just can't spare it at this time. Too, I'd miss all that time in the fields. Maybe I can come in the winter, after the last harvest. I don't know. If I get the property, I will start right away clearing it and getting it ready to plant trees.

" 'I'll work for somebody else for a few more years until my trees start bearing, but as Granny Taylor used to say, I'll be in high cotton then. Or maybe it will be high oranges. HA!' "
He printed that big in the margin, I saw it when Papa turned the page a little to one side to catch the light better.

The rest of the letter went on like that, silly talk, I thought. None of it important. All that mattered was "I'm not going to make it home this summer. I'm not going to make it home this summer."

Papa finished reading the letter, placed it beside his plate, and headed for the front porch. After dinner, he always took a nap in the porch swing. There he slept for a while, waiting for the noonday heat to slacken up before he went back to the fields. Mama started to clear the table without a word. Q.C. pushed his chair back, rough against the floor, threw his napkin in the seat, spilling a big pitcher of tea when he did. He stomped out the back door, trying to get out of the way of Ollie's news. I didn't see him again until breakfast the next morning.

I left Mama and Mattie to do the dishes. Out in the yard, the hot tears came down my face without asking. They plopped into the dust of the yard. As each one hit, it caused a little explosion, just like the one that was going off in my insides. In the shade of the big live oak, I turned and looked back at the neat flower beds and the river-rock-lined pathway waiting for Ollie's homecoming. There was a summer of work and waiting just lying out there under the heat. I ran toward the swing. Ollie's swing. Taking the wooden seat in both my hands, I shoved it with all my strength against the trunk of the tree. Thunk. The seat shouted out as it hit. Carelessly the swing moved back and forth. Back and forth, some ghostly swinger letting the cat die. Maybe I was the cat, dying out there under the tree with Ollie not coming home.

Finally the swing came to a standstill and the August heat held everything quiet. I hated that yard, that summer of working, getting everything back like it was supposed to be, getting the Watkins man worked out of my system, fixing things so nobody could tell. I couldn't stand being in that yard another minute. I ran, stumbling, to the river's edge. A wet wool girdle of air wrapped around me, choking everything good right out of me. I shouted to the log at the bend in the river, "Swings come back to where they started, brothers don't." There was no echo, just the sound pushing itself across the flat, still water.

"*M*ama Eula, you think you gonna be able to eat dinner a little early today so I can get back to my stories?" Jimmie Lee's voice drifts into the air above my bed.

"I guess so, only I'm not very hungry now. A glass of milk will be fine, or buttermilk if you got some."

"I'll check, but I don't imagine there is any." Jimmie Lee shudders when she says it. In a minute I hear her checking in the icebox. She's back in no time.

"Here you go. I found a little carton way in the back of the refrigerator. For the life of me, I don't see how you can drink that stuff."

I work to hold my hand out to take the glass.

"Don't you want me to hold it for you?" she asks, looking toward the door, her ear cocked toward the opening, trying to hear the TV.

"No, I can manage just fine with my good hand," I tell her.

When she leaves to go back down the hall, her bottom

twitches like two pigs caught up in a feed sack. She's more like the Fergusons, though, than any of the rest of them. Fine skin and good hair. "Jimmie Lee, looks like you won't run to fat the way the Taylors or your daddy's folks do." I want her to know I'm noticing her.

Jimmie Lee looks back over her shoulder. "Yes'm, I guess so." She agrees.

I can't think about that too long or I'll spill this buttermilk. Got to work hard, keep from spilling it on the quilt. Buttermilk on the quilt would sure make Mama Two mad. She was mad at me seemed like ever since me and Gus married. Things got off on the wrong foot early with her. I never knew just why. Maybe it was moving in with my mama.

"Jimmie Lee," I call her, good and loud.

"Yes, ma'am," she answers.

"You can come get this glass directly. I'm 'bout through."

"Yes'm."

I hate this hollering back and forth, up and down this little crackerbox. Only a thin wall between me and the living room. I know she's not coming till the next commercial, so I got to think hard about holding this glass straight upright. No buttermilk on this quilt. That's got to be the first thing on my mind.

Me and Gus moved in with Mama right after we got married. Had to do with Mattie and Ollie and Q.C., and Papa, too. We moved in because of all of them.

"All right, Mama Eula, they're selling soap right now, so I can get you settled for your nap. You ready to go to sleep?"

Jimmie Lee has that way of shouting at me, must have learned it from Toy. Folks used to talk that way to the Billingsley boy that wasn't quite right. I try to look at her real steady to see can I tell what she's thinking. Jimmie Lee ain't held down by anybody's look. She's too busy straightening and pulling and yanking these covers this way and that. She stands up right over me, plumping up pillows behind me.

"There, that should do it. Now you call me if you need anything. You hear?" She fixes the cover just like Mama, and her voice is quiet now. I do need something, if only I knew what.

I watch Jimmie Lee twitch out of the room. Now to roll over on my good side. Not too comfortable. I have to stay a little uneasy so I won't fall asleep.

Moving in with Mama started the trouble with Mama Two. Now, I know that it didn't start all the trouble, just the little bit of sorrow that went along with her. Real trouble started that summer with the Watkins man when Ollie didn't come home. The end of that summer dragged on, with me and Mama and Papa living like shadows. Q.C. was there, like a loaded gun, among us. We went through all the motions, plowing, haying, picking, shelling, and canning. But there wasn't any life in any of us. Except for Mattie. She fretted and worried just like she had before the letter came. Mattie's hand cream arrived only a week later. And Mama bought her the material at Alford's. A light green cotton to pick up the color in her eyes and set off her auburn hair. She used it as a going-away dress. Each night, after we finished the dishes, she'd rub the cream up and down the backs of her hands, right out to the end of her fingers. Then slowly, with her thumbs, she'd push the cuticle back on each finger, one at a time.

"They say you can tell a lady by her hands, Eula B.," she told me. "I'd like to have fingernails an inch long. Never shell another pea as long as I live." She held her hand out to the light. A thin half-moon showed white at the ends of her fingers. "There's a place in New Orleans I read about, where even a man can get his fingernails done." She shook her head, unbelieving. "I saw it in the paper." She flopped down on our bed. "Oh, Eula B., don't you ever want anything different?"

"I wanted to go to St. Louis once. They had a world's fair there. People made six hundred dollars a week, they said."

"I don't mean things like money, I mean like for your whole life to be different somehow. Romantic, I guess." She rolled over in the bed and faced me. "Do you ever think that way, Eula B.?" I don't know what I told her.

Mattie kept on fretting, and the biggest part of it came from hoping that Horace Bigham would ask her to marry him. She spent most of her time before prayer meeting on Wednesday and half the day on Saturday fretting over her hair, pinching her cheeks so that they turned pink.

"If you stay in the kitchen and help with these preserves, your cheeks'll get pink all right," Mama said.

They fussed a lot that summer until Horace Bigham came over one night after prayer meeting. He rode up right soon after we got home. Tied his horse to the rope of my swing. Papa was just coming up the steps from unhitching the team.

"Mr. Carpenter, Mr. Carpenter." His voice sounded wavy, like he might be talking underwater. Papa stopped at the top step. Mattie and me were in the front room, hunched down by the window. We could just see them, meeting and shaking hands in the darkness of the porch, moving in stiff shadows toward the swing.

"Hello, Horace, come on up on the porch. I was just about to sit a while 'fore I went in for the night." They both sat on the porch swing. Papa must have started it moving. In just a minute the squeaking started.

Papa's voice started up, with a little drumbeat of creaks from the chain against the metal hook in the ceiling. We could hardly hear Horace. Then Papa said, "Horace, you got a way of earning a living for Mattie?" She put her hand on my arm, closed her fingers down tight against my flesh.

"Yes, sir, Mr. Harlon, I'm gonna farm halves with my papa and he's gonna leave the place to me since I ain't got nothing but sisters." Mattie's new-grown fingernails bit into my arm.

Papa was quiet for a minute. "You know, Mattie's a good girl, Horace, and she's not afraid of work. Her mama taught her that, but she ain't no field hand. None of the Carpenter women have ever gone to the field." The creaks from the chain took over all the space on the porch. Me and Mattie was scared to breathe inside. "She's no slacker, but she's no field hand, neither." Mattie's grip made my fingers go numb, like now, after a stroke. "I don't want you to think Mattie can go to the field."

"No, sir, Mr. Harlon, I don't think that at all. Mattie wouldn't go to the field. No, sir."

Papa thought for a long time again. Mattie's breath was coming in little patches, right above my shoulder. After a while the creaking stopped. The swing gave a little moan, and Papa stood up. Horace must have got up, too, for the swing groaned a second time. We could see the shadows moving toward the steps. The light from the lamp caught both of them and hung them there, looking at each other, just for a minute. Behind their heads, some lightning bugs made sparklers in the night air over the clean front yard.

"Well, Horace, I suppose you can marry Mattie. Ain't nobody else asked me this week." He laughed and swatted Horace on the shoulder. It wasn't like Papa to joke. Maybe he laughed so he didn't have to cry. Then he walked over to the window and said, "You girls can come on out on the porch now. We're finished."

At breakfast the next morning Mama asked, "Well, Mat, how does it feel to be almost married?" Mattie just tucked her head and smiled. Below the edge of the table, I saw her cross both her hands, in a little arch. Then she laid them careful on her knee.

That was early August that summer of the Watkins man and Ollie not coming home that Mattie decided to get married. The year the big war was over. She said she wished she could get married the last night of the revival.

"There'll be the visiting preacher, and special music and the church will be packed out, Mama." We were shelling peas on the back porch when she asked. Mattie shelled with her thumbs now, not using her nails. Mama just kept on shelling, with me watching her. Finally she sighed.

"I don't know, Mat, I'll just have to see."

Ollie not coming home brought some kind of shame on Mama. She didn't stand up as straight after that. I asked her if something was wrong. "Mama, do people think bad about us because Ollie's gone off and not come back?" She thought a long time about that one, too. She answered me slow and careful. "I don't know how other folks judge it, Eula B. For me, it's just an empty place at the table and in my heart. The shame that comes is not from what other folks think." She kept on with what she was doing for a minute. Then she looked out, far into the yard, like she was seeing something that I couldn't see and seeing it clear for the first time. "I just keep thinking that I failed him somewhere, that's all." Young'uns can sure feel like your failures, I know.

That night in the bed I tried to tell Mattie what Mama had said. "You understand that, Mat? Mama saying that she failed Ollie. I don't see how Mama ever failed nobody, do you?" I know a little better now.

Mattie didn't help at all, she just told me, "Eula B., you go on so, fretting about all kinds of things that don't even concern you. You need to shut off all that thinking and get to sleep. You know we got work to tend to tomorrow." I was sure the trouble was with Ollie, and Mattie wouldn't help me figure it out.

Mama always said that she could tell what was going on with me and Ollie, that she could read us like a book. "Mattie's a little harder for me, though, and Q.C. is a real puzzle. I never know what's going on in his mind. Until he gets good and mad, then everybody on this side of the county knows what's got him stirred up." Like that time Papa got to bragging on Ollie. It wasn't long after that, must have been soon after Horace's visit, in August, the summer of the Watkins man, Mama, Mattie, Papa, and me had all gone to prayer meeting. You couldn't keep Mattie away, with all her primping and fixing up. Afterward, Horace would drive her home, the long way. Q.C. hadn't been much on going to prayer meeting for a long time. He always used Ollie for an excuse.

"Since I'm the only hand around here now, I'm too tired from working all day to get cleaned up and go somewhere on a weeknight. Besides, I fall asleep when the preaching gets to going."

Papa hadn't liked it much that he quit prayer meeting, but Mama said that since he agreed to go on Sunday, maybe it was better to leave well enough alone.

"After all, Harlon, he is seventeen years old, going on eighteen." Papa agreed.

When we got home that Wednesday night, it was still as death. The only movement was the lightning bugs flashing in the dark, hot air hanging close around the house. Not a lamp on anywhere.

"Q., Q.," Mama called from the porch. "Maybe he and Mack's boys went frog-gigging." She said it like a question.

Papa grunted, then, "Anybody's got energy to frog-gig can go to prayer meeting."

"Q.C. isn't one to go off without telling somebody where

he's going. Anyway, I don't know, he told me that he was going to bed early since he was tired." Mama was arguing with somebody who wasn't there.

"Maybe Ross and Seth came by after we left for church and asked him to go with them. A boy's got to do a little going every once in a while," Mama decided. I heard Papa grunt again, drop his work boots and, in a minute, I knew he was asleep.

Mama couldn't go to bed so fast. She always brushed her hair. One hundred strokes. She would stand in front of the dresser, unwind her hair, and brush, brush, brush. That was the time she talked to Papa. Lots of times, Papa's snoring would be going strong and Mama'd still be just talking. That night, I could hear her plain.

"Harlon, something just don't feel right. I'm gonna plait my hair and sit on the porch for a while till that boy gets in. I just don't feel right about him leaving without telling us where he was going. You go on to sleep and I'll wait for him." She didn't have to tell Papa that. His snoring was making a soft background for her talking already. She sat there long after Mattie and Horace got home. I went off to sleep that night with the creaks of the porch swing chain keeping time with the brush-brush of her slippers.

Next morning, the sound of the screen door closing woke me up. Q.C.'s home, and it's daylight, I thought. Morning, and he's just now getting in. I waited to hear Mama light into him. The kitchen noises started. No talking. In a few minutes the back door slammed. There, now he's going to get it. She's sent him out for water or wood or eggs or something before she starts talking. Mama'd do that. Put off your talking-to by a chore so she could get her thoughts lined up against you.

I waited for a long time. Hearing the sound of the day's beginnings, familiar as Mama's face. Papa must be milking. A second slam. I got up, started toward the back door, heading for the outhouse. I stopped in the middle of the hall when Mama started talking.

"Harlon, I sat in the swing all night. He never came home. I never saw a wagon or anything pass the house. No sign. Where could he be?"

"Now, Mamie, there's no reason to borrow trouble. If he went with Seth and Ross and decided to stay with them, he'll be on in a little bit, and you can fuss at him real good when he gets here. He'll be in soon, he knows we got to work that lower hay field today. I told him so before I left last night. He knows we got a big day. He'll be on directly."

"I hope you're right. He's just such a puzzle to me the way he flares up so white-hot mad, I don't know, I just don't feel right about him. I told him to make things right with you and he just can't seem to do it." She waited for a minute. "You ready for coffee?"

I couldn't see in the kitchen, but I knew what was happening. Papa nodded. Mama got his big white mug with the green stripe around the top off the shelf. As she poured it full, she said, "Cream and sugar?"

Why did she always ask that? As long as she had been married to Papa, he always took cream and sugar in his coffee, but Mama always asked, "Cream and sugar?" And Papa always answered.

"That'll be fine."

Then Mama ladled some of the cream off last night's milk and the coffee turned a rich brown color. She'd set the mug on the edge of the table while she got the sugar bowl out of the pantry.

"Always put the sugar in the pantry when you finish at night, Eula B. That way you won't have ants on your table in the morning."

No talking now, only the sounds of Mama in the pantry, Papa sitting in his chair at the table. I loved to listen in on Mama and Papa in the morning. It felt safe and comfortable between them. I started toward the kitchen door when I heard Mama, muffled in the pantry.

"Harlon, it's not here."

"What's not, Mamie?" he asked.

"My egg sack."

"Look again, Mamie. The girls probably pushed it to the back when they put things away last night. Just look again."

"I did, Harlon, and I'm sure. It's not here. It's gone."

She sounded just like the angel and Mary Magdalene. He is not here, he is risen. So definite. So sure.

"Mamie, are you sure?"

"Of course I'm sure."

Papa sighed, a long sigh. "Has there been anybody passing by that you let in and fed lately? Anybody who could have gotten it?" Some blame edged into Papa's voice. He was always fussing at Mama for taking in just anybody. Especially when times were bad. "Mamie," he'd say, "you got to be more careful."

"Harlon, it was here last night before I went to prayer meeting. I came in and took a little extra to church because of the special collection for the cost of the revival." I could hear her better now. She was standing in the middle of the kitchen. "I know that it was here when we left." She waited. Then, "It wasn't much, most of the hens are molting. Can't have been more'n twenty dollars. He can't get far on that."

"Shut up, Mamie."

I try to pull the quilt up over my ears right now. I don't want to hear Papa say that. He never talked to Mama that way. But that morning, when I was standing in my shimmy-tail in the middle of the hall, he said, "Shut up," and Mama started to cry. It was that terrible summer. I swept the front yard clean and made a waste place and seven times seventy devils filled it up.

We didn't hear from Q.C. Mama kept saying, "He'll get over his mad and write us a card. Then we'll know what that rascal's up to." Then she laughed, not a real laugh, and looked at Papa. He never did say a thing. That fall, he hired Seth and Ross, my uncle Mack's boys, to help with the haying. Papa talked even less now.

"Maybe he talked when he was in the fields, talked to the mules to get things straight. Mama talked to herself when she thought she was in the house alone. I sure used to talk things out a lot after Gus died." I want those words to stay right there in front of me so that I can decide what I need to do with them.

"Be there in a minute, Mama Eula," Jimmie Lee calls back down the hall.

Right after that, Mama and Papa asked Horace over for supper.

"I'm not changing my mind, Mattie," Mama said, "but it'll have to be just a simple wedding, in the front room, one with just the families."

"Mama"—Mattie sounded like somebody scalded—"you promised."

"That's all I'm saying, Mattie, I'm not up to no show in front of the church," Mama said.

Papa took care of telling Horace at supper. "Family, Horace, is all. No cousins and everything. Just your mama and papa, Mamie and me, Eula B. That's all we can manage if you and Mattie want to be married this fall."

Mattie cried after Horace left that night. But she wanted to be married even more than she wanted a fancy wedding at the church. So on the Sunday before the revival started, she married Horace in the front room. The prince's feathers I planted for Ollie glowed bright red and orange on the table. I made a bouquet out of some summer roses and the dusty miller. Used up the flowers I meant to meet Ollie with on a wedding to lose a sister.

That next week, me and Mama moved Q.C.'s bed out and stored it in the shed next to the chicken house. Mama took an old bedcover and wrapped the head and foot.

"Belonged to my Ferguson grandmother, Eula B. She was Mary Taylor, fine-looking woman. She died when you was two." Mama wrapped it carefully. "It's good wood, Eula B., I don't want no damp getting into it. Maybe someday when Q.C. comes to himself, he'll want to start housekeeping and I'll have something to give him."

I was carrying the slats out to the shed, two at a time, and Mama was rearranging things to make room for the mattress. I saw her crying. We stacked the frame, the slats, and the mattress along the far wall, near the oak split basket that Bob Liggins made for Ollie. Next time I saw it, Mama had filled it with straw for a little banty that was setting on a full nest. I asked her about it.

"No sense in grieving over what you can't change, Eula B."

Mama pretty much lived that way, looking back on it. When it was time to grieve, she grieved, but when there was nothing to do about the grieving, she stayed busy. When it passed, and she got her crying tended to, then she was ready to go on.

That summer, late, after Mattie married, she told me, "Eula B., get your grieving done and then get on with living." I had plenty to work on—Ollie, the Watkins man, Q.C., and Mattie.

She repeated it once more, when me and Gus's little boy came stillborn. I knew it was good advice and important, but both those times I just couldn't hold on to it, and Mama held on for me.

Mattie's wedding was a nice one. She had a pretty dress. Where Mama found the time to make a wedding dress that summer, I don't remember. Standing there in the front room with Ollie's homecoming flowers making a wedding bouquet for Mattie, I looked at Mama and Papa and thought that leaving and grieving and marryings were taking something out of them. When the preacher asked "Who giveth this woman to this man?" Papa said "I do." But when he did, he looked like a sucked-out straw.

The first time I saw a paper straw was when Papa took me into town for the doctor to run a test on my pee. He asked me to drink some juice and wait a while. Then I was to go into his examing room and pee in a cup. Only he hadn't said "pee."

I got hot all around my neck because I didn't know what it was he wanted me to do. He told me again. I looked at my shoes. He sent his nurse in with a paper cup and a straw. She said it plain. "Drink all this juice and then wait until you need to pee. When you do, do it in this little pan."

The cup had a straw in it. When she closed the door, I tried to drink the juice with the straw in the cup. I pushed it to one side and held it there with my finger. Then I put the lip of the cup in my mouth. The straw touched my forehead when I tilted the cup up to drink. I couldn't get the juice to my mouth with the straw on the side.

The nurse came back to check on me. "Like this," she said, "you just suck up and the juice will come." I felt silly. I got it finished right away, and then slipped the straw in the pocketbook Mama always made me bring to town. I wanted to show it to Ollie. I drank my tea with it all that next week. Then one day I let the straw sit flat against the bottom of the glass and it closed down. It never really worked again after that. A sucked-out straw, that was Papa when he said "I do."

Mama said, "We gave Mattie away, lost Q.C., and didn't get Ollie back, all in the same summer." And I lost my trip to St. Louis and the shining Watkins man. It was the worst waste place I ever knew.

When we got Horace and Mattie off that afternoon, Mama and Papa fed the preacher. By dark that night the house started to shrink. Instead of Ollie, Q.C., Mattie, Mama and Papa and me, there was only an old sucked-out straw for Papa, and Mama trying to get over her grieving, and me.

Places and things do shrink when the need for them is gone. I know that. Like my belly.

"Lying there flat as a pond under this very same quilt. After my little boy came, my belly shrank, so did my tits." The words pushed the air out and down toward the foot of the bed.

"No need for milk when there ain't no baby," the midwife told me later. "If your milk comes down, Quester Franklin'll give you something to dry you up." I'd gone to sleep thinking I had a baby to nurse.

"You ain't likely to have much milk anyway, being a red-head. I ain't never seen a redhead yet who could nurse a baby." She was packing her stuff, getting ready to leave, when she said that.

"I'll stop by the preacher's and tell him if you want me to, Miss Mamie. And I'm going right through town if you want me to stop by the funeral home." Their voices kept on coming, against the tiredness in my body, saying words I didn't want to hear.

I turned my face to the wall and heard Mama say, "Please, if you don't mind."

I turn my face to the wall again, trying to pull my dead side along with me. "It started when I swept the yard clean that summer. But I don't know where it ended."

After Mattie left, Mama and Papa didn't talk so much in the mornings. They never mentioned Q.C., and the letters from Ollie came only now and then. But Papa kept markers on the time.

He'd say, "Well, it's January, I wonder if Ollie got enough saved to put down on that hundred thirty acres?" Then he looked toward the barn, not really wanting an answer from me or Mama. Not that we could give him one. Sometimes they talked about Mattie, but we saw her at church, so there wasn't much to wonder about her. She always looked pretty and happy, as far as I could tell. Q.C. stayed a puzzle, a puzzle that nobody ever tried to answer. A puzzle and a failure.

When people at church asked about Q.C., Papa just walked off like he hadn't heard them. Since he didn't talk much anyway, he could get by with it. With Mama it was different. She filled up with tears every time, and then she said, "I don't know, I just don't know." People in the church soon quit asking. I never asked, but I watched Mama. Ollie's leaving was hard and Mattie marrying left a spot, but Q.C. disappearing like that changed the way Mama and Papa lived.

He was their failure now. All that was wrong found its way into Q.C. leaving. February, that next year, Mama took the bull by the horns, as she used to say.

"Harlon, you getting so poor and stringy that none of the Carpenters are gonna claim you. Now, you and me are going to town on Friday and see the doctor. Don't give me any kind of trouble, because I told Mattie to tell him we was coming when she went in on Monday." Mama thought Mattie must be "like that," her going in to the doctor when she wasn't sick or hurt.

They used the matched team to drive in. Mama helped hitch them up. First time I ever saw her do that. Papa still drove on that trip.

It felt like spring that day, and I waited on the swing for

them to come home. I wanted to swing high so I could see out all over things and then have everything make sense.

"Wish I could, I'd try it now, take this old dead half and swing up over all this trouble. Ought to be a place to stand and look at things where they would all make sense. I could see if sweeping the yard clean caused all this trouble."

I sat in the swing until near dark. Pushing with just one toe, the way Mama did. I heard the cow bumping against the barn door. "She's got to be milked." I said it out loud, like I do now. "It's just me and Mama and Papa, and she's got to be milked." I didn't wait to let the cat die. I stopped the swinging with my toe and went through the house to the back porch. Mama left the clean bucket on the outside shelf. I grabbed it and stopped by the shed to get Papa's milking stool.

Star didn't help much, but she only twitched her tail at the flies, not at me.

"I don't know how much milk Papa gets at the evening milking, Star, so I won't know when I'm through." I milked as long as she stood still. Then I loosed her head and finished feeding her. Carrying the full bucket across the yard to the house brought back carrying all those stones to make a home-coming path for Ollie. And of the other pains of that summer.

"Changing hurts, still does"—that's something I want to remember, better get it out in front, out over the top of this quilt—"like coming to live in some little old trailer that ain't big enough to skin a cat. And living with your child and eating oatmeal and having to sit on a potty chair. Changing hurts you, just as sure as hurting changes you. That's a puzzle that works, sure enough."

"Mama Eula, I'll be back there in a minute. Mama'll be home directly, I bet you getting ready for supper. Let me see what I can find." Jimmie Lee's voice overrides the television sounds. The squeals and bells means that the stories are over.

"Something for nothing's not right," I tell the circle on the quilt.

"Jimmie Lee stays with me a lot in the daytime." I want to keep that straight.

"You needing me, Mama Eula?" She stands in the door.

"No, I'm just fine, Jimmie Lee." As fine as you can be when you're living in a trailer with your daughter. But I haven't always lived here, I did live with Mama and Papa, and then with Gus, and we didn't live in no trailer either. I just about always lived with Mama and Papa. Even after everybody else was gone and the place shrunk up to fit just us.

"I'll check back in a little bit, then." Jimmie Lee leaves a wide open space in the door.

The doctor in town told Mama to get Papa to take it easy and to watch and see if he kept on losing weight.

"You can bet if Harlon's losing weight, something is the matter. He's always beeen heavyset, kinda like the Taylors on my side. They all run to fat." Mama told the doctor this when Papa left the room to let the nurse check his blood pressure. The doctor told Mama that Papa might have something bad.

"I can't say just what, Mrs. Carpenter, but Mr. Harlon just doesn't look good. Would take some more tests to find out." Mama said the doctor was just shaking his head when he told her.

"I know he don't look good. His color's been bad ever since the last of the summer." Mama had tears in her eyes when she was telling me that night.

"He's just wasting away, Eula B., just wasting away. I know it's all the trouble with the boys and losing Mattie, too. But your papa just can't seem to get on with living anymore. He's just shriveling up to nothing."

Mama used the corner of her apron to wipe her eyes. Then she stood up, put her hand on the post at the foot of my bed.

"Now, Eula B., we've got to take on more and more of the work around here and try and give Papa a rest. We're both strong and healthy, so it's up to me and you." She tried to hold herself as tall and straight as she could.

"I already started, Mama," I couldn't wait to tell her. "I did the evening milking. You don't have to worry about me. I'm wanting to help."

I milked mornings and evenings after that until me and Gus married. And the rest of that winter we done just about everything except split wood. Seth came down every so often to do that. Resting didn't seem to help Papa at all. He sat in his chair in the front room and looked out the window. We even kept a fire in the front room when we didn't have company or somebody in the bed sick. Mama told Seth to get us plenty of red oak.

"For your uncle Harlon. The front room seems to be the only place he wants to sit. He keeps on looking at the road. I guess he wants to be the first one to see Ollie and Q.C. when they come home."

Every night when we cleaned up the kitchen, me and Mama talked about Papa and how he would get better once spring came. Mattie came to spend Sunday evenings with us. She'd tell him about the singings she and Horace went to. He'd give her a thin, weak smile, like he wasn't really listening. She told him first about her baby. He patted her shoulder and said, "That's nice, Mattie, real nice." Mama watched him with worry around her eyes.

"Just as soon as I can give him a tonic and thin his blood down, I know he'll feel better. And, too, you know what spring plowing does for him," Mama told us, "I've always said that Harlon Carpenter is a new man when it comes planting time."

I knew Mama didn't mean it. She spent too long in the

pantry putting the sugar away. I could hear her blowing her nose and taking a deep breath to stop her crying.

Mama asked Seth and Ross to bring their team down and break up the garden for her. She didn't let on to Papa she'd done it.

"I don't want him thinking, Eula B., that I don't believe he's able, but there's still a right smart whip in the air and I know that after sitting cooped up in this warm house all winter, he'll catch his death of cold if he tries to get out there and work that team."

Seth and Ross came soon after that.

"I surely want to have it ready by Good Friday. You know those beans we planted last Good Friday was the best yield we ever had from that garden spot."

I never heard Mama talk so much about getting the garden ready and getting on with the planting. Before that spring we just done it. First Papa, then Mama, then Ollie, and Q. helped, then even me and Mattie, we just got out and done it. That spring Mama had to talk it all out, to make sure it was really going to happen. The day after Seth and Ross came and broke up the garden, Papa walked out onto the back porch. It was his first time outside since the New Year.

"Mamie, Mamie," he called from the top step, "who broke this garden up?" He was so caught up with looking out the front window that he never even heard them the morning before.

"I got Seth and Ross to come up. They was doing theirs. I thought they could save us the trouble and do ours at the same time."

That was the first time I ever heard Mama lie.

"I was planning to put melons there this summer, try to have a little truck patch there and put the garden a little closer to the house, Mamie."

"Well, that'll be fine, Harlon, we can just get them to plow a little more, later on." Mama kept on with her ironing. Papa walked the length of the porch once or twice more.

"Harlon, you better come on in the house, you've been sitting by that fire all winter, like a sick kitten on a hot brick. You ain't up to being out in that wind." I watched them talk back and forth. Each fooling the other, not saying what it was that they were really thinking, each saving the other from some kind of terrible truth that they both knew. This was not the way they had talked in the mornings, early before any of us got up.

"Mamie, don't be telling me what to do. If it's time for plowing and planting, then it's time for me to be getting out of this house."

I heard the sharp edge in his voice. Even now in this box of a room, the sound of Papa talking to Mama like that cuts across the space in front of me.

"Wasn't long after that we had the snow." It was on Good Friday, 1919. That was easy to remember. Me and Mama and Papa went to town the Saturday before to buy seeds so that we could plant on Good Friday. Everything that bears above ground was to be planted by Good Friday, so the signs are right. Mama checked the almanac and we drove in to get the seeds. Papa drove into town, but Mama had to drive most of the way home. When he gave the reins to Mama, he said, "Ollie never has got to drive this matched pair, Mamie, you think he'll get back 'fore I'm gone?"

Mama fussed. "Harlon Carpenter, you old fool, you and these mules are too stubborn to let a couple of wandering boys get the best of you. 'Course he'll be back to drive them. Probably before the summer's out." Mama was lying again.

The week that followed that Saturday was cold, colder than all the rest of the winter. We burned half a cord of wood in the front room alone and still we didn't stay warm. I slept in my wool underwear, wishing for Mattie and all her fretting to keep me warm. When I woke up on Good Friday, snow covered everything. Mama was already stirring in the kitchen. I ran in there quickly, hopping on my toes so the cold from the wood couldn't bear down on my feet. Mama had put the coffee on but hadn't started any ham or sausage in the frying pan.

"Mama, did you see, it's beautiful, see, everything's just clean and rounded out like make-believe." Mama didn't say a word. I looked to see what was wrong. Her face was white as the snow that covered the yard. The lines there had deepened and she looked so old.

"Oh, Mama, what's the matter?"

"Nothing, Eula B., I was up most of the night with your papa. He's feeling so bad, hurting in his bones, I just hope he hasn't got a touch of pneumonia or something. He just couldn't get easy last night, so I sat up in the chair till he got quiet, along about daylight. I'm not going to fix his breakfast until he starts stirring. Maybe you could get some more wood in the house so we can keep the front room warm. Just don't wake him, he seems so tired." Mama was slumped over, holding her coffee, the steam seeping into her face.

I got dressed in the cold of my room that morning. The kitchen held no comfort for me. I know I filled the wood box on the back porch because when the rest of the family arrived, Seth said that there was plenty of wood on the porch. But on that first trip, when I came in covered with snow and damp bark, Mama was still sitting at the table, half-asleep over her coffee.

"I can feel the cold coming in through the cracks, so we're just going to have to keep the fires stoked up to keep Papa warm." She held the cup with both hands, then pressed it against her temple.

"I brought plenty of oak up." I was proud to know the difference between oak and poplar and ash. I knew what would make a hot fire, which kind would pop, which would make the least smoke under a wash pot. Good sensible things to know.

"Go ahead and build up his fire and then I'll start breakfast."

"Yes'm."

I opened the door to the front room easy as I could. Another cold pushed against me. The bank of coals in the fireplace didn't warm me. That second cold came from Papa's chair. I knew it when I opened the door and looked at him. He was the cause of the cold. Trouble had come against him and it won. Papa was gone.

"Mama, Mama, come here, please come here. Please make it right, don't let this change, too. Stop it, stop it." I cried and cried and Mama took forever getting there. My own voice shocked me when it circled the front room again and again.

"Mama Eula, whatever is the matter with you?" Jimmie Lee came busting in. "I could hear you over the TV." The tip of her lit cigarette looking like a tiny memory of that bank of coals.

"It's Papa, it's Papa." I wanted her to know what happened.

"No, Mama Eula, it ain't Papa or nobody. Nobody but you and me here. Darin's playing with a friend, and Mama will be home directly, but right now ain't nobody but you and me and that TV. Is it bothering you? I can turn it down, yeah, I'll just go and turn it down. Okay? Everything's all right. I'll just go and turn it down. Everything will be all right." Jimmie Lee's repeating things, so they will sound like the truth.

"Papa's gone, don't you understand? The trouble got to him and he's gone."

The tears rolling down the good side of my face are hot and salty. And my mouth on that side keeps jerking down.

"Now, Mama Eula, don't you go to crying on me. You got to look on the bright side of things. You're doing just fine. Mama says you're doing just fine. You got lots of spirit, Mama says." Jimmie Lee is patting me, hard, like getting a colicky baby to stop its crying. Patting away my troubles. Lying to me, all the same.

"There, that's a good girl." She watches me for a minute. I close my eyes to let her leave. She tiptoes toward the door, leaving Papa and the trouble right here with me.

Mama couldn't make everything all right either. Me and her held on to each other, but the house just shrunk down one more notch to hold just the two of us. A house that had held us all, shrunk down just to two folks.

Papa's funeral took place the day after Easter, April 21, 1919. A Monday morning. The preacher said he'd stay over one day. Only if the funeral could be in the morning. The snow was still on the ground, and digging the grave was a job. Long after Papa was dead, Seth and Ross told me, "We almost didn't have the funeral 'cause the ground was frozen solid." Took them most of Easter afternoon to get that grave dug. Preacher kept coming out and saying, "Boys, you got to get that grave dug. I got to have this funeral this morning so I can get on back to town."

Brother Martin was his name. I remember him. Hair sliding back on a perfectly round head, had a wide, flat face like a dinner plate. Served four churches in all, came to us on the third Sunday morning and every other Wednesday night. When he didn't come, Papa used to lead the singing and we didn't have preaching, just singing and Bible reading, some testifying and praying for the sick and needy.

"Wonder who will take over the singing now that Papa's

gone," Mama asked me and nobody. Me and Mama had the funeral that Monday, since Ollie couldn't come and nobody knew where to look for Q.C. I stood between Mama and Mattie. Standing there with the last of the snow on the edge of the grave, I knew that there comes a time when life shrinks down to the size of a grave. Papa didn't need hardly any space at all now.

"*O*nce you start things, it's not easy to stop them." I learned that early. Like starting to sweep the yard and the trouble that came with *that*. I couldn't stop it. Like agreeing to take in those renters. Toy and Edward Earl thought it was a good idea. I let them talk me into it. They meant it for good. But I know that you can mean a thing for good and have it turn out evil.

That first stroke came just after the family reunion, early August. I came home from the hospital with a metal walker and made it fine. Must have done something to my mind, though, because I sure let them talk me into moving into town with them, sometime later on that winter. About February, about two years ago, I think it must have been. February, sure it was, because Edward Earl kept complaining.

"Now, Mama Eula"—I hate it when he calls me Mama—"you can't keep hauling that wood up and trying to keep a fire going. Toy just about goes crazy when she thinks about you using them space heaters. She's all the time saying to me, 'You know, Edward Earl, Mama's gonna back up to one of them space heaters and catch her gown a-fire, and that's gonna be the last of her and the house and everything.' "

"He's right, Mama." Toy always started right up behind him with "He's right, Mama." No, he's not right is what I wanted to say, he's not. Somehow, that winter, this winter, sometime, anyhow, they talked me into renting out my place and moving in with them. And me still up and going. I can't think of why, but it must have been more than me backing up to the fire. There was another little stroke, but not as bad as the first one. I could still get around.

The first renters, coming up in that rusty old van. All of them young'uns. That was what didn't seem right at first. The house shrunk up after Papa died until it fit just me and Mama. Then when that man and woman and all them young'uns moved in, well, it proved that things change to fit the need, that's all it proved.

"Except trailers, trailers don't change to hold folks. Never meant to hold folks."

Hearing me say that out loud stops my thinking. The sounds of the trailer creep right up on the edges of my mind.

Those first renters could've fit in a trailer. They wouldn't have minded. They didn't fit in my place, though, and yet I went right ahead and rented it to them. I don't like thinking about them going into my clean kitchen with those starched curtains and putting their white trash stuff in there.

I made a deal with them.

"Now, every August all my folks come here, that is, the ones that can get here, and we meet for dinner on the third Saturday in August. We been doing it since my brother Ollie went away to California, back when I was just a girl. Every third Saturday in August you got to be away from the house because this is where we always meet. Of course, if that don't suit, then I can't rent the place to you. Me and my daughter, Toy, and Eunice, my sister's girl, will be out sometime during that week before to get things ready. Maybe you want to take the whole week off and go back down to Louisiana and see your kin people. That might be a good idea. Anyhow, I have to have the house then."

I stopped and waited, looking at them both, thinking this would change their minds. The man shifted his chew in his mouth to the other side. Like he could think better, balanced out that way. I never would've put up with a man that chewed tobacco. Right while I was watching him, he spat another brown stream onto one of my white bricks. The dark brown stain oozed over the top and seemed to eat up the whiteness.

"They'll do that to the whole place." I shout the warning to the end of the bed.

"Ma'am?" shouts Jimmie Lee right back, over the squeals of the game show. "You want me, Mama Eula?"

"No," I shout right back. I really never wanted Jimmie Lee. No, that's not true. I was glad about Toy's girls. I was glad to be a grandma. Made me think about things going on. Shirley Earlene, Toy's first girl, was a colicky baby, scrawny. Reminded me of Toy when she was born. Then Jimmie Lee come along two years later, born on my birthday. That was it. I been trying to remember that about Jimmie Lee. Born on my birthday.

Toy told me, "Mama, if the baby comes on your birthday, and is another girl, we want to name it for you." And Jimmie Lee did.

Just barely, though. She got here just before midnight, but when Edward Earl got to the house to tell me and to pick up Shirley Earlene, he said, "Mama Eula, you know Toy said she told you we was going to name the baby after you if it was to come on your birthday. And I thought it was a good idea, too, but we been talking and decided to name her after my brother, Jimmy Lee, the one that was killed at Pearl Harbor." Edward Earl turns his cap round and round in his hands when he talks. "You know I was kind of looking for a boy this time, and since we ain't got nothing to remember him by, no grave or nothing, we decided that we'd like to name this one for him. 'Course it turned out to be a girl again, but we been talking and we think we'll go on and remember him and call this one Jimmie Lee."

That was just what they did. It didn't really hurt my feelings, that wasn't what it was. But there was something that bothered me about it. Naming a lively little girl after a dead brother that Toy never even met. Toy didn't know any of the Johnsons until Edward Earl came home from the service. She never laid eyes on his brother, Jimmy Lee. Somehow it just didn't seem quite right to name a little girl after him.

Toy said I held it against her.

"Shirley can't do no wrong in Mama's eyes, but, Lord, is she always on Jimmie Lee's back." Toy said it more than once. Maybe it was true, Mama always said it's hard not to be partial to one over the others.

Of course, I have to admit that Shirley Earlene was easier to love than Jimmie Lee. Shirley just did as she was told, always. Never had a minute's trouble out of Shirley, but that sure wasn't the case with Jimmie Lee. Something lively about her, a real handful, she was. Gus saw it, too. He gave in to her just like he always did to Toy. He wasn't much account when it came to handling girls.

The screen door's banging shut. Who's coming home? Sometimes I can look at the way the sun is coming through the window and tell who's coming. Darin, Jimmie Lee's youngest, comes in when the rays hit about midway up the pane.

That couldn't be him just now. I guess I slept through him coming in from Head Start. Head start on what? I mean to ask Jimmie Lee what Darin is getting a head start on. I never can do it because she's asking and answering questions so fast and then she's gone back to that TV. Never really any way to talk to somebody like that.

The rays are about even with the sill now, must be Toy home from the shirt plant. Yes, I can hear her moving things around in the kitchen. Must have been to the grocery store.

"Lord, I hope she didn't get any more oatmeal." Is that a real prayer?

"I'm home, Mama, see you in a minute."

She's paying Jimmie Lee for staying with me this week. There is nothing in this world that's right about that. Paying a child to stay with a grandmother.

That shuffling coming down the hall is Toy, she's changed her work shoes, and put on her bedroom slippers.

"Those work shoes just kill my feet. I don't know why they make us wear them things, safety, they say, well, I'd feel a lot safer in something that didn't sit right on my bunions." She's explained that to me more than once.

The shuffling stops outside the door.

"Try to get here early in the morning, Jimmie Lee. Your daddy's leaving to go to court tomorrow and I have to punch in early again. I don't like to leave Mama till you get here."

Jimmie Lee answers back, then Toy again.

"Well, all right."

The door slides open and I can see Toy easing in.

"Evening, Mama, have a good day?" She doesn't wait for me to answer. "Lord, they 'bout killed us at the plant today. We got a new production schedule and they like to have killed us. Then when I went by the grocery, Lord, I never seen the lines like they was tonight. I just picked up what I needed for supper and I'll go back tomorrow or Saturday. I may miss some of the specials, but I can't stand in them plant shoes waiting on the specials. Lord, they kill my feet. Safety shoes, nothing, they're killer shoes for me." She watches her feet when she says this. She says "Lord" too much for me.

"Well, did you and Jimmie Lee have a good day?"

"Don't see too much of Jimmie Lee, but I feel right well."

"Well, what'll we have for supper? Oh, I meant to tell you that the welfare nurse called to say she'd have to come next Tuesday or Wednesday since she's built up some vacation time. Says if she don't use it up, then she'll lose it. Don't that beat all? I tell you, working for the government is something, get holidays, vacation time, sick leave. I swear, it's better than stealing." Toy still watches her bedroom slippers and shakes her head. "Now, what did you say about supper?"

"I didn't say anything about supper." We are both quiet.

"I don't much care. I'm not too hungry right now," I tell her.

"Jimmie Lee said that's what you said about dinner. Now, how are we gonna get strong and well if we don't eat?" The little girl/nurse voice again.

"Whatever you fix will be fine." Toy can leave once I say that. I turn my face to watch the light from the window. Toy waits for a minute at the door and sighs. I hear her sliding those bedroom slippers back down the hall, not picking her feet up, just sliding, sliding, sliding.

Toy adds telephone noises to regular kitchen noises. Her telephone has an extra long cord and she can cook and talk or wash dishes and talk or set the table and talk. I can even hear her dialing.

"Shirley, hey honey, how're you doing? Well, how's the baby? That's good. Just a cold, well, did the doctor prescribe something? Lord, I bet that took an arm and a leg to pay for.

Say, you gonna be able to sit with Mama Eula tonight? Yeah, the league playoffs. Well, I was just making sure. If you want to bring the kids, it'll be all right, just don't let them in the room with Mama Eula. She don't need a virus or cold. You hear? Okay, then I'll see you about six-thirty." All the time she's talking there's drawers opening, grease popping, utensils rattling.

She hangs up and opens the refrigerator. There's a little ribbon of light that slides across the hall when she does that. The pots clinking in the sink mean that supper is not far off. I need to finish up some things before I eat. Jimmie Lee and the renters sort of go together, somewhere.

I stayed on the place until about February, that winter. Edward Earl and Toy drove out in the evening, after Toy got off, to see if I was all right. I thought it was silly, tried to tell Toy that.

"I don't plan to let my body play any more tricks on me, Toy. I promise you that." I figured that I would just keep on going and not listen to it, fool it into thinking it was all right.

She said, "Mama, Mama," and just shook her head.

Toy didn't understand about getting so you couldn't get tricked by your body. Anyway, they came out to check on me, worrying all the time about the firewood and the space heaters. Edward Earl done a lot of the talking. Told me a long tale about something that was real important to him. Went on and on. I'm not used to a man talking so much. Whatever it was, he went on and on about it, like Toy will do about that bowling. It had something or another to do with Jimmie Lee

My good hand pulls my dead elbow over to the middle of my chest and I roll toward the window to watch the changing light.

"Umhph." Sounds like a fart that comes out of my mouth when I do that.

"Supper'll be ready in a minute, Mama," Toy hollers down the hall.

"I didn't say nothing about wanting supper, Toy," I tell her, but my voice goes straight into the pillow.

It was the navy. That's what it was. Edward Earl told me about going to a meeting with some of the men he was in the navy with. Over in Vicksburg.

"Yes, sir, Mama Eula, I seen some old navy buddies that I ain't seen since we was in the Pacific together. We really had us a time. Found out who was where and who was pushing up daisies, who's still going strong. Yes sir, it was something to see all those folks." He shakes his head, wiggling his fat under his neck. Looking down, smiling, like he sees something funny on the floor. "Most of them didn't bring their wives, and we just shot the bull for two days and nights. Funny thing, though, most of the talk was about when we was out there together. Didn't get too much about what we was all doing now. I met a fellow who served with Jimmy Lee. They didn't get shipped out together, though. Told me he just missed Pearl Harbor. Would have been in the next bunch to go. Him and Jimmy Lee was at boot camp together. Real close, he said, they was real close." Here, Edward Earl watched his shoes even closer. I try to edge up on the side of the bed to see, too. "Well, Mama Eula, he said he'd been meaning to look me up ever since he got home. I told him he'd had about thirty years. 'Yeah,' he said. He'd heard about Jimmy Lee and he was mighty sorry. He's been down in Louisiana ever since he got out. Always meant to get in touch he said. But his boy wants to come up here and try his hand out in the country. That's what he said. Asked me if I knew of anybody who could rent him out a small little place while the boy gets on his feet. Kid's had kind of a bad time. Always been a little bit funny. One of those who always gets the short end of the stick, you know? Anyway, he got married, shotgun style." Edward Earl looks up now, straight at me, and winks.

I try to pull myself up, out of his sight, out of the range of that wink. I don't like him bringing his old navy stories to me.

"Anyway, the boy and his wife and kids need a place to stay. He hopes he can get on at the furniture factory or maybe at a gas station, somewhere around here. That way they'll be close to home, but far enough away that the boy might be able to get a job and hold it. Boy's had some kind of trouble with his nerves or something. Needs a little help, that's all."

Edward Earl finally finished.

"Ya'll want some supper?" I asked them both. It was good and dark then.

"No'm," Toy answered.

"Yes'm, if it wouldn't been too much trouble." Edward Earl said that at the same time Toy said "no'm."

"Well'm, what we really come to talk about was whether this boy and his wife and kids might be able to rent out this place for a while and you move in with us, maybe just until the cold weather's gone. I sure don't want you burning up out here and Toy telling me all the while that that was what was gonna happen. She'd never get over it, Mama Eula."

"I'm just fine out here. I don't want to move into town into a house with wheels. Not as long as I can make it here, no, I plan to stay put, Toy. I'll look in the pantry to see what I can find for supper. Toy, you set the table."

"No, Mama, we got to go back into town. We didn't aim to stay this long, but you think about what we said. It would be a lot easier on everybody if we were sure you were safe and everything."

They left and I closed the door, good and hard. On them and on the idea of me moving into town.

"There are worse things than things not being easy," I said.

"I don't know why moving into town seems like such an answer." The sounds from the kitchen are just about over. I was fixing supper that night, too, in my kitchen, Mama's kitchen, her mama's kitchen. Here is Toy, in another kitchen, it don't seem right.

Edward Earl and Toy got their way. Ding-donged me to death about that boy and his wife and kids needing a place to stay. And, too, it wasn't long after that visit that I caught the tail of my flannel nightgown a-fire. Just singed it was all, but the home visitor heard about it from somewhere. Maybe that young man who came out to paint over the smoke damage told them. He was a nice boy, but I never did get it straight who his mama and daddy was. Maybe he called the home visitor and she called Toy, and Toy come out to the house just a spewing.

"You see, Mama, I told you that was gonna happen. Now, I'm not gonna hear one other word. You are coming into town with me. I already called Edward Earl and had him call those people about renting the place and that's that." She was mad and sure of herself. I gave in. The renters came just a few days later. Early March, it was.

That weak-eyed woman with those weak-eyed young'uns. Him spitting all over the yard. I knew it would come to no good end. Like whistling girls and crowing hens. I could bet on it. I have to take the blame. I said yes and they moved in. Oozing their white trash things all over mine.

They came in March. The garden spot was burned off ready to start a new garden. One little patch of turnip greens near the house was the end of the winter planting. Sometime in April, me and Toy drove out to pick the last of the greens and pinch the tops. I wanted to do that before they went to seed. Maybe get one good mess of turnips.

We drove up to the house, and Toy said, "Now, Mama, remember that you rented the house to them. At least till the end of May. You took their money and really we can't be coming out here checking on them every few days. They got a right to use the place just as they want to. We can't be telling them how to keep house or nothing."

I didn't answer. That's the best way to handle a talker. I knew how it was going to look. When he spat on that brick, I knew.

The yard was full of garbage. Cans and papers and disposable diapers hugged the bottom limbs of the azaleas. Their kind of white trash garbage filled up all the places that I marked off with the white bricks. The fences that outlined the garden were draped with clothes, every kind and size. Woman had her step-ins hanging out for anybody passing by to see. I saw the clothesline in the backyard laying on the ground. The yard swing hung to one side, too, one rope dangled loose while the other dropped the seat like a lopsided plumb line. A snotty-nosed little boy was entertaining himself with the rope and the wooden seat. I started over to him. Using the walker made it take longer. He watched me and Toy every step of the way. Pushing the swing seat in and out, watching us careful like. His face looked like snails crawled over it, snot and tears tracing trails in the dirt on his cheeks and upper lip. When we got right close to him, he blinked.

"Youwannaseemama?" The pout on his face moved just a little.

"Is she at home?" I asked him.

"Ithinkshe'sstillinthebed," he answered, not changing his pout still. He talked like his tongue was too big for his mouth.

"Would you tell her that we come to pick some of the turnip greens out by the shed. We don't aim to bother her, we just come to pick that last mess of greens," I explained to him. He never moved. Just kept his eyes on me and Toy and kept the space between us filled with the movement of the swing.

"Sheain'tgonnamindbutIdon'twannawakeherupjisttotellher

that." He kept on watching us, swinging the seat in crazy little circles.

"Well, we'll just go on about our business then and not bother you or her." I shook the folds out of the Jitney Jungle sack and started toward the turnip green patch. The ground felt spongy under the legs of the walker. We'd had a good wet April. The little boy watched me every step of the way. I looked back at him when I would have to stop. He looked back at the swing, like he hadn't been watching. I wanted to shake him. Maybe just because I couldn't get hold of his mama.

Me and Toy went back again in early May. One Saturday afternoon. Their rent was up the last of May. If they weren't going to stay, I wasn't going to rent it out again, at least not until after the family reunion. It would take me all summer to get the place ready. Mattie wasn't able to help me, her arthritis had her down.

It was worse that time. The piles of garbage blown in around the azaleas was higher. A bright pink tricycle sat, one wheel up, leaning on the bias in the dirt. Deep scars in the ground showed where some child pushed the tricycle round and round. The front wheel rolling and the sharp end of the bare axle digging into the yard. Round and round and round the child went, spending up that white-trash energy doing nothing, instead of cleaning up the yard. The rope on the empty end of the swing had raveled some more, almost out of the boy's reach this time. The slats on the porch swing were snaggle-toothed now. Broken up for quick kindling was my guess.

"I mean to go in and talk to that woman this time." I told Toy that just as we pulled out of the trailer park. "I don't intend to rent to them unless she's got the money in her hand. Toy, I knew the day he come to look at it that there was no good coming with them. I don't care if Edward Earl and his brother did know his kin. They're just Louisiana swamp rats and I don't intend to let them ruin my place." Me and Toy rode the rest of the way with no talking. Seeing the place look so bad just wore me out some more. If they left now, maybe I could make a late garden. Maybe salvage something out of this.

Soon as we drove up in the yard, the same little hollow-eyed boy appeared. I wasn't sure where he came from. He just popped out when outsiders drove up. No, that wasn't right. I wasn't the outsider, he was. It was them that didn't belong here, not me.

"Your mama here?" I asked.

"Yes'm."

"Would you tell her I want to see her?"

"No'mshe'sasleeprightnow."

"Well, I'm sorry to wake her up, but we come all the way from town and I need to talk to her about ya'll staying on now that the rent's up. So this time you'll have to wake her up. I guess."

"Idon'tthinkwe'llbestayingherenowthatmypa'sgone."

"Did he go offshore with that new group of boys from around here?" Toy smiled and spoke up for the first time. I looked at her hard, not wanting to change the subject. Toy was hoping that Royce, Jimmie Lee's husband, might get on offshore. She thought that would help. "If he was on seven and off seven, I think him and Jimmie Lee might be able to get back together," she told me. "Steady money'd help, too." The little boy stared at my walker.

"No'mIdon'tknowwherehe'sgone. Jistgones'allIknow."

"Well, we'll be talking to your mama to find out just what ya'll are going to do." I wanted him to get inside so we could get on with our business. I planted the walker hard in the dirt in front of me and looked away from the azaleas with their garbage collars. I wanted to walk steady so the boy wouldn't stare at me this time. At the bottom step I waited a second. Must think about what I'm doing so I don't have to ask Toy to help. Put three prongs of the walker over on the bad side. With my good hand, lift my good leg on the bottom step. Grab the railing with my good hand.

"I hope these folks ain't letting these young'uns swing on the railing and loosen them."

"Ma'am?" Toy yells an answer from the middle of the front yard. She didn't much want to go inside and she was lagging behind, hoping she wouldn't have to help.

"Nothing," I called, "I'm doing fine."

With my hand steady on the railing, I pulled the rest of me up on the bottom step. I felt my good knee straighten and lock in place. There, I made it. Pulling up the rest of me was no problem. Good thing I didn't run to fat like the Taylors. Not so much to pull along after my body started giving out on me.

Got to put the walker on the bottom step and start all over again. Get my good hand, lift my good leg. Pull on the railing. Each of the four steps. A little victory. By the time I got to the top, I was ready to talk to the woman inside. I walked steady to the front door. The screen stood open just a crack. They hadn't figured out how to lift up on the screen just a little so that the door would close nice and tight. Sure would help with the flies in the summer. Having the screen door shut. Me and Gus saved one whole year for new screens. First, he just tacked the screens over the windows, didn't have frames or nothing. Then later he built some frames, but first it was just screen wire over the windows. Toy was just a baby then. A little girl, anyway.

When I knocked on the screen door, my knuckles hit the door facing. Then the top part of the door wagged to one side and slapped against the doorjamb. The bottom of the door held on tight, kept its place because of the high spot on the porch floor. Knock, wag, slap, knock, wag, slap, I kept knocking in that pattern for what seemed like a mighty long time. Reckon that woman ain't gonna get up and answer with me out here just knocking to beat sixty. I started getting mad while I stood there, knock, wag, slap, knock, wag, slap.

"All right, all right, I'm coming. Just hold your horses a minute. Tammy Renée, you hold the baby while I go to the door. Now, don't turn off the TV, I won't be but a minute. I ain't gonna buy nothing from nobody today."

I saw her coming. It was dark in the hall and she made a great big shadow in the light that sifted in through the back door. She was slow in dragging herself to the other side of the screen door. When she got there she said nothing. I waited. Finally I said, "How d'ya do?"

She just kept on looking at me, like maybe she saw me, maybe she didn't.

"I need to talk to you about the rent and if ya'll plan to stay on any longer. If you're not going to be here for any length of time, then I'm gonna have two of my nephews plow the lower garden so I can make a late fall planting." Standing there, just watching me. I was trying to fill up the emptiness that hung there between us.

"I ain't gonna be here no longer than it takes for me to git some of my people from down in Louisiana to come and git me. I sent word about a week ago for my daddy or some of 'em to come on up and git us. My old man left, just up and left, and he ain't been back in over'n a month. So guess he ain't coming back. Anyhow, if he does, I ain't gonna be here."

She was sure about that.

"I don't know why he jist up'n left, but he always was a little curious. The people in Jackson told us that the first time he kinda went off. When he was jist a boy, his mama took him to that hospital out from Jackson and they run some tests on him and they said he was a little off. Not so's you really notice, unless you was around him a lot, but he was a little funny. He's left before, but never for so long and never without so much as a fare-thee-well. He jist left in the middle of the night, drove off on that motorcycle of his, pitching up gravel ever which a way." She kept watching some spot out in the yard, past my shoulder. The gravel from the motorcycle made her head jump back just a ways. "Started them hounds across the way to howling, caused a real ruckus, it did. That motorcycle. Didn't leave me any cigarette money, either. Don't that jist beat all?"

She shook her head over this.

"I bin out of diapers for the baby for nearly two weeks. I jist used up them rags you left in the pantry. It sure does make a difference in the wash, not having them disposable diapers." She looked straight at me to tell me this. Her eyes were gray, washed-out, and her long pigtail in the back seemed to ground her to the spot behind the screen. "Anyways, I won't be here much longer, you can count on that. When my daddy hears that he left me, jist up'n left me, well, he'll come or send one of my brothers up here and I'll be gone, too. You can bet on that." She sighed a wave of air toward me. Bruises everywhere. Those rags in the pantry were my straining rags, bleached out flour sacks, the ones I save for straining the seeds out of blackberry jelly. I always had the clearest jelly in the Home Demonstration Club, extra straining, that's what did it. The thicker rags were for pot cheese. Diapers.

"Well, that was all I was wanting to know. So I'll be checking in the next week or so, to see if you're gone. You can leave the key with Carroll Bickham's boy. He's usually down here right regular checking on the fields that he rents. Be sure you leave it." I waited for her to nod.

"And I'm real sorry that you had such a bad time of it, seems like life's kinda like that. You don't never know, for sure, who you can count on. Until it's too late." I wanted to tell her more, wanted to warn her about not letting her body play any more tricks on her. That had happened to her a lot of times. All them young'uns showed that up right away. I needed to tell her to go home and talk to her mama. Her mama could tell her who down there in Louisiana she could trust. What kind of a man with a yard full of young'uns rides a motorcycle?

Toy was still standing back at the bottom of the steps. I guess she was listening. She wasn't making a sound in this world.

"Yes'm, I will and thank you. I didn't think it would work, coming up here and all, but sometimes you gotta try one more thing before you finally know it jist ain't gonna work." We stood there just looking at one another through that lopsided screen. In the background the TV and the baby kept up a racket.

For a minute or two the space between us had filled up with knowing how life was. I nodded a little nod to her, and stuck my walker out toward my bad side, and started turning around.

I leaned on my good side and dragged my bad foot around.

"Oops, 'scuse me, Mama." Toy bumped into me. She must have walked up on the porch just in time to hear the last of our talking. "I guess you 'bout ready to go, Mama?" Toy was glad it was finished. She didn't want to talk to the woman in the doorway. Never even looked at her, just kept on talking to me, acting like that woman wasn't even there.

She helped me down the steps, making it harder than when I did it by myself. When we reached the bottom, Toy turned her head, almost looked at the woman. She was still standing there, trying to figure things out.

"Well, 'bye now," Toy called out. There was no answer from behind the screen door.

Me and Toy got back to the trailer late that evening. Edward Earl was sitting in the den, as they call it, watching TV. She started making excuses right away about why we was so late. Then I told him.

"We was late because we went to check on them renters that you and Toy wanted me to have, Edward Earl. That's reason full enough to be late. Toy, he ain't gonna starve before you can get some supper fixed. Besides, that beer he's drinking, hiding over there under the couch, ought to keep him going for a while." I wished I could turn around in a hurry and walk back to my room, standing tall and straight, like Mama would have if she'd seen beer in her house.

I heard the sheriff at the door a few nights later. I knew it was the law. Blue light circling in through the window, like some kind of pulse in the front yard. I tried to get up, but in the commotion, nobody heard me calling. Had to wait for morning before I found out what was going on.

At breakfast Toy asked, "Mama, did you hear all that fuss going on here in the middle of the night?" I nodded.

"Well, that was the sheriff, coming to find Edward Earl to ask him about the renters out at the place." Toy wouldn't look at me.

"I wish the sheriff had asked me about them renters, I could tell him a thing or two. Folks that leave their garbage in the yard and don't wash their young'uns' faces never gonna amount to much. I could have told him that."

"Well, Mama." Toy kept on stirring something on the stove. "It don't seem quite that easy this morning. Carroll Bickham's boy, Little Carroll, must have seen something going on down there late yesterday evening, but he didn't go to check, he said. Just saw something kind of going on, he said. He told the sheriff he just felt it in his bones, somewhere, that something wasn't quite right down there, so along about dark he decided to drive down and see if everything was okay. He had a tractor mired up and was going to take the battery out, he said, so he just thought he'd check on your place when he drove by. He told the sheriff that when he drove up in the yard and honked his horn, he didn't see a sign of life. Decided they was just gone, and almost drove off, he said." Toy kept stirring, the steam making little smoky waves between the pot and her face. I waited. "Then he said, he noticed the little boy, the one that came out to see us, I guess. Carroll said he seen him laying on the porch. Well, Mama, it was just awful. That crazy man come back sometime yesterday and killed them all. Just awful was what Carroll said. At least that's what the sheriff said. Killed them all. The sheriff wanted to find out if we knew anything about them, so he came for Edward Earl. They left and went down into Louisiana last night looking for Jimmy Lee's friend, the boy's daddy. Hoping they could find him before the news got out." Toy stopped stirring, started shaking her head.

"We don't know none of the details yet, when he shot them or what. Somebody did say to the sheriff that they thought the boy had been in Vietnam and maybe just had some kind of snap. Thought he was back in the jungles or something. But we don't know none of the details yet."

I sat there at the table, squarely in front of the oatmeal that Toy dished up.

"Bruises," I told her.

"Ma'am?"

"Bruises, bruises, all over my place. How can I ever get rid of this trouble in time for the reunion?"

"Mama!" Toy sounded surprised.

"I don't know how I'll ever get it cleaned up before August.

What kind of cleaning stone would get a young'un's blood off my front porch? What kind of stone?" I felt myself rocking back and forth in my chair, trying to think of a cleanser that would remove the stain of a whole family from the inside of my house. I was crying now, I felt the warmth on the good side of my face. Who was I crying for? I don't know. Maybe it was for the little boy, maybe for his mama, maybe for the place and the troubles going against it still.

"All I know is that it was another time when things didn't work out." That got some of it figured out.

"What didn't work out, Mama? Your supper? You 'bout ready for it?" Toy is standing in the doorway, a towel over her shoulder. "I'm gonna get you up now so you can eat 'fore Shirley Earlene and her young'uns get here. Tonight's our bowling league and we're playing for a place in the finals, so I want to be early, try to get in a practice game. Let's get up and get fed, okay?" Getting ready to go on to the next thing, that's Toy. Moving toward heaven's knows what.

Next she'll want to know if "we" want to go to the bathroom, and then Toy and me will go through talking for another day. At least that weak-eyed woman and me filled up the empty space between us for just a minute. She told me what was wrong and I told her that life was like that. I don't think I've told Toy that. Not that she'd listen, but at least I ought to tell her. Then it wouldn't be on my conscience. Really, you can't tell Toy nothing. I tried to warn her about the soldier boy and then Edward Earl. She wouldn't listen. Maybe if I talked to that woman with the gray eyes before she took up with that man, things would have turned out different. You never know.

"Okay, Mama, let's see if we can't go to the bathroom, okay? Then we can have some supper."

*F*ood talk and bathroom talk. Life don't have to boil down
to that. It wasn't that way with me and Mama.

"Guess we got to hurry a little bit tonight, Mama. Shirley
Earlene and the young'uns will be here soon. We'll finish up
here and I'll get you back in your room 'fore they get here."
Toy keeps busying herself between the stove and the table,
jumping up and down like a little girl, trying to please. She's
always rushing. Going bowling, punching in early so she can
punch out early. Rushing, rushing, rushing. Toy always rushing, Edward Earl never rushing.

Q.C. left, Ollie didn't come home, Mattie got married, and
Papa died. Then the house shrunk down to fit just Mama and
me. We made a late garden that year. He died on Good Friday,
so we planted late. Me and Mama put up nearly everything.
Just like they was all gonna be there to eat it. Like always.
We didn't put the truck patch in, though. I stood my ground

about that. Mama wanted to do it because it was the last thing that Papa ever talked about.

"We don't have nobody to drive the stuff to town to sell, Mama. You can't handle the team and neither can I. So a truck patch won't do us no good if we can't sell the stuff in town. Papa wouldn't want us to be burdened down by a truck patch that didn't make money, now, would he?"

Mama didn't say anymore. But most of the summer she was planning on a truck patch for the next summer, for Papa.

"If we can find somebody to take the stuff to town, Eula B., we' gonna have a truck patch next summer." She looked at me, smiled, and added, "For Papa."

We put the truck patch in the next summer because we found somebody. Gus Freeman. Lived with his folks across the river. The river divided the county. West side of the river went to school in Beat Three, east side of the river went to school in Beat Two. Grew up right across the river from Gus and still didn't know him. Mama knew his mama and papa because of county-wide singings. Papa went for Mount Pisgah church and Mama went along.

Early on in March, the spring after Papa died, Mama sat a long time at the supper table. "Eula B., I talked to Faye Freeman in town last week. I asked her if they was going to truck-farm this summer. She said they was and that their boy Gus was going to take the stuff to town. I asked her could he take ours when he took his. For pay, of course. She said he would. We're gonna have that patch for Papa."

Early in the moist mornings of that summer Gus came to get the produce I picked.

Getting up at first light, I picked the long straight rows, squash and cucumbers covered with a silvery coat of dew, arranging the little crooked necks into designs as I went. The loaded baskets filled the well house up with goodness gathered when the last of the night clouds cast long shadows. Washed, clean, with firm, round skin shining under the water, it felt magic to me. Watching the abundance, growing and producing goodness right out of something as plain as dirt.

Gus wouldn't take nothing for doing this.

"No, ma'am, Mrs. Carpenter, it's the least I can do. I don't mind at all. Glad to do it. Long as you have it ready, I'm glad to take it." Now I know that was a long speech for Gus.

The summer wore on, hot and dry. Only the moist early morning visits of Gus picking up bushel baskets of peas, corn, okra, tomatoes that I gathered interrupted my days. He'd drive up to the back door, unload yesterday's empty baskets, and go in the kitchen to settle up with Mama. They'd sit at the kitchen table, the crumpled money lying between them. I saw them through the back door when I stacked the empty baskets to take to the well house. There I filled them with the morning's pickings. Soon as Gus finished with Mama, he came out to help me finish loading up the baskets. Neither of us said much. I knew he watched me. Especially when I put my hands up over my head to take down an egg basket hanging from the rafters. His looks were simple, though, not confusing or worrisome. Like he liked to watch me stretch and work.

"You work easy like, Eula, and don't waste a single step," he told me. He meant it nice, and I knew it.

"Steady," Mama said. "That's what Gus Freeman is, steady. There are worse things in this life, Eula B. He's a good boy and he comes from steady folks." Mama kept looking down at the peas she was shelling. I kept on looking at the peas in my lap as well. "I think he's kinda interested in you, Eula B."

I felt my face going red, my neck getting warm when Mama talked like this. I knew what she was getting at, but still, it was too soon and the memory of the Watkins man and a trip to St. Louis were too close. How he made me tremble. I never could have lasted those long morning hours in the well house with him.

His looks were never simple. I felt no comfort from him. They were different, those two summers. One was hot and troubled by the presence of the Watkins man. Lying and trouble all around. Ollie lied about coming home, the Watkins man lied about sending for me to come to St. Louis. Q.C. lying that he was staying home from prayer meeting and then just leaving. Not a trace of him for all those years. A troubling summer. It killed Papa.

"Like to have killed me." The "killed" part makes the quilt jump.

"It's just me and the kids in here, Mama Eula." It's Shirley Earlene. Toy's gone bowling. I hear Shirley in the hall. "How you doing tonight?" She has a Co-Cola in one hand, a red, white, and blue bag of potato chips in the other.

"Doing fine, Shirley." "Fine" don't make the quilt jump like "killed."

I didn't do fine that summer, the summer of the trouble and the lying. Lied to Mama. Yet the other summer was a peaceful time. One that let us catch up after all that trouble. Gus was there just as steady as could be, helping me and Mama with the truck patch. Helping, watching, steadying everything. It just seemed natural that I'd marry him.

"That boy's been a godsend, Eula B." Mama said that after supper one night when she was counting the money in the sack in the pantry. Me and Papa tried to get her to keep it somewhere else after the money disappeared with Q.C.

"Lightning ain't likely to strike twice in the same spot," she told us.

"A real godsend. I'm gonna have enough money after this one summer with a truck patch to finish paying for the marker on Papa's grave." It worried Mama that she went into debt to put a marker on Papa's grave.

"Still and all, we can't go on without marking his final resting place. Something about that just ain't right." She borrowed money against her good name at the funeral home so that we could put the marker up. The truck patch settled that debt. It was the only debt Mama ever had. Maybe that was one reason she felt kindly toward Gus. The night she borrowed the money, she sat in her chair at the supper table, slumped over, looking as old as I'd ever seen her. "Owe no man anything is a law of the Good Book, Eula B., and here I am going right against it. But it just ain't right for your papa's grave not being marked proper like. I just don't know what to do. I don't like going against the Bible, but I don't want to dishonor the dead either." I figure that was the night she decided on the truck patch.

The rest of her plan only had to wait for summer and the harvest. We picked and sold lots of vegetables, but we got more than that for our trouble. Mama settled her debt at the funeral home and I got me a husband.

How I settled it that I would marry Gus still isn't clear. But when the moist mornings in the well house were over and the last of the garden gathered, the harvest in and the debts settled, I knew I'd marry Gus.

"He'll be steady, Eula B., he's a man you can depend on." Mama said that over and over.

Gus wanted to get married right away, but I said no.

"I want to wait for Christmas. I want a little more time here with Mama before I leave. It only seems right. She's lost so much so fast. I can't just up and leave without her getting used to the idea."

"Well, I guess we could just move in with her, Eula." He never added the "B." "That'll make it a little easier for her."

So the house grew just a little that Christmas. Enough to hold Gus and marriage and all the changes that marriage meant.

We waited for Christmas. It seemed like a more respectable time since Papa died. Besides, I didn't have nobody to give me away.

"Mama, you think Ollie might come home to check on us? With Q.C. and Papa gone, too?" I saw that other letter propped up against that salt dish, growing again as big as the kitchen. Every word of it pounding against the sides of my head if I would let it.

"I couldn't write him now, with my bad hand." But then I went and found Ollie's letters sticking in Papa's Bible. They was all there, but the one saying he wasn't coming home was in Revelation. Not in the Gospels with the cards showing California gold. He put his new address on the back of the envelope flap. So I wrote him.

Dear Ollie:

You can't know what a hard time it has been here. Me and Mama is all that's left at home. I trust you got the telegram when Papa died. That felt like the end for Mama and me. We still don't know where Q.C. is. It's like the earth just opened up and swallowed him. Mattie is fine, but we don't see her except on Sunday. She has a new baby now, a girl she named Eunice. That's been good for Mama, to have a grand-young'un. Mama and me worked hard this summer and had a truck patch. Gus Freeman took the stuff to town and sold it out of the back of his wagon. Wouldn't let us pay him at all for his time and work. We made enough to pay for the marker on Papa's grave. It was good for Mama to get that settled. She didn't want to die herself with debts against her name. Anyway, what has happened since Gus has been coming over to help with the truck patch is that he asked me to marry him and I guess I will. He wants to get married right away. I want to wait until Christmas. I don't have nobody to give me away. I thought maybe things in California would be so that you could come home for my wedding and give me away. As soon as you can, let me know because that's my only real reason for waiting, I guess. We both miss you a lot and hope that things are going good for you out there. Mama sends her love and so do I.

Affectionately, yr. sister, Eula B.

I met the mailman every day. Looking for a letter with a California stamp on it. But Mattie wasn't there to race me to the mailbox.

"Beating a path to the mailbox ain't gonna get that letter here one day sooner, Eula B." Mama laughed at me, but I noticed that the mornings I got busy, Mama said, "You seen the mailman yet, Eula B.?" We both spent the fall waiting for a brother/son we could count on.

The letter came. Along about the first of November. We'd a hard frost a while before. Everything was dead and gray. I waited to read it until I got to the table in the kitchen. I put the coffeepot on the warming eye, wanting some warmth and strengthening to get me through what the letter was going to say.

Dear Eula B. and Mama:

I was glad to get your letter and to find out that you had a good season with the truck patch and garden. Out here we had a good year, too. I got the down payment on the land and I've been working to get it planted in my off time. A few more years of this kind of work and I'll be working for myself and not the other man. Then maybe I can afford the time and money to come home and see all of you. It's not because I don't want to come, but right now I just can't turn loose and make that kind of trip. I remember the Freeman family from across the river. I'm glad you're getting a good man, Eula B. You will make a good wife for him, I know.

Mama, I would like for you to meet my wife and teach her some of the dishes you cook so good. Not being from down where we come from, she don't know much about corn bread or okra. Still, she's a big help to me and she knows a lot about oranges.

I wish I could be there for your wedding, Eula B. Maybe in a few years.

Affectionately, yr. bro. Ollie

Ollie was married, just like that, we found out. And he wasn't coming for the wedding. That meant there was no reason to wait till Christmas. But I wanted to, and we did.

Married Christmas afternoon, in the front room. Mama made my dress that winter, sewing on it in tiny fine stitches. She pulled Papa's chair over by the window so she could see. I watched her in the late winter afternoons. She poured some of her very life into every seam. I hemmed some sheets and towels and made a camisole or two. Putting lace on them was the hardest part. Not just because my fingers were stiff from outside work, but the lace seemed strange, foreign even, on my clothes. Lace came from someplace with shining charm, not Route 6, Mount Hermon, Mississippi.

"I didn't want to be undressed in front of Gus." I whisper this, surely don't want them girls hearing that. The words didn't even make a ripple in the quilt. A quiet kind of secret, but true, just the same.

I knew he was steady and a godsend, just like Mama said, but he was not a man to wear lace for.

Mattie stood up for me in her green going-away dress. Horace held Eunice, but she cried for her mama. Gus's brother, the one they called Junior, stood up for him. When the preacher got to the part about "who giveth this woman," Mama said "I do." There wasn't anybody else to do it. No man we could count on. No Papa or Ollie or Q.C. or the doctor or the Watkins man. Nobody. Nobody till Gus. He was one I could count on. That in the long run was more important than one I would wear lace for.

After the wedding we drove north along the river to the bridge and crossed over into Beat Two. I lived all my life in Beat Three, but that afternoon Gus's mama and papa had me and Mama and Gus, Mattie and Horace, and all their folks over for supper. It was a big crowd, all of Gus's family, brothers and his sister, uncles, aunts, cousins, a lot of new faces. Not many came for me. Just Mattie and Horace, Mama, and one of Papa's sisters, Aunt Ivy. Down to this, little gathering of women, we were. Not one blood-kin man there.

"I decided then and there looking around that room to be the best wife Gus could ever hope for." I don't mind saying that out loud. Be a good thing for Shirley and Jimmie Lee to hear.

The Freemans offered us a room with them. "Mama made it clear that she meant for us to have her place. That night she went home with Mattie and Horace so that me and Gus could have the house to ourselves." Seemed natural for us just to stay on. Wasn't no sense in paying out good money to rent some other place when the house could swell enough to hold Gus and marriage. After a week or so, Mama moved back home. She left the back bedroom to us and she took the little daybed in the front room.

"Looks like me and Eula B. changed places. She's got a husband and needs the big bed. I got nobody so I'll take the little one." Mama laughed when she said it, but it did seem right the way it worked out.

That started some of the trouble with Mama Two. She never believed that it was all Gus's idea.

A big part of being married and keeping house was just as

natural as it was when Gus came over to fill the empty baskets. "Papa wasn't there to get Gus to promise that I wouldn't have to work in the fields, so I went out in the mornings with Gus, just like a field nigger, but I didn't mind. I liked doing it." I like saying it, too, out loud in the open. Working like that made me feel like I wasn't giving in to nothing. We had a winter garden that first winter, ate turnip greens all winter, and Gus killed a hog before he left his folks' house and we had fresh ham and bacon. The whole thing seemed good to me. The part about the lace and all was only a little part, and I almost got used to that. I never did get to feel like I did with the Watkins man, but I knew that Gus was gonna be there tomorrow when I woke up.

"I thought I heard you asking for something, Mama Eula. You doing okay this evening?" The door is open. Shirley Earlene put her face inside, leaning over at the waist and angling herself in. Her hair is wrapped around pink foam curlers. Toy named her for Shirley Temple and her daddy. When she was just a little thing, Toy kept her hair done up in rags to make it hang in those long corkscrew curls. It was a shame she took after Edward Earl more than Shirley Temple. She leans in at a wider angle.

"I won't bring the little ones in tonight, Mama Eula. Junior has a cold and Jennifer is just getting over something, so I told them that they had to stay in the den. Hear that racket? Lord, they 'bout to drive me crazy. Another year, though, they'll all be in school and I'm gonna take me a vacation." She smiles at the idea of a vacation. "Was you wanting anything particular? Mama said you didn't eat supper, so if you're getting hungry, I can fix you a plate of scrambled eggs or something. Want me to?"

Shirley says all this, leaning on an angle, using her hand on the door facing to support herself.

"No, thank you. I was just thinking out loud. Getting some

things settled before I go to sleep. You tell the children I said hello, you hear. I hope they get to feeling better."

"Yes'm, I will. And you sleep good, you hear." Both of us want the other to hear. But no real talking going on.

Shirley straightens up and pulls the door closed. She won't be back for a while. She and Jimmie Lee both watch that TV with young'uns crawling all over them. Don't see how. A young'un got between me and a job every time.

Like my little boy. He didn't come along that first summer. I went to town with Gus then. Rode the wagon and helped with the vegetables. We put away a good bit. Mama halved it with us. Had two sacks in the pantry. One, her old one, and ours, new, made out of a flour sack, white with pink cornflowers around the top. Mama made a drawstring, "So the pennies won't fall out if you pick it up wrong," she said. She sewed it with fine little stitches, too. Almost like my wedding dress.

We must have used that first money to buy another hog. We killed one sometime the next winter. Took me all night to make the cracklings. First time I done it. Gus scraped the hide with a piece of bone, got it smooth as a baby's cheek. Gus said my cracklings was good as Mama Two's. And me making them the first time. He was proud of me. Said I was turning into a fine cook. He smiled when he said it. Patted me on the butt when I was in the kitchen. I acted like I didn't think it was right. We got along fine. No real fussing or carrying on like Jimmie Lee and Royce, or even Toy and Edward Earl.

The winter gave us that first little bit of time together in the house. I watched it swell to hold Gus and me and Mama and the whole thing of being married. Mama Two pieced us this double-wedding-ring quilt then. Worked on it all winter, gave it to us for Christmas right before that bad spell of weather when Mama got pneumonia.

"Mama, you all right?" I went in her room early that morning. She was lying there just as still as a rabbit. Her face washed out, no color except a little blue line around her mouth. "Gus, Gus, something's happened to Mama. Quick." He come running in, strapping up his overalls, his boot laces hitting the floor like pieces of hail. Tap, tap, tap. "Now, Eula, don't get excited, she's gonna be all right. Just calm yourself down so you can help her." He put his arms around me, holding the terror away from all of us. "You just get her warm and I'll go for the doctor. It'll be all right."

Mama Two told me not to save the quilt. "Go ahead and use it, Eula, I made it to be used. Don't go storing it in no cedar chest. I can make you another one for storing, this one is for using." That's what she said when she brought it over on Christmas afternoon.

So I did. I spread it over Mama on the daybed. I stoked the fire in the front room and moved Mama in there. The shadows of her laying there were falling heavy on top of Papa. The quilt, doubled over on itself, stopped the shivering that first morning.

"She told me to use it, Mama, when she gave it to me," I told her. She fussed about me putting a new quilt on her. But when Mama Two came over and saw it on the daybed, she raised Cain. Toy's a lot like her in some ways.

"Eula B., put this quilt away. Get one out of the box in my room. No quilt is worth having bad feelings in a family. Not even a double wedding ring." I didn't move it for several days, but Mama kept on me about it. "Put this thing away. Save it for your young'uns, Eula B."

I folded the big yellow circles so that they lay right on top of each other. Like we are here, in this house. Me and Gus married and living right on top of Mama and Papa. Keeping blood kin neat and tidy. Not running off to God knows where. I kept the quilt there from then on. Got it out for company, but Mama Two's temper took the pleasure out of it for me. Temper does that.

Mama got all right, but later that winter I found out my body'd played a trick on me. I was trusting it to hard work, never so much as giving it a nod. It wasn't that I was sick on my stomach like I was the summer before I went to see Quester Franklin. Not like that, but something was wrong.

I asked Mama, she knew right away. She smiled, "Bless the Lord, Eula B., you gonna fill up this old empty house and put some life back in it." It brought the color back to her face, knowing that. "You got to start being careful, now, don't overdo." All that spring and summer, Mama kept after me not to overdo.

"I'm as good as ever, Mama. I don't need to stop doing anything. You'll see," I promised her. But she kept on to get me to go in to the doctor.

"Being *like that* is the most natural thing in the world, Eula B., but nowadays folks go on in to the doctor right early, to see that everything's all right. Mattie did, with Eunice. You ought to go on in and get checked out. It wouldn't cost you too much and you and Gus got a good bit stored away. Couldn't be no better way to spend it than being sure that young'un's all right. You go on into town and have it checked. You hear?"

She was sitting in the front room, her chair pulled up to the window, sewing. Like the winter before the wedding. Sewing fine little stitches on clean white cotton. Now she was putting those same stitches along the edges of flannel sheeting. Receiving blankets. Making welcome a little bit of a boy, pushing me to go to the doctor.

"I was afraid." I push that truth right out in front, over the yellow circles. That's one clear thing from back then. Would the doctor know about the summer with the Watkins man, about the time I went to Quester Franklin and bled for eight long days? If I can get this one born, then the next time it won't be noticeable. I didn't go. I didn't lie to Mama, but I just kept putting it off, pushing it back just one more week, until I knew it must be coming.

"I was scared then, too." Frog jumping under the covers again. When the pain started, it was too early. I figured pretty close on the time, and this was too early. Should have been last of November. It was early October now. Too early. It started like the time me and Mattie ate all those green peaches, but it got worse and worse.

"Gus, Gus, you got to get up and go get Quester Franklin. You ain't got time to go all the way into town for the doctor. Ride over there and tell her to hurry. Something ain't right. It's too early." Gus looked scared. He'd put a lot of stock in all this. He waked Mama before he left. She came into our room and started getting the bedroom ready.

"We're gonna need some extra room in here, Eula B." She moved the lamp off the table and set it in the front room. She hung up all the clothes on the chest and straightened the pillows again and again. Then she sat in the rocker and watched. Every time my belly started hurting, Mama stopped rocking. Holding herself in midair, not breathing until I got easy. I heard Gus when he got back, he left the horse by the front porch. Mama went out to meet him. I heard them talking softly, sweet murmurs against the early morning.

Mama sent Gus for the doctor. They decided it before he left. Played another trick on me, they did. I didn't know it until I heard his car chug into the yard a little later. I was too scared now to be mad. The pain got regular. Every so often it would hit. I tried to get ready for it, but it caught me off to one side each time.

"Try to relax, Mrs. Freeman, when the pain starts, just breathe in real deep and relax."

Mama, Gus, and the doctor sat around the bed. Leaving only one at a time to get a cup of Mama's coffee from the warm eye in the kitchen.

They sat while the night air turned pink out the windows. Gus watching with a twisted face. Looking at me, then looking away when the pain came. Mama just sat, nodding every once in a while like she knew what was happening. Every now and again the doctor would interrupt the quiet.

"If you folks will step out in the kitchen for a minute, I'll see how we're coming along." Then he pulled back the covers and pressed against my stomach, with it aching all the way down to my backbone.

"How long?" I asked.

"You never know with the first one. Could take most of the day, even over into the night. You just relax, try to relax against the pain. You're mighty strong. Most on their first do a lot of hollering and fussing." I was glad he said that about the first one. He didn't know. I was glad, too, that he thought I was brave.

"When your body plays tricks on you, you got to put it in its place and not give in." I should have told him that. True today as it was then.

Sometime after daybreak the doctor told Mama and Gus, "You folks better go on and get some breakfast. Looks like we gonna be in for a long day. I got a patient or two I got to see. I'll head on and then check by late this evening. I don't think anything's gonna happen much before dark." He stuck his head in the door before he left. "You just keep on pushing and staying brave. I'll check on you late this evening." He was gone. I heard the car sputter, trying to get going in the early morning air.

Mama came back in the room first, bringing an extra sheet.

"You gonna change the bed now, Mama?" I asked.

"No, honey, I'm gonna make up a puller."

"What's that?"

"Well, I'm gonna fold this sheet on the bias and tie one corner to each of the foot posts and give you the middle part. When a bearing down pain comes, you pull on this sheet and push. Maybe we can get this young'un born before sundown. The doctor says to try that. He don't think this baby's gonna get here anytime soon. But it's here, just in case you need it."

I tried to laugh. Papa had a puller he used to get a calf born. An old cow was bowing up and bellowing, and Papa tied a rope around the foot that come out first.

"You think this baby's coming feet first, Mama?"

"No reason to think that, Eula B., first ones just take a long time to get here." She fluffed the pillows behind me. "You can come on in now, Gus." He pushed the door back just a little ways, like he was trying to slip in through the smallest space possible. I propped up on my elbows between the pain.

"Mama, Gus, I want you to go get Quester Franklin for me. I don't want to use no doctor this time. I want her. She helped me get well before when that doctor was no good. Go get her for me."

Gus looked at Mama. "Mrs. Carpenter?" He didn't know what to do, birthing was a woman's world.

"Well, go on, Gus, it won't take too long to get to her house and she might be just what Eula B. needs right now. That doctor won't be back till nightfall. Yeah, go on. On the first one we need all the help we can get." She kinda half-laughed and half looked scared too. I think Gus was glad to leave. Glad to have something to do. Men get left out when things like this are going on in a family.

He was back in just a little while. I hadn't even used the puller yet.

"Quester is out in the south part of the county, delivering a little pickaninny." I heard him tell Mama in the kitchen.

"Her boy told me about another midwife. I rode down to her place and she'll be here in just a little while." He stopped and I couldn't hear what Mama said.

"She ought to be along in just a little bit. She was finishing fixing her man's breakfast. He works at the mill, has to be there by seven, so she said she'd ride to the crossroads with him and then I'll go up and get her." That was a lot of talking for Gus.

"That's fine, Gus," I heard Mama answer. "We won't be needing her for some time yet. Eula B. is working hard, but she's not having much luck. Guess we're in for a long day."

Gus drove out of the yard soon after that. Must've been getting on toward seven o'clock. Him and Mama had eaten. I could smell bacon and eggs.

When he got back, there was a big, fat coffee-colored woman with him. She was sure and steady. Moved around the bed light as a feather. Like her feet barely touched the floor. And her big and fat. She eased the bed out from the wall and sidled up between the bed and the window. The curtains stretched tight along the sill, pulled by her broad behind. "Mr. Gus, Miz Carpenter, I'm gonna need some extra hands here in a little while, but right now you just give me some time here with Missy." She started talking, soothing me right into having that little boy.

"There, there, now you just let old Della help you push that baby out here so's we all can take a turn at holding him. You just think about knocking the bottom rung off'n the end of this fine bed and push that young'un right out here to Della." It was a kind of chant, and soon I was moving with it and winning.

"It ain't gonna be long now, little missy, you doing fine. Just keep pressing on to glory and you just keep pushing and pushing and breathing and pushing and we gonna have us a little'un. Just you wait and see."

How long that day was, I don't know. But the rhythm came on us all.

"This one's gonna be it, little missy. I can see the top of'n his head. That the best part. Just a little bit longer and you gonna be a mama. You doing fine, just a little bit more and you can roll over here in this big fine bed and get some sleep." I kept playing the game of beating my body and not letting it get the best of me. Pushing, trying to get the swing to go so high that I could see the river. Pushing, pushing.

I heard the puller rip and Della shout.

"That's it, little lady, we got us a baby."

There was more to it than that, but I slept. Mama told me what happened. "We just wasn't able to get him to breathe. Gus run over to the Bickhams to see if they had any ice. Della said that sometime rubbing ice up a baby's backbone would cause it to gasp for breath. 'Get it started with ice. Sometimes it works,' she told us.

"It didn't work for your little fellow, Eula B." Mama tried to tell me easy. "He was tiny and perfect, just didn't have any life in him."

"I'm sorry, Mr. Gus, Miz Carpenter, he just ain't got no life in him. Perfect though. And Miss Eula was the bravest thing. She was something to have gone this long on the first one, never did cry out or nothing. She'd make a good mama. I always say that how a woman takes to birthing will tell how she'll take to raising them. She'd be a good one. Maybe you'll have another chance, Mr. Gus. I sure am sorry."

Della stopped by the preacher's house and told him. He came by later that night. Then she went to the funeral home and told them. Mama told me all about it later. But then, I was sleeping, thinking I had a baby to nurse.

"Eula B., we don't know just what happened. But he just never would take a breath. We did everything we knew, but he just never did even try. When the doctor came back, a little after dark, he checked him all over, real good, and just shook his head. Said he didn't know why either. Maybe it was because it took so long to have him. Maybe it was all that trouble you had with your kidneys when you was a young'un. He couldn't give us no reason why the little thing didn't make it. I'm so sorry, Eula B., maybe sometime later you and Gus will have another one."

"Where's Gus now?" I asked.

"Gone into town, honey. He took the little thing to the funeral home. Bless his heart, it was hard on him. He kept saying to me, 'That's my son, my little boy, my little boy, but he ain't got no life in him.' He wrapped him up in a receiving blanket and put him in that little basket we fixed and took him into town. That's a lonely trip for him, Eula B. You be thinking about him some now, too. He's lost a little boy just like you have."

I listened to Mama tell me all that happened while I was asleep. There was nothing for me to say. I just turned my face to the wall and tried to erase the time. To go back to the pain. When there was some kind of hope.

"Turning away don't work, then or now." But then I could get up and do for myself, for Gus, for Mama. Then I didn't give in to things and I could still win when I had a trick played on me. I could get over a perfect baby with no life in him. "Yes, sir, I could win then." I didn't have no bad side to haul around and I could get up and get things done. That's how to get over trouble, keep on doing things you have to do. Somehow you get through it. That's what I done. Worked, too. Mama and Gus wanted me to stay in bed half that next month. Till I could get my strength back. That was a bunch of foolishness. As soon as I got a good night's sleep, I was back on my feet, trying to do everything I done before. I just didn't have no baby to take care of, that was all.

"You'll pay for this, Eula B., getting up and doing around

while you're still bleeding like a stuck pig," Mama warned me.

This old stroke may be what Mama was talking about. I don't know but seems like I won more fights with this old body than I lost. I sure hated losing that little boy, though. He was a perfect little thing. Round and pink, Mama said he reminded her of Mattie. She came to see me the next day. I was sitting in the kitchen, peeling pumpkin for pies for the wake.

"Eula B.?" She was at the hall door. I looked up at her, her face, white and drawn. Her eyes were red. Mama stood behind her. They'd been crying together.

"Eula B., I'm so sorry. So sorry. I left Eunice at home with Horace's mother. I wanted to come be with you. Gus came by the house on the way back from the funeral home. He's such a pretty little boy. I stopped by to see him on my way over here. Oh, Eula. I'm so sorry." Mattie wrapped her hands round and round her handkerchief. Her nails were short, for doing wife and mother work now.

"Thank you, Mattie. Funeral's tomorrow. We're waiting for Gus's brother, Johnny Mack, to get back from Jackson." I put the bowl with the pumpkin on the table. "I think I'll rest awhile now, Mama. You and Mattie can visit." I stood to go to the bedroom, and the room swam around me. Mattie reached out to catch me.

"Lord help us, Eula B. You're gonna faint dead away with us standing right here." She put her arms around me, held me close. Her body shook in time with mine. Mama stood to one side, then joined us. The three of us crying out our losses in that old familiar place.

I rode into town that night with Mattie and Horace when he came to get her. I saw the baby all laid out in the basket Mama made for him. Gus was sitting up with him. His little white skin shined like some kind of magic light was going off inside him. Still as a picture.

We brought him home in the cold night air, me and Gus. He couldn't feel a thing. He spent one night at home with us before we buried him right next to Papa. It was cold, even for that time of year. Maybe funerals bring out the cold. Putting that little thing in that wide, dark hole about killed Gus. It was almost more than he could take. We never talked about it though. But on Sundays, after church, when I was fixing dinner, he'd go out to the graveyard and stand by that little grave and just look. He wanted a boy, somebody to work with.

"You okay, Mama Eula? With these kids acting like wild Indians, I can't hear it thunder in there. I thought I better check. You sure you don't want to come in the den and watch TV with me and the kids? I won't let them crawl all over you. I promise. There's a good show just fixing to come on."

"No, Shirley, I'm 'bout ready for bed. It's been a long day for me." I turn to face the wall. "You can turn out that light."

$\mathcal{I}$ feel the door slam when Toy gets home. Then space. Another slam and a car's sound. This car is smooth, not like the metal tapping of the doctor's car. Shirley and her young'uns are gone. Toy'll be in soon. Tiptoeing down the hall, pulling herself up small so she won't disturb anything.

The sound from the TV gets louder. Toy must be getting hard of hearing. She'll be here in a minute. I'll pretend to be asleep. The door is opening, a ribbon of yellow light slides across the far wall.

"Mama," Toy whispers, "you awake?"

I don't answer. The circles on the quilt make slow, steady rises. The door eases closed and the wedge of light leaves the room.

"Mama, you 'bout ready for breakfast?" Morning sounds, not late-night planning sounds. "We got oatmeal again this morning, but the doctor says if you eat this all up, then tomorrow morning we can have an egg. Don't that sound good?"

I turn to look at Toy hard.

Toy, I don't never see you eating oatmeal at all. It's always me that gets the oatmeal, and you eat them little fried pie things that come in a box and you put in the toaster oven. That's what I need to tell Toy. But she don't give me any time to answer.

If she gave me some time, we could talk about something besides food and bathrooms. Like how come we was never we. Never together like me and Mama.

"Now, come on, Mama, help me just a little bit and we'll get up and go to the potty and then we'll have some breakfast. Don't that sound good?" Toy's grunting and straining, trying to get me and this body up and in the bathroom. "Come on, Mama, give me just a little help. There we go, up and at 'em. You doing good this morning. Just a little bit more. There, now. I'll be back soon as you finish peeing."

She hasn't always talked to me this way. Not when I had a place of my own and there wasn't a rent check. She's not a bad daughter.

Gus was soft on her. That was a fact. He never would make her do nothing. Guess that was because she wasn't no boy and he just didn't know what to do with a girl. When she was born, he said, "Eula, I declare, I don't know what to do with a girl. Me and all my brothers never did know much about them. Sister was always Mama's job. I guess raising this one will be up to you." Gus still went to the graveyard on Sunday after preaching and looked at that little grave right next to Papa's.

He never did get over losing that little boy. And Toy just couldn't quite take his place. Not that she was supposed to, but he always longed for a son. Too bad, too. Toy needed him to tell her "no." She was headstrong and needed a man to deal with her. Gus just couldn't do it. He left it all up to me. Maybe that's why me and her never got around to important things, never got them settled. I was too busy telling her all the little things and we didn't get around to the others.

"I don't know."

"Mama?" Toy calls from the kitchen. "You 'bout through in there? Just a minute. The water's 'bout to boil for the oatmeal. Hold your horses."

Wonder why she says that. Mama Two used to say that. Every time we'd go over and get supper with them. Gus and Mack would get into it over something and Mama Two would say "hold your horses." Seems like a silly thing to me to say. But she always said it and now Toy says it too. Funny thing the way some things follow one after another.

The bathroom door squeaks when Toy comes in. My head starts shaking all on its own.

"What's the matter, Mama, ain't you through?"

"Yes, I'm 'bout ready, I just think it ain't right to have a young'un helping a mama in the bathroom. I think that every time I come in here."

"Well, that's a silly thing to think. Who's gonna help you if it ain't me? You always told me that you pay for your raising. So I guess taking your mama to the bathroom comes under that, don't it?"

Toy looks straight at me. What she said was important. It's something we can start with. A slice of open time hangs there between us, waiting to be filled up. So many things I need to say while I watch her looking strong at me. She holds still, like a good pointer, for just a minute.

"And you've been a good daughter there, Toy, paying for your raising." She watches me, still and quiet for a long minute. I think she heard me.

Then the time passes and Toy starts fussing with my nightgown and robe.

"Now, let's just put our feet back into these slippers and go see what we can find for breakfast.

"These next two weeks or so, Edward Earl is gonna be gone more'n he's home. You know the trial of the renter just started. They finally got the jury picked and Edward Earl is a witness. He'll be over there every day until they call him. Lord, he is scared to death. You know how a lawyer can get you to say just about anything he wants you to. Asking all kinds of tricky questions and trying to trip you up. Edward Earl was so nervous this morning that he 'bout couldn't eat a thing." A laugh puffs itself right out of the good side of my mouth.

"Oh, I know what you're thinking, Mama. Edward Earl ain't never had anything upset him so bad that it hurt his appetite. But this thing has come as near to it as anything I ever seen. I don't know what they'll do to the boy. I reckon they'll wind up sending him down to Clinton to the pen for the criminally insane. That's what he is. In-sane." Toy makes the *in* part heavy. Like being *in*-sane is worse than being *insane*.

I don't know if he's insane or just no good. Seems like a lot of folks nowadays get away with being insane that in my day would have been just plain "no good." I reckon that anybody'd kill their young'uns would have to have something mighty bad wrong with them. We talked that day at the door, though, that weak-eyed woman and me. At least she knew she didn't know nothing and she listened.

"I can't stand here all day watching you like a young'un, Mama." Toy waits a second, then, "You gonna eat some of that oatmeal by yourself?"

I lived alone for a lot of years with nobody around me and I made it fine. Made it better out there in the country with my work and my land than any folks I ever saw living here in this trailer park. I need to tell Toy that, but it will take too much out of me. I don't want to waste my good thinking time arguing with Toy. I nod yes. She goes on about her business at the sink. Wonder if she tries to get things settled while she works.

If I fiddle with this oatmeal long enough, she'll give up and put me back to bed. I won't have to eat it. My good hand pushes the gooey stuff from one side of the bowl to the other. It slides back into place, filling up the hole my spoon makes. I push it again. Up the side of the bowl. It laps over the edge and falls on the plastic place mat. A gray spot on a yellow daffodil. "Like some big chinch bug, gonna suck that bud." Will Toy scold me?

"Lord, Mama, you worse'n Darin when it comes to messing with your food. No wonder you ain't big as a minute. I'm gonna tell that doctor that I can't do a thing with you and this oatmeal. Maybe he'll give you something else for breakfast. You sure ain't taking to this oatmeal. He's only trying to keep your cholesterol down. But I'm gonna ask him to think of something else. I can tell him for sure that you ain't gonna take to this." She picks up the bowl, opens the bottom cabinet with her knee, and slides the oatmeal into the garbage can. It hits the bottom and makes a soft thump against the plastic.

You can tell that doctor all you want. But no doctor's gonna take care of your body. You got to do that on your own. They won't help you sometimes even when they got the chance.

"We got to get on back to bed, Mama. Breakfast or no breakfast." Toy comes to help me up and like some wounded three-legged dog we make a slow procession down the hall. We've done it before. Short, jerky movements. Toy grunting and straining, as much from her own weight as mine. I drop onto the bed, angled to one side. Holding myself up with my good hand. Toy gets a clean nightgown and underwear out of the chest of drawers. She sees herself in the mirror and pulls her blouse down over her stomach. Stands up a little straighter. She speaks to the mirror.

"Mama, the health nurse is due today and she's gonna bathe you and change your bed. I've put out some clean things for you. Try to be nice to her. She's doing me a big favor and you know your Medicare pays for it, so you might as well let her help us."

There she goes again, talking loud and treating me like I don't know a thing. Like I don't know how to treat folks. Still in all, I don't like that little nurse. She does all that "we" business and talks to me like I don't have good sense.

"You hear me, Mama?"

I nod yes. I want to turn my head to the wall. But I don't want to get Toy going about needing to be nice. Soon it'll be "now Mrs. Freeman this, and now Mrs. Freeman that, and let's move our little leg and let's wash our little back." Who in the world can think about anything important with that kind of silly talk going on. And she never shuts up, goes on and on.

I heard them once talking in the kitchen. After she finished with me. Toy asked her to have a cup of coffee. What would Mama say about Toy asking a nigger girl to stay and have a cup of coffee? 'Course, Mama stopped that afternoon and had a glass of tea at Quester Franklin's.

Toy told me what she said: "I don't think your mama likes me coming here and fooling with her. Some whites still feel that way. Your mama's probably one of them. Mrs. Kilpatrick, the white home nurse, doesn't visit this part of the county, or I'd send her. I don't mind coming, but I don't think she likes me very much."

"I told her you don't mind her not being white, Mama, but that you just don't want nobody fooling with you." Toy said it in a hateful way.

How does Toy know what I like or don't like. She never asks.

"She interrupts, is all. I don't care that she's not white." I want Toy to understand. She's already leaving the room though.

"Ma'am?"

"Nothing."

Toy goes on scolding down the hall. "You already paying for her, Mama. We need to keep her coming, Lord knows we need all the help we can get." Toy's loud voice trails away, and the trailer shakes. It is quiet now.

The trailer shakes again. Heavy steps along the hallway. Not the nurse. She never stomps.

" 'Morning, Mama Eula." Edward Earl's voice comes in the room first. "I don't aim to scare you, but I've got to go over to the courthouse this morning, and I forgot to take my blood pressure medicine. I bet I didn't sleep two hours last night. Wish this thing was over. I ain't never been one to talk in public much. I sure ain't looking forward to being on that witness stand."

I don't answer. I never got used to a big talker in a man. I just keep on looking at him. Waiting for him to wheeze back to the kitchen and get his medicine and another breakfast. He waits a minute, seeing if I'm gonna talk. Then pulls the door to. Pushing it back open, he sticks his head around the edge.

"Well'm, I guess I'll be back about dark, or whenever they decide to let us go. That judge don't seem to be in any big hurry to get this thing over with, and them lawyers keep jawing at each other most of the time. Well'm, 'bye, Mama Eula."

I nod, short like, to let him go. I hear him in the kitchen, moving glasses in the cabinet and pouring another cup of coffee. I bet I'll smell bacon in another few minutes.

" 'Bout took his appetite, indeed." The yellow ring on my

stomach bounces on " 'bout" and makes a little ripple over to the edge of the bed.

A kind of uneasiness settles on me this morning. Feels like July and August. Mama called them "not enough time–too much work" months. The garden comes in all at once. Feels like something pushing all the time. Today is like that. Toy scolding me to be nice, Edward Earl coming in on my thinking time, and that nurse will be here any minute now. I got to get it straight about Gus. Planned my work a day ahead. He used to laugh about that.

"Eula's got enough planned for tomorrow that if they was planning on having the rapture, they can just as well put it off." Laughed at me and all my plans and work. I know work eases a kind of pain that nothing else will cure. When my heart hurt, I'd work it out. A day's work ahead drove away the thoughts that bothered my nights. I learned that the summer of the Watkins man when Ollie didn't come home.

"Edward Earl would never understand that." I puff again and the cover jumps. The trailer door closes and pushes the air in the trailer against the walls. The curtains move just a little. I bet he didn't wash a dish. Just makes a mess and expects somebody else to clean up behind him.

Gus was neat as a pin. Never did leave nothing behind for anybody to have to tend to. Didn't leave me no boy to try and train. Just one girl and told me from the start that he wouldn't be much good with her. He was a good man in lots of ways though. But he was part of my failure. Not just that we didn't have no boy, but some other kind of way. Like deciding he wasn't a man you would wear lace for. Kind of shortchanged him. When he watched me in the well house on those early mornings. I knew he felt for me, probably in a better way than the Watkins man. But I just couldn't feel it back.

He was glad about Toy. He never got in the way of me and

Mama and our doings. Never once complained about living in the house with us and a baby girl. One man, three women. He just went his way and did what he had to and never complained the first time. Like the old song Papa used to sing. "And he never said a mumbling word." That was Gus.

Quiet and easygoing. Took a lot to get him mad, but he held on to his anger. Like Q.C., there. Got mad all over when he was mad. He didn't know much about women, so he just mainly left them alone. Just having one sister and all, and nobody messed with his mama. She ruled the roost at their house, Mama Two did. So Gus learned early not to cross women. He just kept quiet around them and then pretty much did as he pleased. Never talked much about what he thought or how he wanted things to be. Just seemed to go along, steady and sure.

"And that's a fact."

"Well, good morning, Mrs. Freeman, how are we doing today? I've come along from the county health office to check on you and to give you a bath and just see how well we're doing these days. Your daughter let me use the table in the den to catch up on all this paperwork for your case, so now I'm all set to see how we're doing."

I'll never get Gus settled with her here.

"I guess your family's all up in the air about the trial at the courthouse." She kept looking in her bag, like she was going to find some answers in there. She put a little plastic tub, a bar of soap, towels on the top of the chest of drawers, talking all the time. "Since the killings were over on your place, I suppose that everybody around here has a pretty good idea what happened." The inside of the bag still didn't answer her. I sure wasn't going to either. "Wasn't that something? Wonder what they gonna do to that fellow. I tell you, I don't know what this world is coming to. Must've been the war, don't you think? That's kinda what the paper said." She cracked a towel and looked down at me. "Now, let's hold up our little shoulder and try to get some good old warm soap and water under there. That's a good girl. My, aren't we doing just fine today?" She smiled out at the circles on the turned-down quilt. "Like I was saying, I guess you all must know pretty much what went on out there with them. Them living on your place like they were. Knew Edward Earl from the war is what I heard."

I keep trying to move my good leg over on top of the towel at the side of my body. Maybe if I think about this hard enough, I won't have to look at this girl who's jabbering in my ear.

"I mean I don't want to be nosy or anything, but I was just wondering if maybe he'd been loony all the time and something just caused him to go off the deep end. You know, I saw a program on television about men who were in the war just going off the deep end sometime. Don't even know who they're shooting, just remember the war and how to shoot and something just happens to them and they just go off. Don't you think that's what happened, Mrs. Freeman?" She still doesn't look at me. She's washing all over me, everywhere, and not really looking at me at all. "I mean, your daughter said that you talked to them a lot when they was first out there on your place. Don't you think that's what might have happened? Somebody at the office said they were gonna have a psychiatrist from Jackson and one from the insane asylum down in Louisiana come to the trial one day this week. Said they both said he was just plain crazy. You think that's so, Mrs. Freeman?" She stops for just a minute, working to lift me up a little higher on the pillow. She doesn't grunt or strain like Toy. But she's slender, nice-looking for one of her kind. "That's a girl, Mrs. Freeman, just lift that leg up for me and we'll have this little old body clean in no time. We're getting along just fine today, aren't we, Mrs. Freeman?"

I pull my head around. I look her right hard in the eye. She stares back for just a minute, not saying a word. Good, I want her to stay quiet. She starts lifting the sheets on the far corner of the bed.

"Well, I told your daughter that I felt like if I just kept on coming out here we could work something out. We can get this old bath and changing this bed down to a matter of minutes. Then we could sit and visit for a while. Now, wouldn't we like that?"

I look hard at her again.

"Soon as you get through here, I got some thinking to do. I need the rest of the day to do it." I nod to her. The kind of nod that tells Toy to leave. Doesn't seem to work on the nurse. She laughs a little laugh down into the pillowcase she's holding. The pillow's under her chin. She pops the pillowcase into the air, filling it like a cloth balloon. She can't talk much, locked onto that pillow. Gus had a squirrel dog that used to grab the sheets on the line and shake and pull till the sheet came floating down on top of him. This nurse with the pillow under her chin looks like a terrier who missed the mark. That one of Gus's used to sneak up under the house when he finally got away from the sheet. Maybe a falling sheet'll make her go away.

"Probably not."

"Probably not what?" she asks, dropping the pillow down into the case.

"Nothing."

"Well, I won't be much longer. Soon as I fill out my time sheet and figure out the mileage from the health office in town out to here, then I can leave a record for your daughter to sign. Then I'll be heading on to my next patient. I have five or six to see today, so I don't want to be too long in one place. You can tell your daughter I put the papers on the table in the kitchen."

She stoops over and rolls dirty sheets, gown, and towels into an envelope. They make a neat little package, and she kicks it in the corner. She picks up her bag and turns around, looking at me head-on for the first time.

"Well, that finishes us up for this week. I'll see you when I get around this way next week. And don't you let that trial at the courthouse worry you one bit. I mean, you couldn't help it that it happened on your place. You didn't know that he was some kind of loony when you said you'd rent it to him." She swings the purse over her shoulder. "You didn't have no way of knowing that he'd been in the war and was just gonna go off the deep end one day, now, did you?"

She doesn't wait for me to answer. Just opens the door, shaking her head. "Don't know what this world is coming to?"

I puff a big sigh when I hear the trailer close again. Maybe now, in the quiet before Jimmie Lee arrives, I can get back to thinking. About Gus. He's been gone a long time. Fifteen years, I guess.

"There's different kinds of men." That was true. The words stay just above my chest so I can watch them. The steady ones, and the shining ones, surely somebody marries them and lives with all that light.

I hear the trailer door close. "Plain ones like me, though, have to be around the steady ones. That's the only kind I could stand." Must be Jimmie Lee. "That you?" I call out.

"Yes'm, it's me, Jimmie Lee. I ran a little late. Had to go by the welfare office and sign up for another program. I swear, they make it hard on a person. Always asking for forms and papers and stuff. Why, the one today had a line for Mama's maiden name. Don't that beat all? I filled it in and handed it to the woman." She comes in talking, in a big hurry. "And do you know what she told me." Jimmie Lee swings her purse to the floor and flops down in the chair at the end of my bed. "Mama's name, Etoile, means Star in French. Did you know that, Mama Eula." She looks down into the wide space at the top of her purse, rummages around. "Asked me where in the world we got such a name. Heaven only knows, I told her! Ask my Mama Eula where that fancy name comes from." Jimmie Lee draws a cigarette out of her purse and sticks it between her lips. A little click from her lighter makes a fire shoot up near her nose. She leans back, sighs, and closes her eyes. "Lord, it must take me two, three days a month just to get all that stuff I need so that I can draw my check. Then it ain't enough to live on. Well." Jimmie Lee finally takes a breath. "How we feeling today. Did the health nurse come already? I guess she must have since I see all them sheets and things rolled up in the corner. Guess you're glad to have that over with. Mama said she don't think you like her coming too much. But then, after all, you've paid for it with your Medicare so you might as well get your money's worth."

"There's all kinds of men, Jimmie Lee, all kinds." Got to beware of those who come with too much light, too many stars. *Etoile*, a star bursting all over that Mississippi summer. Jimmie Lee's face is lost behind the smoke. I hear her clear, though.

"You can say that again, Mama Eula. I seem to be able to find the rotten apple in every barrel, too." She throws back her head and laughs. She finds it funny. Toy found the wrong ones, too. The Camp McCain pretty soldier boy, just like the Watkins man for me, a pretty foreign boy, one just passing through. Then Edward Earl. I forgot to tell Toy.

"There sure are different kinds of men."

"You're something else, Mama Eula." She pats my leg, smiles at me.

Sometimes Jimmie Lee sounds like a record of Toy, just in

a little younger voice. A cigarette voice, crinkly and hoarse. But she touches me.

"Jimmie Lee, was you born after the war?"

"Now, Mama Eula, you know I was, on your birthday. I was named after Daddy's brother, killed at Pearl Harbor. I had to come along after the war. Mama and Daddy didn't even get married until he got home from the war. Lord, you'll have me half in my grave. You know I'm not that old." Jimmie Lee laughs over the idea of being old. I keep watching her, head thrown back, mouth open wide, laughing. She laughs easy. I like that.

"Your voice is old, older 'n mine because of them cigarettes."

"Now, Mama Eula, don't you start in on me again about them cigarettes. It's my nerves. You know since me and Royce separated I just can't get myself straightened out. Cigarettes is all that calms me. Too, it keeps my weight down. If I didn't smoke, I'd be big as Mama. Lord, I gain so easy now. I'd be big as the side of a barn if I didn't smoke."

"There's more ways to keep from getting fat than smoking. Besides, you're built like the Fergusons, you most likely won't run to fat. Still in all, smoking ain't the way to keep from getting fat. Work is." I look down at the little ridge I make in the bed. "Reason I don't take up no more space than I do now is because I always worked. Work's what will keep your body in line. Cigarettes is no way."

"Okay, Mama Eula, okay!" She backs toward the door. "I'm gonna go on into the den and watch some of my stories." She shakes her head and laughs again. "Looks like that nurse got you fixed up just fine. You want me to put those sheets and things in the wash?" She waits just for a second. Then, "Naw, I guess Mama can do them when she gets in. That washing machine makes so much noise and jumps around so much that I can hardly hear the TV. Yeah, I'll just wait and let Mama do those when she gets in. She knows just how she wants them done anyway." Jimmie Lee gives the sheets a little push, jamming them hard into the corner. "You call me if you need anything. You hear?"

I keep my eye on the sheets, pushed partway up the wall in the corner. Slowly, they settle, spreading out like the white of an egg. Left there, they look tired. Like me. Pushed up into this trailer and just lying here, having to wait for every single thing to be done for me. Somebody got to help me up, somebody got to help me down. No way for a grown woman to live. How was it I got into all this? Wouldn't be here if Gus had lived. But he's been gone a long time. It wasn't the war that got him. Though, he'd been steady in war, too. They just didn't call him. We got some kind of letter 'bout the war though. Not about Edward Earl's brother, we didn't know them then. But about somebody we knew. Not Gus, not Jimmy Lee.

I look hard at the ceiling, looking for a sign. Gus wasn't the kind to go to war. Q.C., now, he was a natural. Hotheaded, looking for a fight. Guess he got it too. That's what the letter said. Mama said he almost missed it. Almost was too old. When Pearl Harbor came, he must have been almost forty. But they let him in. That's what killed Mama, I know it for a fact. Losing Q.C. for so long, getting almost used to him being gone, then hearing from the government, kind of like finding him again. Then losing him all over again for the second time. It was too much for her. That's what did it.

Mama knew Q. was gone that summer Ollie didn't come home. He didn't see no way out then. He knew he was stuck on the farm forever, unless he got out soon. He didn't love it the way I did. Funny. Thought he had to run away. Mama knew he was gone. Papa kept looking for him to come back.

Still in all, maybe somewhere deep down she thought that

after he run far enough and long enough, he'd get tired and want to come home. You never know. After he took the egg money and all, he had a lot of shame to think about and coming back was so hard. He had to pay Mama back. Couldn't have come home till then.

"Eula B., you and Ollie, that's what Mama sees." He told me that, sitting on that log that stretched out from the sandbar into the middle of the river. He strung trot lines from it to the other side. "Yeah, you know when the preacher talked about alpha and omega. That's Mama. She loves the first and the last. Me and Mattie, well, she hadn't got much time for them in the middle." Q. found me sitting there on the log, watching the river. "And Papa, he's the same. Nothing I do is good enough. Why can't you plow like Ollie, how come you can't sing like Ollie, you don't know numbers like Ollie." He'd left the fields, mad. Come to run his trot lines. Found me there, daydreaming. Last big flood got that log, I guess. It was a perfect sitting spot. Put my feet in the river and cool off. Q. was wrong about Mama and Papa. They loved him and Mattie. He just never believed it. After he took Mama's money and left, he must have figured there was no way back.

After Papa died, folks never asked any of us about Q. Not even at the family reunions in the summers. What could Mama say anyway? When the rest of the cousins and aunts and in-laws told of their boys and how they was doing, how they was going up in the world, how could they ask about Q.? They didn't know about the money, but they knew that his leaving was enough to kill Papa. Only one time Mama ever mentioned him was during a revival. The visiting preacher came by to pay a pastoral call.

"Evening, Mrs. Carpenter. Hot enough for you?" We was in the kitchen and Mama kept right on with her canning.

"Have a seat, Reverend. Can't leave this steamer right now.

You'll have to excuse me. Can I get you a glass of tea? Eula B., see if there's any ice on the porch." She kept right on at her work. He sat down, sweating in his suit. He arranged his big black rectangle of a Bible just so on the white oilcloth surface. Like a square black eye staring around the kitchen it watched Mama adding jars to the steamer. I fixed the tea. Set it, cool and brown, next to the Bible. Lined it up, like a soldier.

It was the summer of the bad drought. Dust covered the azalea's leaves after the preacher drove up in his car. I wasn't trying to listen. Went back to shelling peas.

"Mrs. Carpenter, sometimes it falls the lot of visiting clergy to call on folks he doesn't know so well. I been looking forward to getting a chance to talk with you. I haven't seen you too regular at the evening services, so I thought I'd drop by." He settled his glass on the table. The wet circle it made now touched the edge of the circle it made when I set it down, a wet figure eight on the cloth. "I hope you don't think I'm meddling, but I did wonder what was the trouble. Since your folks have been pillars of this church for years. Well, I just have to tell you right out, Mrs. Carpenter, some of the brothers and sisters at Mount Pisgah have mentioned it in our prayer times. They wondered what was wrong. Some even felt led to have me come and talk to you. That's the main reason I'm here." He put his fist to his lips and cleared his throat. He wore a wide gold ring. His glass made a separate third circle on the oilcloth. Right beside the Bible. "Mrs. Carpenter, it grieves me to ask, but it grieves the Lord more to have a straying child." His hand went to his face again. "Are you right with Him?" I watched the peas from the purple shell drop one by one into the bowl in my lap. The end of my thumb pushed them out, set them rolling. The kitchen held me and Mama, the preacher, the steam, and that big black eye of a Bible. I made my breath go shallow, not to disturb the air around me. Mama didn't say a word for the longest time. She fitted the last jar into the canner. Touched the sides of her hair with her fingertips. Her face pink with the steam was fixed. She dried her hands on her apron and sat down.

"I reckon I am. Getting up and down the steps at the front's beginning to worry my knees."

"Well, Mrs. Carpenter, that's for sure. The failure of the flesh catches up with us all." He smiled, wide, and leaned back a little in his chair.

Mama sat up tall in her chair, like she was growing under the weight of what she was fixing to say. "But that ain't the real reason. For a long time I dreaded going because I didn't want anybody asking about my boys. Then folks stopped asking, not wanting to pry into why and where and if and what, and I got so that I was mad every time I came from church. I lost my husband to the grave, one boy to California, and one boy to God knows where, and I was mad, mad at the Lord for taking every decent man out of my life. So I lost all interest in going."

The preacher caught his breath up and it bounced around that still kitchen like a bird flying with a broken wing.

"It took me a while to get over being mad. Then I found a way of being with the Lord that don't include much church-going. That's what I been doing lately. So to answer you, I think I'm all right with Him. But I don't know about some of the sisters at Mount Pisgah. I guess they would have to speak for themselves."

Mama pushed her chair back, scraping it hard against the floor. She walked through the front room and pushed the screen door open for the preacher. He followed like a little puppy, carrying his Bible up under his arm. "I do appreciate you coming out here to check on me. I know you meant well, but there's some things in this life that a body's got to work out for themselves. Losing a son like I lost Q.C. is one of them. Just to have him disappear without a trace, without a good-bye. It's worse than a death. Every day I wonder when the mailman comes if there'll be a letter telling me of something that's happened to him. Telling me he's in trouble, in jail, or dead. I got to work out this part of my salvation all by myself." The door stood open behind her hand. "Thank you for checking."

"Well, I'm glad to have met you, Mrs. Carpenter, but I want to remind you that the Good Book—" here he waved the black eye in the air in an arc around Mama—"says that we are not to forsake the assembling of ourselves together. You think on that and I hope to see you at church one night before the revival is over." With that, he was down the steps and in his car. As he drove out of the yard, he sprayed a fresh coat of dust on the azaleas.

Mama turned to go back into the kitchen. "You wanna glass of tea, Eula B.?" That was all she spoke of Q.C.

It must have been late in 1942, or early '43 when we got the first letter about him. It came with official signs and told Mama how proud she must be to have a son who would volunteer to serve his country when he didn't get drafted.

"And him better'n forty years old, joining up with a bunch of kids." Mama sat on the porch, reading that letter over and over. She was a good reader. It didn't take her nearly as long to read that letter from the government as it took Papa to read the letter from Ollie. The letter said that Q.C. had volunteered for service right after Pearl Harbor and requested "extremely hazardous duty." Later on in the letter it said that he was missing in action and presumed dead.

The next letter told us how he was in some part of the war that couldn't be talked about in the open just now, but we could rest assured that he had served well and was a hero in fact. The letter talked about how he had done "outstanding service to his country in times of peril." How his family could be awful proud.

They didn't send him home to be buried next to Papa and the baby. There went Q.C. again. Disappearing without a trace. Leaving us to wonder and to hope, knowing all the while that he wasn't coming back.

Mama went down fast after that. She got to where she sat and looked out the window, like Papa did before he died.

"You know, Eula B., it's different having boys and then having girls. I can't put my finger on it exactly, but there's a difference. Both my boys left me. I don't know why that makes me feel so bad, but it does." She kept watching the side yard through the window. "I got you and Mattie, but I just feel so bad."

We heard from Ollie only every now and again. Knowing where he was didn't do us much more good than not knowing where Q.C. was. Ollie was lost to California just as much as Q.C. was lost to that dark August night.

"Be sure to save a spot for Q.C. on the other side of me, Eula B. On resurrection morning I want to see him the first thing," Mama asked me.

"Okay, Mama," I promise her again, this morning, in this cracker box. With no more breath than I had when that preacher come to ask about Mama's soul.

"I want to save that space for Q.C.," I whispered. "Mama won't rest easy until she knows he's there beside her."

The day worked out better than I thought. With that nurse and Jimmie Lee both to put up with. "Nothing makes me fret more than a day where I don't get nothing done."

"You need something, Mama Eula?" Jimmie Lee yells from the front room. Den they call it. I won't answer. She couldn't hear me if I did, and she won't come back if her show's any good. Don't seem right to have to hide from your own when you want to get something done. It's this silly trailer. All boxed in with nothing growing on the whole place.

"Huh." The wrinkle on the sheet jumps up. A cracker box, part of the trouble with all them is that they all scrunched up here in this trailer, rubbing up against one another, getting on one another's nerves. That's a good part of the trouble. Not near enough room for folks to live.

Still in all, can't say that having room always means that you ain't gonna have trouble. You do. All that room in the country didn't help those poor young'uns and that woman.

She needed half the county to get away from that loony. Bet the trouble'd come a lot sooner if they'd been cooped up in a trailer park. But, Lord bless them, what a terrible thing to happen. Bruised my place. We'd had trouble there before, but nothing like a killing. And it being his own, too. Just lined them up in the front room on the settee and shot them. All but that oldest boy, the one that talked like his tongue was too big for his mouth. He must've run for help. They found him on the front porch by the door. Couldn't get out any faster 'cause of the way that door would hang on the high spot on the porch floor. That slowed him up and his daddy had time to catch him. Terrible thing, killing your own. Gus never would have raised his hand against a woman or a child.

The place saw some dying, though. Just in my lifetime. Mama Taylor died there when I was less than two. That started it, I guess. Then that first one of mine, the one Quester Franklin took care of. I guess it died there, too, in a way. Then my little boy, and Papa and Mama and Gus. Lots of dying there, but a lot of living went on there too. Up to the renters it was pretty even. But not after that, that old loony messed it up good.

I should have said no when he drove up in that van and spit on that white brick. Never should have listened to Edward Earl. In a way, though, I'm to blame. The nurse said I wasn't, but I feel like I am. Folks are supposed to take care of what goes on on their place. I didn't and now, look at who had to pay for it. That poor weak-eyed woman and all them young'uns. I don't know how to get that part settled. It's not like Gus and Mama and Q.C. and Ollie. I can't figure this one. All those lawyers and judges will have to settle it for me.

Edward Earl's the only one I got who's even up there at the courthouse, and Lord knows he can't do it. He come home from the courthouse yesterday, plumb wasted.

"I never seen anything like it in all my life. Courthouse full, Mama Eula. Folks standing out in the hall and the television folks from Jackson and New Orleans there with their cameras and microphones. Making tapes for the news in the vans outside. Talking to everybody that'll talk to them."

Toy and Edward Earl was watching the news. I was sitting at the table eating my supper. They showed a picture of him. That old loony. Hair hanging down on his shoulders. He had handcuffs on and two policemen had him under the elbows half-dragging him into the building. His beard was longer than I remembered. Something about him looked like Jesus to me. Getting dragged in to see Pilate.

"They bring him in to court every day, Edward Earl?"

The television man told about how folks in Richardson feel about the tragedy. He had a wide face with no expression. He don't seem to care one way or the other. Says nothing about that poor woman and all those young'uns.

"Yep, they sure do." Edward Earl waited for the commercial to start talking. "They been bringing him over from Angola every day. It's too far to drive him down from Parchman, so the State of Louisiana's keeping him at night. 'Course, he is a Louisiana citizen, so they got some right to him. The driver from the Angola prison sat next to me in the witness room. He said that he has to get him before rap up and leave Angola before daylight to get here when court starts. Don't nobody over there want nothing doing with that loony." Edward Earl shifted in his chair to look at me. Wants to see if I'm listening. I just nod to him.

"Driver said they got one man to drive and two men to sit in the backseat with him in case he gives them any trouble. Can't get no breakfast or nothing at the prison since they leave so early." Edward Earl shakes his head, the fat under his chin waves back and forth. "They been stopping at that little store in Clinton to get a honey bun and a cold drink every morning about daylight. But then the fellow that runs the store found out who was in the car and he told them not to stop there anymore. Said he didn't want no money from a child murderer. They been coming all the way to town here before they can get a thing to eat. Driver said that loony just kinda looks at his feet and shakes his head all the time they're driving." Edward Earl looked down and shook his head. Acting it all out. "Said sometimes he kinda wails, kinda like that Billingsley boy used to do, I guess. Said it was real spooky driving with that fellow wailing in the backseat. Said he'd be damn glad when this trial was over. 'You think they'll give him the chair?' I asked the driver. He said, 'Hell, no, them head doctors'll prove that he's *in*-sane and he'll be free, walking the street in less'n two years. You wait and see if I ain't right. Yes sir, it's got to be where there's more criminals outside the prison than there is in.' " Edward Earl turned up the volume to hear who was going to testify tomorrow. He pointed to the screen. "That's his lawyer right there, from up at Jackson." The scene on TV moved to show the courthouse with the war memorial in front. There, the man with the wide face and no expression smiled with his mouth and said, "Good night, from the courthouse in Richardson, Mississippi."

I bet Edward Earl is telling everybody who'll listen in the witness room all about what he went through in the war. How he lost a brother and how he never had no reason to shoot his family. He's huffed and puffed about that around here enough. When he gets up on that witness stand, he'll be dripping wet and they won't be able to hear him past the first row. He ain't no brave man, he'll be scared to death in front of all them lawyers and judges and fancy doctors from the *in*-sane asylum. No, Edward Earl won't take none of them family boasts into the courtroom. Still in all, he's enjoying that money he's getting from the state every day for sitting up there and waiting to be called on. Said that first night that they all got paid since they were being kept away from their regular jobs.

"Now, there's a laugh." He's been doing that ever since I met him. His regular job is not having a job.

"You say something, Mama? You need some more tea?"

I shake my head to Toy. I wish I had somebody else up there at the courthouse to tell them what I know about this thing. Somebody needs to tell that she was getting ready to go home. Just waiting for her daddy to send somebody up to get her. She almost made it out of there. I know her daddy must feel awful, thinking if only he'd come a day or so earlier, maybe none of this would have happened. Life can sure play mean tricks on you. That poor thing and all them young'uns. Don't seem right that they have to pay for some old loony who got all messed up in the war. Sure was a terrible thing. I carry his face in my mind back to bed with me. I kinda hope he really is insane so he won't have to hold all this terror inside himself. "The two children I lost come back to sorrow me, even now—and me an old woman."

"Mama Eula. You want something or you just talking to yourself?" Jimmie Lee's back here, standing in the door. Must be morning again.

"I'm all right. I was thinking about that trial. Out loud. Never does pay to put things off. You need to go ahead and settle them. Don't you think so?"

Jimmie Lee pulls her shoulders up and tilts her head to one side. She smiles and shakes her head. "I guess you're right, Mama Eula. I don't think I've got much important to settle. I just get the kids off to school, wait for the mail, see if that no-good Royce decided to send his child support, and then come over here to take care of you and to catch up on my stories. That don't seem like much to get settled to me. But I could be wrong." Her shoulders go up and down again, and she looks down at her hands, spread out by her sides. "If you don't need me, then I'll go back to the den." She turns toward the door facing.

I do need her somehow. How can I tell her I need her to see how things can start off good and then go wrong. She ought to know that, ought to have learned that from Royce. She loved him once enough to marry him and now she calls him "that no-good Royce."

Jimmie Lee stops and turns around, facing me. "Say, you want part of a Co-Cola? I was fixing to open one for lunch. Since it's getting so hot, I thought you might want one too. How 'bout it?"

"Co-Cola's not good for your kidneys. I never had much of that kind of stuff. Mama always said it was bad for your kidneys."

"I tell you, Mama Eula, you'll take away everything I like, my drinks, my cigarettes, Lord have mercy, I couldn't get on without them." Jimmie Lee's a right pretty girl, nice hair. She don't fix up much, more like me than Mattie in that way, but she's all right. "Oh, listen, I'll fix your lunch in just a little bit and come and get you. Or you want to eat in bed? Well, you decide when I get it ready, okay?" This time she closes the door completely and I hear her shuffling down the hall. Toy and Shirley Earlene and Jimmie Lee all wear bedroom slippers in the house. Never put on working shoes. Just slide around in those slippers all day. I asked Toy about it. "I don't see how you stand wearing them slippers all day. Just slip-slopping around the house. You got to change every time you want to go outside. Lord, that seems like a lot of trouble. Just put on some good working shoes and get on with the day." I told Toy that.

She laughed. "Mama, I don't have to be running out every few minutes to see about chickens or gardens or drawing water or any of that stuff. I moved to town, remember? I stay in the house all day. I don't need to have a bunch of working shoes. Bedroom slippers suit me just fine. Besides, they're comfortable. Anything's better than them safety shoes we have to wear at the plant."

I thought about that after she said it. She should have figured all that out before she went to work at the factory. How she'd be living all on the inside.

"Well," I tried to finish up that talk, "I don't know how you feel about it, but when I pass on and you get me ready for burying, I want you to bury me with some real shoes on. I couldn't rest with those little flimsy things on. No way to go into glory without a pair of real shoes."

"Oh, Mama," Toy said.

"Well, it's true, folks need to make arrangements for what's important to them. Shoes and going on to glory is important to me. So you do what I say, you hear?"

"Okay, Mama." Toy sighed and slumped down in her middle.

"I got shoes for burying stored in a suitcase with some remnants, don't you forget, Toy."

"All right, Mama," she sighs heavy and long.

Even Edward Earl gets up and puts on his cowboy boots every day. He don't sit around in slippers. That's one thing I can give him credit for.

"Can't figure out for the life of me why he wears cowboy boots. He wouldn't know what to do with a cow if one was to come in the front room." It makes me feel good to say that. To find out something good about Edward Earl. I hope Toy remembers about them shoes.

Toy didn't learn about bedroom slippers from Gus either.

He wasn't a man to spend no time at all undressed. Like he wasn't the kind to wear lace for. At night, when he went to bed, hooked one strap onto the bib of his overalls, then hung that loop over the foot post. Next he'd put his shirt over the knob on the top. When he got up the next morning, it was right back into them clothes for him. Made it in to get the first cup of coffee already dressed. Shirt, overalls, and boots. Not cowboy boots though. He wore those tall, lace-up working boots, summer and winter. The kind to do real work in, nothing fancy and dolled-up. Boots for plowing and haying cows and hauling fertilizer. Gus never did even own a pair of bedroom slippers until he got sick that last time.

It was strange for Gus to be sick. He never had an ache or a pain. Then all of a sudden he just sort of started going down. Not that he ever complained for one minute. He just kind of quit eating and quit doing much of anything. Like he just sat down and waited for the end to come. He did his dying the same way he did everything else, slow and steady, just like a rock. He got so thin there close to the end, I knew he wasn't gonna make it. The doctors didn't say much. Mama used to talk about folks just wasting away. That's what Gus did. I can't say what caused it. Never did know. He might have been worrying over them papers he signed. That might have caused him to go down like he did.

I knew when that man came by. Asking Gus a lot of questions. It was a good long time before he got so thin. That whole thing, though, carried over to his dying. It was the only time I knew him not to carry everything on just out in the open. Kinda like me and the Watkins man and lying to Mama. Everybody's got something in them that they wish wasn't there. That thing with that man and those papers was like that for Gus.

Toy's girls was still at home when he came around for the

first time. They was visiting, swinging on the porch, in the summer, when he drove up. They came running in to tell about a man looking for Papaw. Called Gus "Papaw." Him and Gus talked for a long time that evening and then he come back two or three more times. That last time, he brought some papers and Gus signed them and so did I. I didn't even look at them. I was too busy putting up pepper jelly.

"Eula, this fellow's got some paper's we got to sign about the place."

"Just a minute, Gus, I just got this jelly to the boil and I can't leave it right yet."

"Well, Mr. Bacot isn't going to wait for you to get finished there before he heads back for town. Soon as you can, you come on and sign these for him." Gus kept standing at the kitchen door. He was out of place in the kitchen in the middle of a summer afternoon. My face burned with the pepper steam.

"Ask him to have a seat. I'll be out directly."

"Eula, we can't ask him to set around and wait all afternoon. He's a busy man."

"Well, all right, Gus. You stand here and stir this jelly so it won't boil over." Gus acted like I poured the hot syrup on him when I said that. The spoon didn't want to do right for him. Kept sliding off the sides and rushing into the middle of the pot. I dried my hands good so I could write. That Mr. Bacot was sitting, sweating in the front room. I nodded to him and he brought his handful of papers to the kitchen table. The steam from the pepper jelly got in his eyes. They watered and watered. I had to get him a clean straining rag to dry them.

"What you cooking that's burning my eyes so?" he asked.

"Pepper jelly," I told him. He showed me where to sign, pulled out a monogrammed handkerchief, and commenced snorting into it. Fussing with his eyes and his nose all the time I was signing. My straining rag and his fancy handkerchief both flying like flags around his face.

"Mr. and Mrs. Carpenter, you say you signed this paper of your own free act and deed?" Still dabbing at his eyes and nose. "That you know the contents thereof, and that this is your signature?" Gus stopped stirring and nodded. I took the spoon from him and nodded to Mr. Bacot. I didn't even ask Gus what it was all about. Summer's too busy for worrying about papers.

Later, that lawyer in town said Gus didn't know what he was signing and did I want to take them to court.

"I'm not about to go to court and spread my business all over the county," I told him. Toy and Edward Earl was with me.

"But, Mrs. Freeman, you have a right to these minerals, and with the current oil boom, you might be a rich lady if we could set aside that deed that you and Mr. Freeman signed. I am certain that your husband thought it was a lease, not a deed. That sort of thing happened all over the county just about the time Mr. Freeman negotiated with Mr. Bacot." His hands made a fleshy pink tent under his chin. He waited for a minute. I nodded for him to go on. "Several others out your way did the same thing. All of them have said that they thought it was merely a lease, not a deed. They thought the money they were paid was for leasing the mineral rights, not for selling." He held his palms up, soft, pink palms, with no hard places from a hoe or an ax. I nodded quicker this time. "We are attempting to get these deeds set aside so that the income from the oil that's around here will go back to the landowners. Not to the company that tried to trick a lot of you folks." He was a nice young man, and he leaned forward in his leather chair. Trying to get me to see how right he was. He talked for a long time that morning. We all listened real careful. Trying to follow all he was saying.

He didn't know his office was in the same place as the doctor's. He had unstained hands, city hands, too. 'Course I wouldn't have known it on the inside. Rugs on the floor and curtains and shelves made of walnut, I guess, or maybe cherry. A radio playing off in another room somewhere, soft music. Not a thing like that Sunday morning that Papa took me in all wrapped up in a feather comforter in all that heat. Him saying I was tall for my age and that belt buckle shining and leading him around. *Etoile.* That lawyer visit was not the same. It was like the room was tamed down by the soft music and the soft floors and the little bit of light easing in around the window dressing.

"Mrs. Freeman, we are simply waiting to help you fight this thing if you should choose. Of course, our firm would require a retainer and we would hope that we could represent you on a contingency fee basis after the initial matter has been solved." On and on he talked. I looked at the walls. Did he ever touch them? Or sit at the window and wonder whether I was going to get well or not? I couldn't tell from looking. I stood up while that nice young man was still talking.

"Is something wrong?" His smooth face wrinkled up.

"No more than this," I told him. "Whatever me and Gus signed, we signed. If we didn't know what it was, then that was too bad for us, but I don't aim to get all mixed up in no court business or spread my affairs all over the county. I told you that. Gus is gone now and he can't speak for what he thought was on that paper. Him and me never talked about it, so I can't say for sure what he thought. I was making pepper jelly when that fellow brought the papers in the kitchen for me to sign. Gus said it was all right, so I signed them. I don't know nothing else about it. Since I can't say for sure, then I have to believe that they were all right for us. Now I got to be going since the day is wasting away with me sitting here, doing nothing. I do thank you for writing me that letter, but I don't think I want to have me a lawyer right now."

I led the way out. The young man was leaning over his desktop, his hands spread out flat now on the papers in the middle. Toy and Edward Earl followed me. They didn't say a word the whole time we was in there. Soon as we got in the truck, it was a different story.

"Mama Eula, you know what that lawyer was saying is probably right. Papa never was one to sell anything. Not land anyway. I think he just might have been tricked into thinking he was leasing the minerals. Not selling them. If that's the case, then you could get some of that oil money that's coming in to everybody's got land in that forty over there that borders the creek. Sure would be nice to get a hold of some of that easy money."

"Edward Earl, I don't want to hear no more about this. I don't know nothing about no papers. What I told that lawyer is what I mean. If we signed them, then we're bound. No two ways about it." I put my teeth together and pushed hard, in and out.

"Well, Mama, all's Edward Earl was trying to get you to see was that you might be in for some money. Lord knows you could sure use some. It's not like you got a satchel full under your bed these days."

"I got plenty to keep me going. Toy, I don't want to hear another word about it."

"Lord knows, Mama, me and Edward Earl only wants to help you do what's best for you and for everybody. Everybody else is taking theirs to court and you could be helping your neighbors if you'd join in the law suit. That's all we was trying to get you to see." Toy turned sideways in the truck seat to look at me. Her lips were pooching out like a pouter pigeon. I kept on looking straight ahead at the road. Toy made the space between her and me bigger than before.

"Toy, I told you and that lawyer that I'm not about to spread my business all over this county. Besides, I told you before that there's some difference in some folks' mind between what's best and what's right. When you put your name on a piece of paper and agree to something, then you're bound by it. You can't go changing your mind and going to court just because you don't like how it turned out." The last curve before we got home was right ahead. I held on to the arm on the truck door. Steadying myself.

"Well, Mama, you could think of your grandchildren. Some of them might be entitled to some of that money. It might make rich folks out of them. That might happen if you'd be willing to go to court."

I sighed as Edward Earl slowed into the curve. "It takes you a long time to get things straight, Toy, but I am not going to court. Me and Gus signed that paper in the kitchen over the pepper-jelly steam. Now I ain't gonna hire no lawyer to try and weasel out of something we both did."

Toy kind of swelled up, pulled a little closer to Edward Earl.

"You could think of us a little, too. Not be so hidebound with all your what's right and what's wrong. You could bend just a little, Mama, for us. You could think about us for once."

"Toy!"

"Well, it's true, Mama, you always doing what's right. What makes the most sense. Never a new dress unless you outgrow your others. Always so practical. When I was singing at the school, in the program, and I asked you and Papa to come, Papa said sure, he'd be there. And you, you, Mama, you said—" Toy was crying now, leaning hard against Edward Earl's shoulder. He put his arm around her, driving with only one hand. "You said, well, if your daddy's gonna go, there's no point in me going too. I'll stay here with Mama and we can finish ironing the front room curtains." She looked at me, across the front seat of the pickup, her nose running and her cheeks turning splotchy red. "You stayed home and ironed, Mama. And me singing in the school program." She left a little space between each word. Edward Earl patted her shoulder with his big, meaty hand. There's curly hair on his knuckles. There wasn't enough room in the truck's cab for all Toy was saying. Her words pushed right against the windows and into my ears.

The truck pulls up in the front yard. "Thank you for driving me into town, Edward Earl." I pull the door handle up toward me. "I'm sorry me and Toy spoiled the ride home."

I took my time getting into the house, stepping solid on each foot, hearing Toy all over again. The pickup was back on the road by the time I was on the bottom step.

Looking back, I think I know why Gus done it. It was a good while after Toy and Edward Earl married. Their girls was still little. Mama died and me and Gus kept busy with the gardens, but we didn't have nearly the work we once had. It was after a family reunion. Shirley Earlene was twelve or so, I guess. Gus asked me, "You think Ollie's ever gonna come back home, I mean even for a visit?"

"I don't know. I think he always aims to. I don't think he meant to be gone so long. Somehow, he ended up putting his life there and it may even seem like home now. You know he's been there, let's see, how many years has it been. Nearly forty, I suppose. Maybe it just seems like home now."

"I guess maybe it does. You'd think he'd be a little curious about how things are here, wouldn't you?"

I looked at Gus real close, trying to figure out where he was going with all this. "If he hadn't been sick himself, I think he'd been here for Mama's funeral. But that spell he had with his heart came right before she died. His doctor wouldn't let him come no way except by airplane. You know Ollie couldn't do that. Not that I blame him one bit, of course. I don't think I'd climb on an airplane with a good heart, much less with a bad one." I was rocking in the front room when I was thinking about Ollie and a plane ride. Gus didn't say no more about it just then. Week or so later, though, he brought up seeing Ollie again.

"Eula, you like to see Ollie?"

"Now, Gus, you know I would, but we talked about that just a day or so ago and you know I got no way to get him to come home. That's up to him." This time I was washing dishes. Gus was sitting at the table, waiting for his supper.

"I know that. But what's to keep you from going to see him?"

"Lord have mercy. Gus, you must be getting crazy in your old age. However in the world could we get off to California? Besides that, it would cost an arm and a leg." The bubbles in the sink popped around my hands when my fingers looked for the silverware. Later, when I was ironing, I thought about it again. I snapped the idea right into the pillowcase I was doing up.

He kept coming back to it, though. Two or three times. Him and Toy was like that. Worry you half-silly about something, till you came around to their way of thinking. Finally, one day Gus just said it outright.

"Eula, I want you to plan to go and see Ollie. I been thinking about it for a long time. I think I just may see my way clear about it. Now, you start planning to go, you hear?"

I didn't answer him right off. Go to California, by myself, to see Ollie? Thinking of it was like trying to understand the labels on some of Gus's medicine. I just couldn't make out the words. Still in all, if he meant it, I'd see about it. But I didn't tell a soul. I almost made another long trip once. Didn't make that one, so I didn't plan too much on this one, either.

"But I did." Started putting my clothes out on the bed and looking at them. Wondering. What kind of weather do they have in California? Must be hot. They grow oranges. Wonder what his wife is like? She sends us a card at Christmas. Been doing it for Lord knows how long. Puts some pictures of their young'uns in every once in a while. They would be up good-sized now. Mostly grown. Ollie said she could make corn bread now without putting sugar in it. I guess she's learned something about cooking.

I got lost in my plans. Finally told Toy about it.

"You know, Toy, I might decide to take off from here and go and visit your uncle Ollie. It don't look like he's gonna decide to come home. I want to see him before I die." That's all I said. Toy thought it was a good idea.

"I'll take you to New Orleans to catch the plane, Mama, if you want me to."

"Plane? I'm not going on no plane. I'll take the train, thank you. You couldn't get me up in no airplane, no sir. It'll be the train for me."

Toy argued, just like the lawyer and the court business. But I wasn't going up in no airplane. The train was the only thing that could take me to California.

Toy finally sighed. "Well, Mama, if that's the only way you'll go, then I'll call the ticket agent and see what kind of ticket and everything I can get for you. Lord, it'll take you a week to get there. But ain't nobody able to tell you nothing. You will be dead when you finally make it. But you've made up your mind, I can tell. I know there's not one thing in the world that'll change your mind."

She went to Columbia to get the ticket.

I had a little leather-looking case that a pair of Gus's eyeglasses came in. I put the flat black-and-white ticket in it. For a whole week after Toy brought the ticket out to the house, I got it out every night and read the names of the places listed on it. Some of them were the same as those talked about in *The Indians of the American West*.

"I don't know how long I had the ticket when Gus had his first spell." Not too long. After that I left it in the case most of the time. A lot of time I was sitting with him, listening, waiting to make sure he'd draw another breath.

"You ready for some lunch, Mama Eula?" Jimmie Lee calls in over the TV.

"I guess I could eat a bite now," I call back.

"Can't hear you," she answers, "I'll be there in a minute."

Gus got worse after that. Little by little. Got so you could notice it from one day till the next. Dr. Simmons in town would just shake his head.

"It's his heart," he told Toy. "He's just worn it out. Working like he has since he was just a boy. In the heat and cold, never really taking care of himself. It all adds up. He's just slowly losing ground. I prescribed some things to keep him comfortable when the pain comes. Try to keep the fluid from building up around his heart. But outside of a miracle, he won't last much longer. I'm sorry, Mrs. Johnson." I couldn't make out what Toy said. I was giving the girl at the desk the information about Gus, seeing how much I owed them.

"I'm glad you want to eat now, Mama Eula." Jimmie Lee has a plastic TV tray in her hands. She sets it beside the bed. "Hey, I halfed the Co-Cola with you anyway. Beats oatmeal and prune juice, don't it?" She flings her hair back and laughs. I feel my face smile at her.

"It probably does, Jimmie Lee. Don't guess one little glass will hurt my kidneys either."

"That's a girl, Mama Eula, a woman can't always just do what's good for her, now, can she?"

"No, not always." The fizz from The Co-Cola goes right up my nose, little stinging bubbles. Tastes sweet, sweet on the good side of my mouth. Sweet pleasures of sin, Proverbs call them.

"Thank you, Jimmie Lee, you're a good girl." She sits at the foot of the bed while I eat. Not being fussy or trying to help me keep the crumbs from falling. She stays the whole time. I put the fork down, wad the paper napkin up, and put it on the plate.

"If you're through, I'll take that tray and get back to my stories." She stands up, tall and proud, a real Ferguson.

"I'm through." She pats my foot, leans over, and tucks the covers in again, tighter this time. Making a snug little case for me. "And thank you." She forgot the tray. She'll come back and maybe we can talk.

When we got home from the doctor's office that evening I went into the house and got out the black case. The ticket looked as good as new. Fresh and unused.

Gus had a bad smothering spell just a few nights later. I called Toy. "You take this ticket back to Columbia. Tell the man I won't be needing it. I can't be running off to see about Ollie right now." Toy came to get it, stuck it in the big purse she always carried, and sighed.

I cried that night. It had been a long time since I'd done that. Maybe when Mama died was the last time. But that night I got all those lost trips cried out. St. Louis, California, places listed in my geography book, all of them filled up with people that you couldn't count on. I best stay right here, where I knew folks and couldn't be fooled.

After I got the ticket out of the house, I got on with taking care of Gus. It took some doing, but I was there right up to the last. Edward Earl wanted me to get somebody else to do it. That was like him.

"Edward Earl, as long as I have one breath left in me, I'm gonna take care of Gus. Don't you forget it. When I want you to tell me what you think, I'll ask you." It was easy to get mad at Edward Earl. When they left, going back to town, I wanted to push a little of it over on to Gus.

I stood in the doorway of the bedroom. Looking at him wasting away in the bed. "Try, Gus, try. Don't let your body get the best of you." I hollered it at him from way down inside. But it came out as a little, puny whisper. He didn't even look toward me.

That night I thought I heard him call me. Real low. I waited from the daybed to see if he was just dreaming. Nothing. I lay there a little bit longer. Then I found my robe over the chair and pulled it up around me. I could sit for the rest of the night beside him.

"Gus, you calling me?" I put my hand on the side of the bed. The same kind of cold that come from Papa was standing all around that bed. The doctor had showed me how to use the oxygen tank. I put the plastic cup over his face and turned the faucet on the top. He didn't move. I moved the cup away and waited. He wasn't breathing. I kept putting the cup over his face, turning the faucet. I could hear myself hollering. "Try, Gus, try. Don't let your body get the best of you. You got to try. It'll play a trick on you if you don't. I know, Gus, I know. I had it happen to me, Gus. It was why I couldn't give myself over to you like you wanted. I'm sorry, Gus, I'm sorry." My voice sounded far away, strained. I could will him to live, just from what I had inside of me, if I could just reach down far enough.

"It was why I couldn't wear lace for you. I know what a trickster your body can be, I know, Gus." His eyes blinked just a little, I thought. "Oh, Gus, Gus, try. You got to try."

He never did open his eyes again. I kept working till daylight. Then I called the funeral home, no point in calling the doctor then. We'd got our business settled.

Folks started coming right away. Didn't want me to be alone, they said.

"Some things you got to bear alone," I told them. Losing Gus was one of them. Nobody could help me with that. With as few folks as I had to count on, losing Gus was something I'd have to reckon with on my own. No smooth words or hand pressing would get me through. I just had to reach down somewhere inside and pull up what was in me and lean hard on it.

I got through the wake and the preaching all right. But going to the graveyard was the hardest. I leaned on nobody when I walked up that hill to the open grave. From the edge of the road I saw the mound of fresh dirt. Beside it, four markers. Four of my own were up there now. Gus would make it five. More up there now than down in the house. Me and Mattie all that's left. Her, sick and crippled up, and Ollie good as gone.

Of course there's Toy. Her young'uns. But that's a different thing. The hill held more of me than the house now.

I watched the hill and walked a path around the edge of living after Gus died. Trying to feel like life was really happening again. There was enough busyness to put off getting things settled. Toy and Edward Earl kept after me because I was staying out there by myself. I had a time with them, but I won. I stayed. At least until those strokes got me. I outsmarted them for a while. That summer with the Watkins man I learned that I could win out over my body, but I couldn't teach it to Gus, not when it mattered.

"With so many things that can go against you, you got to get in charge of the things you can." That's a fact I need to tell Toy and her girls. Jimmie Lee and Head Start and government programs. She can't do one blessed thing about those, so she better find some way to get in charge somewhere. Always waiting for Royce to send a check and the government lady to get her eligible for this and that. She's always at the mercy of somebody else. That's a bad place to be. "Get in charge where you can, Jimmie Lee. Get in charge." She's not listening. Got that TV shrieking out over the air, filling up all the thinking space in this house that's not a house. "Jimmie Lee," I call to her. "There's too many places where you got no choices. Things go against you and you got no choices." She doesn't answer me.

"Act of God." That's what the insurance man called it. Sitting on the front porch with his little stack of papers bunched up under his arm. He showed up soon after the storm. Called it an "act of God." While he was explaining, I was counting up on that hill. I nodded up towards it.

"Now, Mr. Brock, that's an act of God." Not tornadoes.

"Ma'am?" He kept on shuffling papers. They slid to one side and he opened his knees to stop the motion. The papers dropped through the hole. Leaning over the scattered mess, he looked up at me, pitiful, like a puppy. "Ma'am?" he asked me again. The sweat stood out around his mouth. He's probably a sweet boy at heart, but frazzled by this storm and trying to explain it to people.

"Losing family. That's an act of God." I tried to get him to see the difference. "You got no chance to change that."

"Well, yes'm. But what I'm talking about here is fixing the roof on your house. The insurance that Mr. and Mrs. Johnson, your daughter and your son-in-law, got you to take out? Well, it doesn't cover acts of God. And tornadoes are considered, by our company, as an 'act of God.' That's why I brought all these papers. To show you how the company decides all these things. Right here"—he held up one of the stapled-together sets of papers—"it lists all the circumstances that 'acts of God' cover. Now, if you'd had lots of rain damage inside the house as a result of the tornado blowing the roof off, well, then"— here he smiled, seemed glad to find some other hard thing—

"the policy would have *paid in full* for that loss." His smile got bigger and he wiped the little beads off his lip.

"I don't know why in the world I need insurance anyway. I been living here all my life and nothing's ever happened to this house. It was my daughter's idea. Mrs. Johnson. She talked and talked about it until I just gave in." A limb from the live oak stretched out across the walkway. I need to get that thing pulled around to the burning pile behind the shed.

"Well, Mrs. Freeman, we certainly do hate it when a brand-new policy holder like yourself has damage and then we discover that the coverage was not complete. Of course, we do offer an extended policy that would have granted you protection in this very instance. You realize that you bought only the most basic of coverages and that explains some of the problem." He was stacking the papers neatly on top of his knees. "There is a very good comprehensive policy that I could write for you which would extend your coverage considerably and grant you more protection for just pennies a day more in premiums." He turned the papers on their side and patted the ends.

I stood up and the porch swing gave a little creak. "You are mighty nice to drive all the way out here, Mr. Brock, to tell me this. But I won't be needing any more insurance. I don't hardly feel like I need the little bit I got. Like I told you, it was Toy's idea. But trying to buy protection against the hand of God kind of feels like spitting in the wind to me. So, if you're through looking around at all you need to, I'm needing to start back up on some of this cleaning up. Tornadoes may or may not be an act of God, but there's plenty of mess that goes along with them. And thank you for coming." I headed for the steps, giving him time to stack his little papers in the black briefcase and snap the fasteners shut with both thumbs at the same time. Click.

I wasn't afraid that night. Spring storms tell me only that

the weather is changing, fixing to bring in a good growing season. We had storms all along the river ever since I can remember. Nothing to be afraid about. This one was a bad one. I heard it coming up that bottom pasture long before it hit.

I always heard folks say that a tornado sounded just like a freight train. They were right. I heard that thing coming up the bottom sounding just like a train. Roaring to beat sixty, I felt it when it touched the chicken house. Got a good bite there. Then took just a little nick out of the house. Pulled the tin up on the corner over the back porch. Soon as it passed I heard that tin just flapping out there, like the sole of a worn-out shoe. That was all.

Toy wanted me to move out the next day.

"Mama," she said, "one day we're gonna come out here and find you dead from one thing or another. Lord, you drive me crazy, wanting to stay out here. All off to yourself and everything. Suppose that tornado had touched down on the house and not the chicken house? Now, just suppose that? You'd ended up just like a chicken, plucked clean and squawking." Toy got louder and louder. Her voice all tight and high. I tried to see myself blown featherless like a chicken. Looking all plucked and cold. "We could've lost everything." She shook her head and the tight beauty-parlor curls wiggled.

"Now, Toy, I can't go running off every time some bad weather comes along. And I'm not all by myself. The Bickhams are down the road and somebody told me that the Graham farm is gonna be rented soon, so I'll have some neighbors down that way. I'm not gonna move into town and be all cramped up, not able to see daylight. It'll take more than a blown-down chicken house and a few pieces of rattling tin to move me off the place that was my mama's and then her mama's before her."

"Oh, Mama," Toy said. But she let me alone.

My mama always said, "It's an ill wind that blows no good." That was true about the tornado. The insurance man said it was "just an act of God," like that was something bad. Something I had to insure against. Still in all, it had been just that. An act of God, but not the way he meant it.

The morning after the storm I started cleaning up. I'd been through storms before. Toy and Edward Earl showed up about noon. Driving up slow, looking all around like they had never seen the place before. Lord, here they come and Edward Earl will be wanting some dinner. I don't have a thing in the world cooked. Took everything out of the refrigerator first thing this morning.

"That's the trouble with electricity." I said that standing in my kitchen that morning. Talking to God, I guess, since everybody was blaming the storm on Him. He was sure getting the credit at the insurance company. I took the food to the well house. "Electricity goes out in the first little bit of bad weather. Well house don't never go off. It's gonna stay cool. Won't lose nothing if you got a well house. Can't say the same for electricity." What I got out there to feed Edward Earl?

When Toy saw me out in the side yard, she jumped out of the truck and came running over to me just a crying and hollering. "Lord have mercy, you all right? I just been worried sick. Me and Edward Earl got out here as fast as we could. Couldn't get any answer on the phone. Called the phone company and they said that all the lines on this side of the county was down and there wasn't any way to get you until God knows when." There He goes, getting some more of the credit. "Then I called the county barn to talk to the road crew. They didn't know what kind of damage was on this side of the river. I have just been sick worrying about you. You okay, Mama?"

" 'Course I'm okay. You can see as much. I don't have a

thing fixed for dinner though. Had to put all the food in the well house since the power went out." I started back around the side of the house. The yard was covered in branches and leaves. A good day's worth of sweeping and raking. The sun was getting up hot and I needed to start.

"Mama, we don't need nothing to eat. We're so glad you're all right. You want Edward Earl to get one of those boys from down on the Bickham place to help clean up this yard?" She was walking real easy like around the branches. Had on her bedroom slippers. Couldn't walk just straight out over the mess.

"I reckon they got their own mess to clean up. Seems like to me in a time like this everybody needs to take care of his own." Toy and Edward Earl stayed for dinner. Cold leftovers out of the well house, leftovers after the storm.

The yard took me several days. The chicken house was over on its side. Two legs sticking out. A turtle on its back almost. I decided to tear it down. It had been there since I could remember.

"I'll put it further back, down toward the creek. Use that spot for some climbing roses," I told the Bickham boys later. "Leave those posts standing, run some wire between them." Florabundas would do fine there. That ground will be rich. Grow me some winners for the fair. Tearing down that old house and building a new one was a good choice. Wonder if the insurance man would call it an act of God?

It was several days before the Bickhams got there. They had lots of damage to their milking barns. Lost a bunch of freshening heifers, they said.

"Sorry we was so long in coming back, Mrs. Freeman." The oldest one, Jeff, told me that. "But we had to wait to do the repairs on the barn till the man from the government got there."

"Did he call it an act of God?"

"Ma'am?" He looked at me over the top of the lumber he was stacking. "No'm, he didn't call it nothing. He just had to fill out some papers to file with the government so we could get our money back. We got some kind of dairyman's insurance with the U.S. government. You got anything to cover your damage?" he asked.

"None at all. Just got to depend on myself. Stack that lumber over by the creek. We can reuse a lot of it when we rebuild."

"Yes'm." He started off, swaying under the lumber's weight.

The boys strung the wire tight between the two posts that the tornado left. I gave them a little early supper, the rest of the leftovers, before I went to get my pocketbook. They said they didn't want nothing.

"No, ma'am. That's all right," Jeff said. He did all the talking for the two of them. "Daddy said for us to come over here and help you just because we was neighbors. And you living alone and all. No, ma'am." He shook his head, but his brother just kept looking at the two dollar bills folded up in my hand.

"Well, I don't aim to be charity just because I live by myself. Now, I know you boys can use this. So take it. If nothing else, put it in the collection plate on Sunday and call it an act of God."

"Ma'am?" They both said that. The younger boy took it. Never looked at my face. "You boys check back with me the beginning of the week. Soon as the wire and the new tin get here, I'll be needing you to put up the new house."

"Yes'm." They said it together and slid into the truck. The place was beginning to look like itself again.

Looking over what they done, I figured I had room for seven or eight good-sized florabundas. They'll look nice there. I like having roses near the house. They smell so nice. A good thing about the country. Change plans, grow things, without asking anybody.

I started digging the first thing the next morning. There was something about digging.

"Yes sir. Digging is one good way to get on with living." That's one thing I know. First the flower beds for Ollie after the Watkins man. Then after Papa died, me and Mama started that truck patch. The summer after the little boy died, Gus didn't want to do much, but I talked him into buying muscadine vines. Got forty or fifty jars of juice and jam from those vines just last summer. "See, it works."

Seemed sensible to do that after the tornado too.

Toy and Edward Earl didn't understand that. All they wanted me to do was get comfortable, stop working so hard, move into town. That's all they could see to do.

"I wish Toy could understand about digging. And bedroom slippers." Cartoon sounds. Darin must be here this morning. There's some stirring closer though, in the kitchen. Toy said it was March already. If I get things settled soon, I can get back before the muscadines make this summer.

"Toy, Toy." The wedding rings don't bounce much now. Must be giving more air than sound.

"Toy, Toy."

Kitchen noises stop and the shuffle starts down the hall. Bedroom slippers.

"You all right, Mama?" Toy's voice comes in over the quilt. Her hair, still in pink foam curlers, followed.

"Uh-huh, I'm all right, but I was trying to figure. Is it March already?"

"Yes'm, it's March, Mama. Along about the middle. Still feels a little cool, though. You thinking about planting your garden?" She stays stuck at the door. Not really coming in.

Like she might get caught in something she didn't want if she gave herself over to the room.

"I was wanting to tell you that gardens help you get on with living. You know, every time I had a bunch of trouble, I went back to digging and planting, and it helped. Toy, it really helped, do you know that?" I hoped I was giving all this enough air to get over to the door where Toy was standing. The idea didn't seem to quite get there.

"Mama, I know for you that's the way it's always been. I just don't feel that way myself. I guess I've worked inside at the plant too long to change over to digging and planting. I don't know." She pulls her shoulders up so high that they touched the edges of the bottom roller. That sets a little ripple off, going up the side of her pink foam cap.

"Mama, I tell you what, I'll see if I can figure out some way for us to have some tomato plants right around the edges of the trailer. Would you like that?"

I nod and close my eyes.

"I'll go ahead and get your breakfast ready since you're already awake. The doctor wants me to try you on some cream of wheat since I didn't have no luck with you and that oatmeal. I don't reckon cream of wheat will do much better. But we'll try." Toy lets her voice trail after her when she closes the door.

"Darin, get your feet off the couch." Toy shouts her way down the hall.

She sounds tired. She's looking after both ends. Helping raise her grandyoung'uns on one side and got me on the other. Edward Earl in the middle just dragging her down there too. etoile. She toils. Sitting in that plant all day, putting collars on shirts. Don't seem like that would make her tired, not like it's real work. Outside work, now, that makes your muscles holler at night. But still in all, she's tired. Living all jammed up here, folks pulling on her from every angle.

"If I could just get some way to get back home, Toy could come and help me. She'd learn about digging and planting and what it will do for you. Get over this silliness about bowling."

The tornado hit about this time of year. How many years ago? Sometime in March. The live oak just started getting that funny yellow-green halo about it that comes just before the leaves pop out. The rain and the warm weather after the storm made the leaves spread like little fans. Hid the place where the limb come off. It's like that outside. One scarred spot's soon just covered up. Like that old dumping spot near the river. Soon as folks stopped dumping there, the grass covered it over, and by the next fall, black-eye susans grew over everything. Yellow double wedding rings cover me now.

I don't suppose folks is entirely that way. When that old loony spit on the brick, the rain cleaned it off. No way now, though, to clean off the mess he made on the place. Me and Mattie could take all summer, not fool with no garden at all, and still we wouldn't be able to clean up all the harm he's done. No amount of digging and planting would cover that up. I don't guess. Edward Earl did say that they put him away for ninety-nine years.

Now, that seems silly. Everybody knows that he ain't gonna live that long. Why they put a body in for longer than he'll live is more than I can tell.

Digging and planting saved me many a time, but it was the work I did right after the tornado that I was figuring out. About that "act of God." Sent the Bickhams home to wait for the lumber. I started digging for new roses.

The tornado left the roof damaged and the chicken house about gone. More than that, though, it added fuel to Toy's fire about me coming into town.

"Mama, you just got to move off the place and get somewhere that we can know you're gonna be all right and not worried every minute that you gonna catch a-fire or get blown off to kingdom come or some other such thing."

I knew she was working up to renting out my place and squashing me up in that trailer. The tornado was just one more vote against me. I started that digging to get over all that fuss about me moving into town.

Pushing down on a shovel. I could still do it. I move the end of the quilt there with my toes. I can see that block move, like it's waving to the bedposts. I can still step on a shovel. You need a good pair of shoes. Can't step down hard on a shovel top in a pair of bedroom slippers. A good hard sole will get a hole dug faster than anything.

It was easy digging in that chicken house dirt. Rotting hay and chicken droppings don't smell bad to me. I can close my eyes tight and open my nose right now and almost bring up that smell. Rich, ready to grow something. I stepped down hard, shovel slid in easy, right through summers and winters of roosting White Leghorns. I heard the point of the shovel bite. Scraping, made my flesh crawl.

"Made a goose walk over my grave, yes, it did." The flesh on my arms jumps up now, just for remembering that sound.

"You don't keep house for fifty years and not know what breaking glass sounds like." Not supposed to be glass under that chicken house. It's been there for years and we never built nothing on top of a dumping spot.

I kind of felt around with the tip of that shovel, pushing the dirt to one side with the toe of my shoe. Then I saw it just boiling up. That rich, rotted spot, like some kind of deep kettle of turmoil. Money and lots of it. I pushed the shovel first one way and then the other. It kept hitting and bumping glass. I got down on my knees. Didn't wait to get a paper to put down to keep from soiling my dress. Just dropped right down in that rotted mess and scratched the dirt away. Like I was some terrier bitch after a rat. Scraping it back with my hands, chicken droppings and all.

Ended up being five fruit jars full of bills all rolled up into tight little pipes. I set the jars in a line. Preserved money. The gold mason lids rusted brown in the grooves. I sat there, watching. Finding lost treasure in my own chicken house. Toy'd never believe that! Ollie went to California for it. Q.C. found his somewhere in the South Pacific. Me, I find mine in the chicken house. Right here at home. No fancy places or people for me.

I dug the whole floor up, shovelful by shovelful. Then I worked the dirt back down so it looked like I was just making a rose bed. Took me to near about dark. When I finished it looked just as natural as you please. No treasure spot at all.

After I took the jars inside and set them in the sink, I fixed a little cold supper. The jars standing guard around the drain. I rinsed my dishes and set them to one side. Then took a cleaning rag and washed each jar, easy like, in case the shovel had cracked it. I dried them and put them in the center of the kitchen table. Took me a while to decide to open them. The lids had rusted shut and I had to bang the edges with a case knife to get them to turn loose. The money was packed down tight inside. Wouldn't just roll out. I had to pry it out. Table covered with little green pipes. Like peppers that didn't get full and ripe. Deep inside each jar was a piece of white paper covered with Gus's handwriting. Told how many bills was in each roll. How many twenties, fifties, hundreds. How many of each kind. Then in one jar there was a longer sheet of paper. Looked like some that Shirley Earlene or Jimmie Lee took to school. Ruffledy edges, like it was tore out of a schoolbook.

Gus done his big figuring on that piece. He listed how much

was in each jar. Added that all up. Put "TOTAL" at the bottom of the page. Then he divided into that. Another number. Put the answer down. That figuring took me a long time. He put the answer down and put "per A." beside it.

Per acre. It was per acre. It was the money that lawyer gave him for signing that paper. He got some money for every acre that was on that paper. Put it all under the chicken house. That was how he was gonna pay for the trip to California. I couldn't tell that lawyer in town that I was gonna go to court about that paper. I found all that money from Gus. That was California money.

"When he got so sick, he must have just forgot to tell me. That's all I can figure."

"What you saying, Mama?" Toy pushes the door open. The curlers are gone. Bet they're in the bathroom sink. They'll have ridges in them where the hair was pulled so tight. Leaving a mess in the sink don't seem to bother her.

"Nothing. I was thinking about your daddy. How he was so sure I was going to California. We both might have. But he took sick so quick."

When he got sick, he just forgot about things. Forgot about that ticket for me to go to California, but he sure planned for me to go.

"Yeah, Mama, I know. Papa sure had planned big on you going to see Uncle Ollie. Just didn't work out that time, though. Shame, too. We haven't heard from them in a long time. Maybe I can get a card off to them sometime this week. Need to keep in touch. Aunt Jeanette said that Uncle Ollie wasn't doing too good last time we heard. You know on the Christmas card. Lord, has it been that long? I'd better see how they're doing." She pulls her high hairdo back out the door and starts down the hall.

I pulled the curtains that night. Undone those tiebacks on

the kitchen curtains. Don't reckon I ever let them curtains down another time in all my life. All the sorrow that kitchen seen and never once had I pulled the curtains shut. But with that money strowed out all over the table, I shut myself in, like I was ashamed, having all that money and not knowing where it came from.

"Per A." told me though. Told me it was ours. I knew Gus hadn't stole no money, but for the longest time I couldn't figure out where that much could have come from. I thought all kinds of things, like maybe it was an earnest on my inheritance, made up from what we lost from Q.C. and all those years of interest. Like a miracle, Mama's egg money gone to seed, and here it was now, springing out of the chicken house floor. It could have been that sort of miracle. Brother Martin always said, "The ways of the Lord are mysterious as the whirlwind." Maybe He multiplied the money under the chicken house.

Act of God. That tornado. "Finding blessing out of cursing" was another thing Brother Martin talked about. Tornado turned out that way. Toy's words in the truck, no blessing out of them yet. But it'll come, it'll come.

"I'm glad to get that settled." I use my breath to push the words to the front of me to let them stay for a minute in the air so I can be sure that they are right. Seems like they hang there shorter and shorter and the hump I make in the quilt is less and less. Not much ridge in the covers. Kinda like I'm fading into them. Fading away. Maybe that's how dying feels. Fading into nothing.

"I never did put it in the bank. Gus warned me about them."

"Better not put anything in a bank that you can't afford to lose." He said that. He didn't believe much in banks, not since his papa lost his money in a crash. I kept it in the grip under the bed. Had to move my quilt scraps again. Put them in a box in the pantry. Stored the clean straining rags in the top of that box.

I feel myself sigh, but the ridge doesn't rise. That poor, weak-eyed thing must have found that box when she was waiting for her daddy to come after her. Don't want to think about them renters. The hard parts of remembering wear me out. The Watkins man, well, I was just a young thing and didn't know a bit better. But after that I never did make no more mistakes about who you can trust as far as a man went. I learned my lesson there. Ought to have known better then, but I let myself get talked into that one. But after him, and Ollie, and Q.C., and even that shining doctor, well, I just put my feelings off to the side somewhere. Didn't let them trick me either.

Part of the money went to the Bickham boys for labor and part to the lumber company. Spent the first little bit to build back the chicken house. I paid it all out in cash, from the grip. Pulled it out from under the bed. Pushed the little gold bars to one side. The fasteners slid over and I pulled one handle one way and one the other. The grip yawned open into a wide, toothless hole. The money was still in little pipes, wrapped inside a pillowcase. Didn't have no money sack big enough for that much. Drew out just enough to count out the wages at the end of every day. Didn't want to go to bed owing no man. Paid the driver of the lumberyard truck the same way. Soon as he was unloaded. I left the grip in the middle of the bed until I got ready to go to sleep. Then I slid it underneath. Safe.

"Seemed only right that the tornado money should rebuild what it tore down. The wind that blowed it down was the same wind that stirred up the money. Seemed only right." That much talking and thinking's got me down. I'll try again to get a toe wave to the foot post. Seems the first step in digging and planting again.

I used that grip only a few times. I got it out when I got that ticket to California. One night after Gus went to bed, I took it out from under the bed. Emptied it of all the pieces of cloth I got at the remnant house in town. I stacked the folded squares of color on the end of the bed. Scraps waiting to become something useful. They was a lot like some folks. Waiting to become. All the clothes I planned to take to California fitted in. No trouble. I stood back from the bed. Saw how easy they all went in. Gus was asleep, but I said out loud to the walls, "That's a good sign. Maybe I am supposed to go. Everything's working out just too easy. Don't want to read circumstance into the hand of the Lord, but it seems to be working out." I took the ticket in the eyeglass case and put it in the top of the suitcase and put all of my readiness under the bed. Next morning I got a box out of the store house to put all the remnants in. Just a little while before Gus started going down so fast.

I began to get ready in little ways. Almost a month of planning and packing before I noticed that Gus was wearing thin. Getting weak or sick. Nothing you could put your finger on. I had seen enough of dying by then to know it was beginning for Gus. It took me a while to give up California. "I gave it up as slow as I got ready to go." The walls of the trailer don't soak up me talking to myself the way the spare room did.

One night, early fall, Gus had a terrible smothering spell. Couldn't get his breath for the longest time. After I got him settled, I slid the grip out from under the bed. Took a while to hang up the dresses and replace my Sunday stockings and step-ins in the drawers. The mouth of the leather grip smiled toothless at me again. I took the ticket out of the eyeglass case, laid it on the chest. The remnants, waiting in the pantry, fitted right back in the grip and slipped under the bed like they were born there. The box I left in the pantry with the straining rags in it. Next morning I called Toy. We had a phone by then because of Gus and his smothering. Doctor said we had to.

"Toy, I want you to come get this ticket and take it back to Columbia to the depot agent there. Get Gus's money back. You hear?" I shouted at her since she lived all the way in town.

"Okay, Mama, but Daddy might get better, a lot better, real soon. Then you can go." Toy was always dreaming that things were gonna be better than they ever was. She came right away, took the ticket for a refund, and brought me the money back on the same day.

"There," she said. She held her hand out like she wished it didn't belong to her. Like she wanted to disown it some way, bringing back something as simple as money when she took away something as grand as a trip to California.

"I thank you for all your trouble. You want some supper?" I should have told her about the time I almost went to St. Louis. She would have understood that. She hated it so bad that I couldn't go. Toy had a way of feeling for folks, feeling what it was that was going on inside. Hating to see their hurting. She did have that about her.

"No'm. I guess I'll head on back to town. See about the girls and Edward Earl. They both going to a basketball tournament in Clinton tonight. Got to get them off on the pep bus." She still held her hand out, pointing to me and to my lost trip. "I'll get them off to Clinton, even if I can't get you off to California." She laughed a little hard laugh. Came more from a place of weeping, though, than laughing.

"Well, you and the girls hurry back out to see us. Your daddy ought to be feeling better once the weather breaks." I heard myself lying like Mama.

The truck pulled out of the yard and I saw the lights switch on. They caught shadows across the road. Chased them down, opening up wide yellow pools.

I slipped the refund into Gus's money box in his top drawer. I didn't know where it come from. When he died, I used some of that California money to pay Brother Griffin for saying the words at the cemetery. Brother Felton had the words at the church. The deacons paid him, but I felt that I ought to give Brother Griffin a little extra. He wasn't serving the church any longer and he came quite a ways to be here for the funeral. I thought it was only right.

Later, I counted that money three times to be sure I had it right. I put the cost of the ticket under "total" and put a takeaway sign and figured. Even money. Right down to the last dollar. Gus never used one bit of the California money.

I washed and scalded each jar, dried it with a clean towel. With a little nudge from the heel of my hand, each bill rolled back into itself, into a green roly-poly. I dropped them one by one back in place. Put the jars into the grip. Since it was traveling money, that seemed the right place for it.

Every night for a week or so, I took it out and looked at it. Opened the grip with a snap, lifted out the white pillowcase, and sat the five mason jars on the table. Waiting for Gus to speak out, tell me what to do with all the rest. Seeing if I could will myself an answer. I didn't put the curtains back in the tiebacks after the second night. Just left the kitchen dark and shadowy. Waiting for some kind of light to come on inside to give me peace about what was left.

As slow as sunrise in winter, I worked through the puzzle. That money was holding me some kind of way. Keeping me from getting on with living, from getting on with being something useful. Like those remnants. That night I took the biggest remnant, a piece of lilac gingham, and made a money pouch. Took the pillowcase off those jars and set it aside to wash and bleach in the morning. Each one of the jars gave up its treasure, one at a time, fed it into the lilac gingham. I put the kettle on to boil. Scalded those jars and used them next summer. They was good canning jars. Some extra scrubbing took the rust off around the mouths.

"I still got the sack."

"Mama, I'll be there in just a minute. Edward Earl's got to leave early this morning. I don't go until the second shift. You and me can eat a little later." Toy stops shouting for a minute. Says something low and quiet to Edward Earl. Murmurs like a healing. "Just hold your horses."

Toy always did say that about hold your horses. She never held a horse, or a mule or nothing. She always been scared to death of our old milk cow, Rahab. Never did take to none of the animals we had. Maybe she was just skittish from birth. Not much like a farm girl. Mattie had some of that in her. Mama Two always said that about holding your horses, not that she knew much more about horses, either. Most she just knew about complaining and bellyaching and having her own way. I believe to my soul she was the hardest woman to get along with I ever saw.

She must have come to stay with us sometime the year or so after Mama died. Her own children had to pass her around. She was that hard to get on with. And Gus, he treated her so good, but she never could see him for that brother of his. He never let on that he minded one bit. Of course, she always called on Gus when she wanted something done. Knew she could depend on him, not on that flashy Johnny Mack. Hard for me to see how a mama can be so blind when it come to her own young'uns. And that baby girl, Lord, she babied her to the point that she never could make her own way to save her. Mamas have a way of making or breaking their young'uns.

"I went wrong some way with Toy. And I can't see it."
Words that cut me right in two. Did I say that out loud?

"Don't want Toy to hear none of this."

I don't remember much of her growing up. She was there.
I was busy. That was about it. I was too busy to notice that
she wasn't getting all she needed. That school program business, I don't even remember. Must've been in the spring. I
always did up the front room curtains in early spring. Somebody else could best tell me where I went wrong. Mama said
I gave Toy her head too much.

When Mama got sick, after we heard about Q.C., that was
when Toy started going on and on about that job in the plant
in town. Mama warned me. "Eula B.," she said, "now, you
mark my words, going to town and working in some plant is
just letting etoile"—Mama always did call her, etoile—"walk
straight into the devil's playground. You mark my words. No
good will come of it." Right as rain, that's just what happened,
Toy went right in there, got herself involved in everything
going on in town. She and Esther Mayfield and the rest of
them, painting their faces and chewing gum, going back into
town at night, especially after soldiers started coming over
from Camp McCain. Just walked straight into the devil's playground. Toy really didn't have nobody like Gus to choose
from. Camp McCain boys during the war were here today and
then off somewhere else tomorrow.

That one she brought home, a pretty boy with a Yankee
accent, sat there holding hands in front of me and Gus. I told
her off right there. She ran right out of the room crying and
carrying on. Didn't speak a word at home for days. He never
showed back up. I tried to tell her that he was one you couldn't
count on. Toy's eyes stayed red for a month.

Not one of them was the kind you could count on. Least
not while they was soldiering. Some of them might have gone

back home and been worth something. Not while they was soldiering, though. Most of them girls married somebody during the war. Esther married some fellow with a funny name from up in Minnesota or Michigan. Somewhere like that. She went with him for a while, had a young'un or two, but Toy said that it didn't work. She's back home, still working at the plant. Lives out in Beat Two with her mama and papa. Nope, those boys weren't studying staying put when they came down here.

Q.C. might have found somebody during his soldiering. Old man like that joining up, volunteering, just asking for trouble. Mama said it was kind of a way of taking his own life. She always likened it to David and Uriah the Hittite. Getting yourself put out in the front lines, in the heat of battle, the Bible says, knowing you ain't got a chance. Only difference is that Q.C. chose it for himself. Be nice to think he found some nice girl who cared about him before he went off. Mama always wanted to think so. She liked to think that he got married and was happy somewhere and that was why he never got back home. That's what she hoped. But every time she said it, she'd look away because she'd start to cry. Thinking of Q.C. sleeping in some old flophouse, living off restaurant food, not having anybody to wash his clothes, well, Mama said that just hurt her to the quick.

"I like to think, Eula B.," she said, "that in one of those towns where Q.C. stopped for the night, it was a Saturday, and when he woke up the next morning, he heard somebody singing "Bringing in the Sheaves." And he followed the singing to a Baptist church. There he saw a pretty girl who had the sense to see that Q. had been raised right, even if he did have a bit of a temper. And she was willing to love that temper right out of him. And he married her and she sent him off soldiering. He told her he had to be part of that war if he was any man at all. She said, 'Well, if that's what it takes for you to be happy, Q., then you just hightail it right out there and fight.'

"That's why he went, Eula B., because he wanted to fight, not because he was tired of living. I know it in my mama's heart." Mama and Q., Mama Two and Johnny Mack. Me and Toy? All part of a mama's blindness.

"Okay, Mama, I'm back. Finally got Edward Earl off. Ever since that trial, he's got so he goes down to the courthouse every morning and listens to the police and sheriff reports. He thinks he'd like to go into law enforcement. That's kind of what he was doing when I met him, remember? Security guard. He might be good at that. I can't see them hiring nobody his age. Lord, he'd probably draw the night shift for years. He couldn't take that. Have to give up his TV programs." Toy laughs, spreading her hands out, helpless. "Still, he mentioned that if Toady Walker runs for sheriff, he might work for him. What do you think of that?"

"Toy, I ran that soldier boy off for your own good. You know that?"

"Ma'am?"

"You know why I ran that pretty soldier boy from Camp McCain off?"

"Oh, Mama."

"But do you know? I didn't want you to wish all your life for some kind of man you never could have."

"Oh, Mama." Toy looks at me like she's scalded. A pink rim rises out of her collar. "That was a long time ago." She starts to pull at the bedclothes, straightening them over and over. "You think Toady Walker could carry Beat Three?"

She's not really talking to me. When she really wants me to answer, she talks real loud and straight. Forcing her words like a wedge right into my face. Her voice is tighter and higher than it is now. No, she's just talking, going over things in her own mind. Trying to decide how she feels about it. I don't have to answer. Toy draws her words in closer and directs them down at me now.

"Well, I guess we better get up and get our breakfast. To-day's the day for the nurse to come and give us our bath and check on how we're doing. Can you help me get us going?"

She puts one arm beneath my knees, the other around my neck. Straining and pulling me up to sitting on the side of the bed.

"Now, Mama, you put your toes against the side of my foot, yeah, like that. Now, I'm gonna take both hands and pull you up so you can walk into the kitchen with me. Okay?" Every few days Toy tries a new method for moving me. Each one leaves her breathless. I know the ridge I'm making in the bed is getting smaller and smaller. I know I'm not any heavier, but Toy gets more out of breath as the days go by.

"You ain't taking up smoking, have you, Toy?"

"Mama!" Toy sputters near my ear.

"Well, I thought not. I could smell it if you did. Cigarette smell goes through everything. I could tell if you did." Mamas can tell. I'd know it, even if I couldn't smell it. Did Mama believe the lies about the Watkins man?

"I guess she did. She never asked me nothing about the time I was gone when I went to find the conjure woman." That's not just straight. The words want to come out the bad side of my mouth and they won't stand still, get in line so I can handle them.

"Mama, I sure can't be trying to lift you up and you mumbling about me smoking and your mama. Now it's all I can do to get you up. I can't do no talking now."

I try to think about putting my toes against the side of Toy's foot and pulling up. In spite of all, the smoky pattern of mamas and young'uns fooling their mamas swings around right in front of where I need to place my foot.

"Now, Mama, you got to help me just a little. I'm getting older and tireder every day myself. Pay attention to what you're doing with your feet. Come on, there, that's better. Lean against me and let's try to head up the hall. Our nurse will be here directly, and we want to be able to tell her what a good breakfast we ate."

I turn my head to look fiercely at her. But she is so caught up in all her "we" business and breakfast talk and bathroom talk that she can't just stand here and be a part of the "we" that's really here. Busy, busy, getting things straight and taken care of. Big part of every woman's life. Still in all, Toy has taken care of me mighty good since that second stroke. Some folks has young'uns that put them away in old folks' homes. I'm proud that Toy never done that. But if she'd just left me alone, out at the place.

"Never would have had those renters. That's for sure."

"What's that, Mama? Lord, are you still stewing over that renter family? I told you, you can't take up no part of what happened out there. Lord, if everybody took up the cause for stuff that happened on their land, why, they'd just never get over it. You can't go dwelling on that again. Me and Edward Earl figures that the judge and the jury took care of that. We just got to go on with our living and try to forget all about that. Though it's gonna be hard for Edward Earl. Him having to set there day after day listening to all that terrible testimony. Hearing all about the way that loony acted. 'Course we had no way in the world of knowing what he was like. Lord help us if we'd had any idea. You know we would have never let them have the place. But his daddy did serve with Jimmy Lee before Pearl Harbor. And we was trying to do them a good turn. Sort of for Jimmy Lee's sake. Makes you wonder if you can afford to be nice to people these days. Lord knows we thought we was doing the right thing. Still, you can't tell anymore what is the right thing, can you?" Toy does all that talking, out past my shoulder somewhere, with me hanging on to her like some Christmas tree ornament left way past the season.

"Now, Mama, let's get this good old breakfast down and wait for our nurse." She's back to shouting at me. Must have those renters settled enough to satisfy her.

"Before she gets here, we want to have time in the bathroom and finish up all that. Then we'll be ready for a good bath and maybe some time for her to give you a good rubdown so we won't get bedsores."

She sits me down, rag-doll style. I feel one side of me going down, slowly sliding toward the floor. My good arm keeps waving in the air slowly. Like a flipper trying to right a sick fish.

"God-a-mighty, Mama," Toy shouts as I go over, flipper waving. Thunk. I make a dull little sound on the floor. I don't feel a thing. Landed on my dead side. "God-a-mighty, Mama, you all right?" Toy's knees make little half-moons of fat right beside my head. She grabs me under the arms and sits me up, both of us looking right under the kitchen table. A big black crayon marker says "Jones Furn. C.O.D." and a white label has rolled up toward the center like a cow's tongue.

"Here we go, Mama, up in the chair. We'll skin this cat again. You hurting anywhere? Mrs. Toney said I was gonna have to use restraints on you before long. Lord, that like to have scared me to death." I rock back in the chair. "You wait right here, Mama." Toy has her hands on my shoulders. "Hold on with your good hand." She puts both my hands on the table to brace me. "Just a minute, you hear?" She runs out of the kitchen, into her bedroom.

"Here we go." She holds up a long black belt with a square silver buckle. "We'll strap you in so you don't get away this time." She puts the belt over my head and down around my middle. "You sure you ain't hurt?" She jerks the belt behind me. "There, that'll keep you straight."

She goes back to the stove. Shaking her head. Starts back on the cream of wheat. Nurse's day again. Seems like it was only yesterday.

"I got a lot settled, Toy. Did you know that?"

Toy keeps stirring. "Yes'm, I guess so."

"Now, Mrs. Freeman, you gotta promise me that you're gonna try a little harder for me these next few days. You been just lying here in this bed fretting over all kinds of things. Now, this next week, I want you to practice moving every thirty minutes or so. You can roll to one side and then the other. Change around every little bit. Do that for me, okay?"

The nurse does like Toy. She looks hard and straight at me and talks loud when she wants me to answer. They talk natural like when they speak to each other, but when they get around to me they look straight at me and holler. Must think that stroke took away my hearing and my reasoning.

I wish I could tell them that. I need to tell them, too, that I'm tired of bathroom stuff and cream of wheat over and above oatmeal. People think those are the kinds of things that old people want to talk about, but they're wrong. That nurse and Toy will find out when they get old and their young'uns talk only about bathrooms and cereal.

"Now, Mrs. Freeman, are you listening to me? Now, be a good girl and show me how far over you can turn without any help from me or Miss Toy. Come on, that's a girl. Give me a good roll." She stands back, away from the bed. Hands on her hips, waiting. "Come on, Mrs. Freeman, cooperate with me this morning." Sounds like she's talking to some show dog. "Roll over." I want to look fierce at her. Make her see what she's doing to me. I can't tell what my face is doing these days. Only one side works. Trouble with depending on your body, it plays tricks on you. That's one thing I want to tell this nurse and Toy. If I do, though, they'll think I'm not working very hard on turning over. If I try to tell them, they'll both get right over this bed and talk hard and loud and right at me. I'll keep my thoughts to myself. It's their own fault for not listening to my advice. "Well, I think you can do better than that. Miss Toy here has told me that every once in a while she'll come in here and find you all turned around in this bed, and you wide awake and just squirming. Worm in hot ashes, you are. Now, you show Mrs. Toney what you can do."

Calls herself Mrs. Toney. Now, that's something. I wonder what will they think of next. Bad enough her coming here and fooling with me like she does and then calling herself Mrs. Toney.

"Mrs. Freeman, I'll give you one more chance to show me how much you can move around. If you are not partially mobile in bed"—she turns to Toy—"that's what the guidelines say. 'Patient must be partially mobile in the bed in order for the home health nurse to continue treatment.' Once she gets so she can't get around at all, then she gets another kind of patient rating and you'll have to qualify for another kind of home care. Rules say I can come only as long as she can do a little for herself." She turns from her soft talking to Toy back to me. Toy goes around to the other side of the bed. Shouters standing on both sides now. I look first at Mrs. Toney, then at Toy. Guards. I try to pull up my good shoulder and throw the dead side over. Like throwing a feed sack into the back of the wagon.

"Umph." The circle right over my belly moves up.

"There now, ain't that good?" Mrs. Toney just beams. "It looks like we'll be able to keep on having our little times together, Mrs. Freeman. You done that just fine." She nods to Toy, real proud like, and Toy smiles first at her and then down at me.

"I'll be back next week. Try to keep her moving in the bed so that the bedsores don't develop. I'll get the office to issue a requisition for some of that stuff that you spray on the parts that look red. Makes a kind of callus so that the sore doesn't come. It's the best we can do when they get this old."

She's talking to Toy now. Talking regular, not shouting. I heard her and I'm not even trying to listen.

They both ease toward the door, carried by their soft talk of everyday things. When Toy shuts the door, the voices fade down the hall, and in just a few minuutes I can feel the front door slam. Makes a little jerk of air run through the whole trailer.

Toy is in her room now, getting ready for the second shift. Jimmie Lee will be coming in a minute. Turning on the TV and smoking. After all that settles down, I'll have lots of time.

Ollie, the money, this thing about Q.C. finished. I know he's out there. He's come home. Or was it just the letter? No, can't bury a letter, and there's a marker out there. Next to Mama. I kinda wanted to be buried next to Mama. Have it Papa, Mama, a space for me, then Gus and the little boy. Seemed it should have been that way. But Q.C. took the place next to Mama, I think. I'll get Toy to take me out to the cemetery to check on it. When we go out to put in the garden. She said it was late March already.

"Toy, Toy, do you know how late we are? We've got to get out there and burn off all those weeds if we gonna get a thing in the ground. When is Easter?" I wait. Toy isn't answering.

"Toy, Toy, is it Good Friday yet? Things that bear above the ground got to be planted by Good Friday. You remember that, don't you?" Still no answer.

"Toy, Toy, can you hear me? It's important."

The front door slams. Toy's bedroom slippers shuffle down the hall. She comes to the door.

"Lord, Mama, what are you getting all worked up about? I walked out to the car with the nurse to get some of that stuff to use on your bedsores until the requisition comes through. Just hold your horses. You know I'm not going off anywhere. Jimmie Lee will be here before I have to go. You want some lunch? You need to go to the bathroom?"

I shake my head. I'm all asked out.

"Well, if you don't need me for a while, I think I'll go watch my stories. Working these odd shifts like I been doing, I am so behind. I don't know who is doing what. Jimmie Lee tries to keep me up, but when I'm home I like to watch for myself. You call me if you need me, you hear?" She is hoping I won't call, hoping that I won't think of what it was I was gonna ask. I do need her, mamas need daughters—to tell things to.

I hear the TV voices and I start thinking again. Now, even if I talk out loud, they won't come nosying in on what I'm doing. That's a good feeling. I still got to be careful what I say.

Mama went first, after the little boy. He really didn't count though. It wasn't like we knew him or counted on him at all.

So really it was Mama first. But in some ways, Q.C. was first. If you figure that he died in the war, then he was first, after Papa. But if you figure that he was gone after that summer, when he stole the money, then, if you figure that way, then he really went before Papa. Either way, he was gone a long time before we knew for sure. People from the war said they'd try to ship his body home. Soldiering has a lot of fright in it. One of the main ones must be dying and being buried some-place so far away. With not one soul to memorialize you. Must be awful. Waking up on Judgment Day in a place you don't even know. Terrible. That worried Mama. She finally figured that Q.C. was really dead, not MIA. That stood for Missing in Action. When she decided that, she wrote them a letter saying that if there was any way at all for them to send Q.C. home, she would be most appreciative. I copied the letter over for her, but she signed it herself. She told them she wanted Q.C. to greet the resurrection from a place he knew, a place that was familiar.

They sent him home. At least I think so. It was after the war, though. Sent him home with a flag over the coffin. Couldn't open the coffin. That was what took Mama. Sent him home in a wooden coffin with a brass plate on the top. Quintus Cincinnatus Taylor Carpenter. Some more things were written there. But the soldier that came along with the coffin told Mama that she couldn't open it. He made a long speech to us all about how Americans don't sleep in foreign soil. But we still couldn't open the coffin.

"You understand, of course, Mrs. Carpenter, too much time has passed." He stood up straight and lean as a slat to tell us that. Mama just broke down.

"How will I know if it's Q.C.?" She really carried on. It made the soldier step closer to the coffin, like he was trying to get the box to reassure Mama somehow.

"The United States of America guarantees it, Mrs. Carpenter. We guarantee it."

In the end we left the coffin just like that soldier boy brought it. Closed. We never had a closed-coffin funeral in our church before. Seems like when the Billingsleys' grandson was sent home from Vietnam, they had one for him. Said he was all-to-pieces from stepping on a bomb. That closed coffin killed Mama. She didn't last any time after that. She had him put up on the hill, next to her place.

"Maybe that'll make up to him in death, Eula B., what he didn't have in life. Being right next to me." She wasn't no time in joining him.

It wasn't any problem with his marker. The government put it up for us. They had one that they put up if we'd put him in a soldiers' cemetery. But Mama said, "No, thank you. The least we can do for Q.C. is bury him among his own and pay for his marker." Still in all, she got a check from the government. We paid more for it than the check was, but the government was willing to do their part. Guess it was the least they could do, seeing how Q.C. gave it all. That was what the soldier boy that came with his coffin said. "Yes, ma'am, Mrs. Carpenter, he gave it all."

There was still a place left for me and a place for Ollie even after we buried Q.C. and Mama. I never did think about Gus. Or Mattie. Didn't know just where we was going to put them. Maybe I thought he'd go back across the river and be with his people and Mattie would stay on with the Bighams, just like she'd done since the day she married. Seems like in dying you go back to your real people. But Gus got to be more like us and less like his own. He moved over here when we married and he farmed our land and he just got to be more and more like us. Was us before it was through. Seemed only right that he be buried right near the place he farmed all his life. Got so he was just part of us, too. Earned his place there all right.

That was what had me worried, though. When we buried Gus, it looked like we took up Ollie's place. I can't have it so that Ollie don't have a place.

"Toy, Toy, come here a minute." I call. Then add, "Please."

I wait for the shuffle of her bedroom slippers. No sound in the hall.

"Toy, I need you for a minute."

The second time, I hear her start. A minute later, "You calling me, Mama? Lord, I thought you'd be asleep. Usually Mrs. Toney's visit puts you right to sleep. What you wanting, lunch? Bathroom?"

"No, Toy, come on in all the way. I need to ask you something important. You need to listen." Toy slides further in. Looks at me straight.

"Well, what is it, Mama?"

"Give me a minute, I'm trying. I was just thinking of it and I need to know." Seems like these things kinda slide over onto the dead side of my mind and I got to get over there to find them.

My face begins to pull. "I know, Toy. It was about a place for Ollie. Did we save a place for Ollie. We didn't use them all up, did we?"

"Lord, Mama, you still worrying about that cemetery? There's plenty of room on that hillside for half the county. I don't know of nobody beside you Carpenters and Daddy that wanted to be buried out there. You got room for a crowd. Now, you try to get some sleep, you hear?" She tries to make her getaway.

"Well, that's good news. Plenty of room. And Mattie, I forgot to ask about Mattie's place."

"Well," Toy says, "I don't know about Aunt Mat, I don't know what she wants." She keeps her hand on the door.

"Mama, like I said, there's room for half the county up there. But I don't see nobody else busting to get in. Now, don't you keep on fretting, you hear?"

"Toy, there wasn't no room for a pretty boy soldier or a Watkins man, you understand that?"

"Ma'am?" Toy waits a minute, looking soft at me. "What's that, Mama?" Then she finishes her question by closing the door behind her.

I don't know about Mattie, either. Maybe she's been a lady over on the Bigham place too long and she's gonna be buried with them. You can't tell. Some women do that. Leaving and cleaving, Mama called it. She'll be buried in a fancy dress, I bet. Still in all, I'm glad that there's room for Ollie. I never meant to give his place to Gus. You could count on Gus, but Ollie was blood kin and I got to make allowances for that.

Feels like the dead side is taking over again. Can't let this come over me. It's fine to sleep when work's done, but working comes before sleeping, or feeling or anything. Some folks just sleep their life away, and poverty slips up on them. Good Book says that, too.

Things keep slipping right out of reach though, can't keep up this thinking.

"Mama, Mama." Toy is standing over me, shouting. "I wondered how long you was gonna sleep. You been sleeping most all the day. Jimmie Lee said you never even woke up for lunch or nothing. I was just checking to see if you was all right. I've been in from the plant for a good little while, and you kinda worried me, sleeping so long like this. You okay, aren't you?" She's standing right over me.

I nod, trying to get her face to come out of the wavy air in front of my eyes. I know it's Toy talking. But I can't get her face to be still. The outlines of her jaw make me think she's underwater. She wasn't like that when I went to sleep. I'm trying to tell her okay. My neck doesn't want to nod. Seems like my head just settled back on this pillow like a rock.

"Mama, you hear me? You don't look like you're quite at yourself yet. Slept too long? That it?"

Toy's face keeps on being watery and her voice kinda disconnects, like a telephone during a thunderstorm. My telephone used to do that. Every time a spring storm would come, sounded like bacon sputtering when I tried to talk on it. One time when Ollie called, long time ago, the phone crackled like that. I couldn't hardly hear him. Must have been when Gus died. He called then. I didn't think to tell him that I kept a place for him. He might have wanted to know. But I forgot to tell him.

"Mama, Mama, can you hear me? Let me know if you can. Lord knows, I believe to my soul that she's had another stroke. That's why she slept so long. Edward Earl, Edward Earl, call the doctor, Mama's had another stroke."

Toy goes flying out of the room, bedroom slippers slapping down the hall. She has her bowling shirt on. I guess she was gonna tell me how it was her night to go out bowling. Wonder if she was gonna leave me with Edward Earl?

I hear him coming now. He eases into the room, huffing and puffing. His belly comes around the corner first. That's all I can see when he stands over me, by the bed. I look up at the underside of the shelf of his stomach. He's taken to wearing his belt and buckle under the shelf. I can't move my head back far enough into the pillow to find his face with my eyes.

The Stetson on the buckle stays at the same place. But it's wavy and underwater, just like Toy's face. I can't get my sights to move. I'm just under here watching the hat on that belt buckle.

"Mama Eula," the voice above the Stetson puffed, "you got to talk to me, you got to tell me if you can understand me. You hear? You hurting anywhere? You feel any different? Mama Eula, you hear me?" He wheezes out every question and I watch his shelf above the belt wiggle and twitch as he talks. I try to find his face again.

It takes the ambulance only a little while to get here. I hear the siren before I feel that pulse of the whirling light outside the bedroom window. It shoots through the darkness like summer heat lightning. Toy sits on the side of the bed. Wiping my mouth. She's tending me like I did Mama.

I guess that's what she's doing. Got a washrag in her hand, keeps putting it on my face. I can't feel much that's going on, though. Can't tell just what she's doing. I try to smile to tell her she's doing right.

The young men from the ambulance bust into the room. Three of them. Wavy like Toy and Edward Earl. I can see their starched white uniforms. Shirts tucked neatly into stiff, bright pants. They move from one side of the bed to the other. Pushing something between them. Three pair of hands rustle the covers. The yellow rings fly backwards, up and then down, in a heap at the foot of the bed. I can feel them just a little on my feet. Hands look for me under the cover. They lift and push and shove. Not feeling any touching yet. Not like at the doctor's office when Papa took me. Three sets of hands. Two are white, one black. The black hand slides a cold, starched sheet under my middle. Slicker than the sheets that Quester Franklin had. Same black hands. The voice belongs to the black hands.

"Just slide her over onto the draw sheet. We'll lift her with the sheets, easier that way, and we can support her better. She'll be dead weight." He kneels beside the bed. The first face I see. Still watery and wavy. Toy is standing by the dresser, the hem of her bowling shirt is even with my eye. Her crying makes the shirt jump and jerk.

The voice beside me starts again. "There now, you gonna be all right. We're the team from the hospital. We're gonna take you in so you can be a little more comfortable. You hear me? You having trouble breathing? Lon, get the oxygen just outside the door there. Listen, I'm gonna put a little mask over your face so you can breathe a little easier. Probably like the one you had when you had your babies. You hear me? Now, you just breathe into this little white cup. It'll make it go easier for you."

He puts his hand behind my head and slips a long rubber band over it. A little white cup pops across my nose and mouth. I need to tell him that I never used any such a thing when Toy was born. All I ever had was a pull sheet. What's he talking about?

I can feel the difference in my breath, almost hear the sounds of living hissing inside the little white cup. Pulling all of living down into this small space. Shrinking life down smaller than a trailer.

The hands lift me, high over the bed. Onto a stretcher. One set of white hands and shirts and trousers on each side. The black one at the back holding a slender silver tank up over my head. They start for the door. Tubes swing from overhead along the side of the stretcher. We go marching down the hall.

With a quick move or two we're all locked inside the white stillness of the ambulance. Like a hearse, only white. Are hearses and ambulances different? I never saw the inside of either till tonight. We brought our little boy home in a wagon. Must be the lights from Edward Earl's pickup glaring in the back window. Did Toy have time to change her shoes? The waves come over me when the ambulance starts charging out on the highway.

The hospital room isn't too much different from the room in the trailer. Feels little and square, no sign of life. Hours of talk going on around the bed. I can hear it when it doesn't disconnect. I can tell what's going on. Most of it's the same—bathroom, food, aches-and-pain talk. Nothing important.

Toy sits in the plastic chair at the end of the bed during the late afternoon and early evening. Jimmie Lee sits in the mornings and Shirley Earlene comes in from time to time to help out. Edward Earl shows up in time to go with Toy down to the hospital cafeteria. Nothing too different.

Can't help but believe that they'd be better off if they'd stayed on the place with me. Ollie, too. But maybe he really did like it out there in California. I hope he knows he's got a place saved for him here. I got to tell Toy to get my old grip out and help me get ready. My burying shoes are in there, with the money.

It's that grip that's got me worried. The money from the floor of the chicken house was in it when I moved into town. I meant to send some of it to Ollie. I think that second stroke got me before I got it off to him. I need to ask Ollie if he got it. I know you can send money through the mail. You just give it to the man at the post office and he writes out something, then when that gets out to California, Ollie can take it to the post office man there and he'll give him the money. I don't know how they know to do it, but it works. I know all about it. Sometimes Jimmie Lee gets some money from Royce that way. Money order or some such thing. Order money just like you can order from Sears and Roebuck. Yes, you can. I know because Jimmie Lee says Royce done it. When it suits him, that is. I'll ask Jimmie Lee about it when she comes to sit with me in the morning. I need to get that money out of that grip and get it sent on to Ollie. It might be the only way he can get home and get to use his place. He might be out there in California with no way at all to get home. That'd be terrible to be off like that and not able to get home. That might be just what's wrong with Ollie.

"Mama Eula, you trying to tell me something?" Jimmie Lee's red lips wave over the top of the railing of the bed. Must be morning. I don't remember sleeping. I didn't hear Toy leave for the plant. Must have been sleeping good. I got to ask Jimmie Lee about ordering that money. Maybe if I could sit up just a little and get my head out of this pillow, she could understand.

"You need the bedpan? What about a little sip of water?" She pours a little water into a paper cup with a crooked straw sticking out of it.

"Jimmie Lee?" The voice doesn't sound like mine.

"Ma'am?"

Wonder if I can work that straw any better than when I tried that drink in the shining doctor's office. Never had seen one of them before. Awfulest time trying to get it to work. That nurse had to tell me how to do it. Never did get any better then. Had to wait for Quester Franklin and the uva-russel tea. Probably won't get no better here neither. Feels like that to me.

"I wish Mama was here. She'd go and get some old conjure woman with some real curatives. Not like the Watkins man, either." The voice cracks and starts above the sheet.

"Oh, Mama Eula, you gonna be fine." She's lying to me now. Like Mama about Papa, me about Gus. Lying about dying.

"Can't get well all cooped up in a place like this. Cut off from everything that's healing. Little old box of a room with no real living in it. Same as with a trailer. A body can't get well in a place like this." I say this long speech.

I can see Jimmie Lee's face right above me, bright red lips shaking, eyes all outlined with black, blinking hard. Wonder if Ollie's found that out. He needs to know it. Two things, he's got a place here and you can't get well cut off from living.

"Living things is healing. I want to tell Toy that. So you girls won't bring her here. She ought to know that you can't get well when you're all cut off from living." Tears from Jimmie Lee's face hit the top of the turned-back sheet. I can't feel them, but I can hear them plop like fat August raindrops against the starched whiteness. "I wish I could have told her so much, in time so that she won't make mistakes."

Ollie's all cut off from his people. Has been for years. Ain't no way to live. But Ollie could come back. I got the money. I meant to send it to him. I kept it in that old grip. California money, I called it. I just eased that cardboard lining away from the leather outside. It was just pasted, so I eased it off and put that money between the lining and the cover and pasted it right back. Made my own paste. Flour and water. Held good, too. I was careful. Didn't get any paste on the money. Weighted it down with mason jars while it dried. Same ones I found the money in. I got plenty to send Ollie so he can get home. Be back with his own people. Need to be with your own kin, living and dying, I believe. Especially dying, you need your own. I meant to send that money. I got to ask Jimmie Lee.

"I'll lift your head up just a little, Mama Eula. Try to take a little sip of this water. Your lips are so dry. I know a little sip would feel fine. Just try it for Jimmie Lee. There, that's it. That's a good girl." Jimmie Lee goes on and on about a little sip of water. "Mama'll be proud of you, taking a big drink like this, Mama Eula."

Talking to me like I'm not quite all there. I can hear her. I know what she's saying. Don't have to talk like that.

"Here we go, Mama Eula, try a little more, that's a girl, big sip." Jimmie Lee works steady with the cup, the tears still forming in the corners of her eyes. "Mama says you're something else, Mama Eula. A woman to be reckoned with is what she said. Yes ma'am, a woman to be reckoned with. That's sure what she said."

I want to catch her eye as her face waves back and forth in front of mine, look fierce to stop her talking like that. "Remind her about my shoes, you hear." She nods, holding the cup just below my chin. I take a big breath and try to pull in a long swallow. I am thirsty. Long draws of summer well water sure would taste good now. The hospital water doesn't do right. It works against the muscles in the back of my throat. Won't go down. I feel the cold running down my chin. The rest of it starts down my windpipe. Headed for my lungs. Body playing tricks on me still. I can see the jerking in the sheets, knotting up with the coughing. I can't stop it. It's happening again. Tricks. Here I am, trapped in this lifeless place, with no living at all, and my body is still playing tricks on me.

Jimmie Lee slides her arm from behind my head and scoots me toward the center. She yanks the silver tube of railing up and it snaps into place. "Mama Eula, I'm gonna go get the nurse. Lord, you 'bout to scare me to death. You're gonna choke to death with me standing right here beside you."

The sheet jumps and knots. I can see it plain. Cats fighting in a slick white sack. I'm coughing but I can't even feel it. Can't do a thing to stop it. Like labor. I can just go with it or not.

Lots of things are like that. Go with them or kick against them. Some folks got to do one. Some folks do another. Gus just kinda went along. Ollie and Q.C., now, they was ones who had to make their own way. Couldn't do nothing the easy way. I guess that's the Ferguson in us. Mattie, she was more like Papa and Gus. I must be kinda mixed up, part Ferguson, part Taylor. Fighting sometimes, taking it as it comes sometimes. Getting rid of one baby, fighting to have another one, losing him and then not knowing what to do with the girl I had. I'd fight what I could, accept the rest. Mama couldn't take losing both her boys. She fought that, and when Q.C. was really gone, well, she just gave up. Couldn't fight anymore.

The bed is still shaking. Feels like more than coughing now. A big shiver runs through me. I can feel it, keen and bright like the dead part of me is waking up again. My heart is knocking like a woodpecker. Jimmie Lee will be able to see it through the sheet. She was crying over me. The shiver comes again, and I feel all the life inside rushing to the outside of my skin. Like the night in the wagon with the Watkins man. I can almost see what's going on inside my body. It's having to give up all its secrets. I'm looking in on the tricks and understanding them now. If Toy will hurry, I can tell her.

"Hurry." The word doesn't come out right.

The door opens. I need to tell Toy. But I can't turn far enough to see who it is.

"Tell Toy," I call to them.

I feel him in the room. The bright, shining presence comes in first like I'd known it before. It's not just a belt buckle this time. The room is full of shining and glowing. If only I wasn't sunk like a rock in this pillow. I need to lift my head and see his face. It might be Ollie, if he got the money. Or the doctor. Or the Watkins man. He always said he'd send for me. Most likely it's Ollie, he said he'd come if I ever really needed him. I don't want to go out all by myself. I hope he got the money. I hope I sent it. He can go out with me, pick out the place he wants. I'd let him have the first pick. When we was little, he always gave me first choice. This time I'll give it to him.

His shining fills the room. I want to see his face so that I can tell him to take the first pick. I think he's calling my name.

"Who's there?" I call back into the fierce glow. The words fall flat against the cold sheet.

The shining comes full around me. Wrapping me in its heat, but bringing a freeing lightness. Not heavy wrapping like a quilt. I want to smile, to get my face to work right. I'll smile and then I'll know I won. The tricks are over.